In Search of the Golden City

Mia Lutsch

In Search of the Golden City

ISBN: 9780996663427

Library of Congress Control Number: 2016931216

Cover Design by All Things that Matter Press

Cover photo by André Koekemoer

Published in 2016 by All Things that Matter Press

Acknowledgements

This book started with a dream I had in my early teens, but only really became a possibility when I learned about shamanism. Thanks to Ross Heaven, who taught me a lot about healing and accessing those other realms where inspiration can be found. I couldn't have asked for a better teacher. I am grateful also to the unconscious forces that caused me to become ill when I wasn't keeping my commitments to myself, thus nudging me to actually start writing instead of dreaming of doing it someday.

Thanks to André Koekemoer and Wilma Lutsch for their continuous support and encouragement, and for reading my work and providing feedback. Thanks to André for putting in time and effort to create a beautiful cover design for me. Thanks to all the other friends and family members who expressed excitement about the project.

Thank you to Phil and Deb Harris for editing my work and supporting me through the publishing process.

Chapter 1

He was born in a cave. The owl watched intently as it heard the mother crying out in pain. From inside flowed multitudes of color as the new being came into life. The owl knew that the new one would be a listener and a seer. He would have the power to change people's minds. Knowing this, the owl called its brother the eagle who took upon itself the task of protecting the newcomer. It let out a cry to forge a bond between its own spirit and the new-born baby. From then on they would be connected; as the eagle saw, so the boy would see. It would guide and guard the boy through life. The courage of the eagle was imprinted in the boy's heart. This would carry him through hard times, whether he was aware of it or not. The boy's name was Akim.

Ten years later the boy was a young sprout with a sharp mind and a fiery personality. He had far too much energy for his young mother to handle, so she often sent him outside to play where he immersed himself in his own little world in which the trees could talk and where nature spirits lived. Sometimes he could see them. They were shy at first but also eager to share their wisdom—stories of old and how to survive in the wild. They taught him about what was important in life: love, happiness, and courage. They warned him not to get burdened by other people's notions of who he should become, but to protect the world of happiness inside him.

"How do I do that?" he asked.

"By believing in it," they said, "by believing in it."

"As soon as you allow what others think of you to be more important than what you think of you," a wise old Oak told him, "you give away your authenticity. Authenticity is the power and the will to be yourself. It is the life blood that flows and reminds people of who they really are, that there is something infinitely greater than what can be seen when looking on the surface. It is what makes people bounce back against the odds. It is the invisible force behind the answer, 'I don't know,' when people are asked, 'How on earth did you do that?' It is what enables people to look back on the other side of a storm and say, 'I have survived, and I'm a better person for it.' Because of it, they can thank the storm for the gift it brought and acknowledge the hand that guided them through it.

"We are all connected, son, and the good that you see in a brother or sister is also in you. The bad that you will experience in the world is your reminder of what you want to create. It will push you never to settle for less than your highest vision. Keep building on the world outside so it might be a reflection of the magical world on the inside. Because you have the gift of nature within you, you have the power to transform."

Six years later things have changed. Akim had a growing restlessness inside him that he couldn't get away from. At times it felt like something was pressing on his chest, threatening to suffocate him. Where had the innocence gone? Being imaginative had been acceptable when he was a child, but somewhere along the way, gradually, all children were initiated into the world as grown-ups. Dullness would take hold of their souls as they were taught to think about how they would fit into society. How would they serve the world and make a living? More importantly, how would they be true to their background in social distinction? Nobody could see the spirits in the woods the way he used to, so it was no use talking about them or sharing what they had taught him. It just wasn't relevant. The village kids were concerned about school work and which kid would win the next contest. The girls would huddle in their own little corner, giggle together, and share their own secrets. They were quiet and shy and he didn't know how to approach them.

There was one that stood out more than the others and she caught Akim's attention. It was because of her eyes. If any person would look at them they would see a strong reservation, almost timidity, with a playful spark dancing in them whenever she laughed. But when Akim looked, he looked deeper and could see in them promises of a soft sensuality and a strong, yet enigmatic, will. He could see that when she cared, she cared deeply. She would stand up to a tyrant or a monster if someone she loved were in danger. Her name was Metis.

Chapter 2

Akim wondered, what was this strange, uncontrollable fire that seemed to have a will of its own?

Akim wasn't familiar with it and it overwhelmed him. He had heard stories of people being in love and had thought, here and there, that he felt it when he liked a girl. Yet, this was different. His expectations couldn't have prepared him for the unfathomable experience of falling in love the first time. It was also very different from the love he saw between the married couples in town. It was strange, exciting and mysterious. He didn't know whether he could trust the feeling. People had warned him that he should never trust his heart. If he did, it would be his downfall because he would lose touch with reality. Akim could see how that was true, but suddenly the dull world of "reality" didn't hold much appeal anymore. The only important thing was the magical world where power of the spirit resided. In that world, love, courage and sincerity were more important than being rich, popular or successful.

It started out with a few friendly glances, then smiles. Akim thought she was pretty and that he liked her, but the infatuation hadn't knocked him out cold, probably because it was still unknown to him. Nobody could be prepared when encountering this force for the first time. It always snuck up ever so slowly from the shadows and wrapped its arms around a person. Only when it had permeated one's being entirely, starting with the cracks in one's soul, did one recognize that there was something strange going on.

Akim didn't quite know how to approach her. He wanted to talk to her, but he didn't know what to say. He thought, why did talking to girls, especially one you liked, seem so easy to other boys? How did anyone manage to get a girlfriend if the idea of approaching her terrified him and made him sweat?

As hard as it was to approach her, the thought of staying away from her was even worse. He tried to create a situation where they would be alone in the same place coincidentally. But if he succeeded, he still didn't know what he would say to her. However, he could deal with that when it happened. Finding her alone was very hard—girls their age didn't normally walk around on their own. When they did, chances that nobody would be in the near vicinity were almost zero. So far the most he had managed to do in his quest for getting to know her was to say hello. His failure to get close to her drove him to despair. Yet, on some level, he felt that thinking of her, knowing she existed, and having the pleasure of looking at her were enough, even if he couldn't be with her.

When he woke up in the morning, the first thing he thought of was Metis. Suddenly, nothing else really mattered anymore. She was in the air he breathed; she was in his dreams when he went to bed at night. She was everything in the universe. His love for her was all that existed. This state of being happy and in despair at the same time lasted several months until one day he grew tired of it. Something had to happen or he had to move on. He couldn't yearn for her forever. He went to sit next to the village river to clear his mind. Talking to the nature spirits about his despair was a last resort and he wasn't even sure he believed in them anymore. Besides, sometimes looking for answers just generated more questions. But being completely lost, he was willing to turn to his old companions.

On this day, Akim sat on a rock on the riverside and allowed himself to feel his despair. He didn't feel like yearning or begging the universe to show him the way to win her heart. He just sat, feeling tired and lost. It was then that the river spirit approached, wanting to show itself. It was wispy and looked like an old man with a long beard. Its cloak was covered with slimy water plants. Underneath the cloak, Akim could make out images of spooky fish. In its hand the spirit held a torch that glowed not with flames, but with a pale light that emanated from the torch itself. Akim wasn't sure that he could trust the spirit, but it beckoned for him to watch the river below where he was sitting. He looked down to the place where it was pointing. A yellow and blue glow radiated from a certain spot in the water, forming an enclosed light basin. Inside it were the most beautiful fishes Akim had ever seen. They appeared in all sizes and shapes and were swimming in every direction. They were colorful. It was like a little magical universe of brightness in the middle of an ordinary river.

The river spirit came closer to Akim until it was staring him in the face with old, somewhat sad eyes. It continued to watch him until it seemed satisfied that it had found what it was looking for. A slight smile appeared 'round the corners of its eyes. It talked to Akim even though it didn't have a voice. Akim thought that he could understand what it said, as if the river spirit were communicating through its eyes.

"I am glad to see that you have courage, boy, because you will need it. Those who have courage will find that it is tested at some point. If you don't want to walk the path of the warrior, the one of the true heart, then you had better turn around now. You can have a life like everyone else; it's your choice. The question is, do you really want it?" At this point the spirit looked into his eyes again with a very stern expression, as if searching his soul. Then it turned around and floated away a few meters, continuing its conversation.

"I didn't think so. You have chosen the path of the warrior before you were born. You can choose to stop walking it at any point to live a life like everyone else, going through the motions of what is expected of you and accepting the *normal* reality that most people subscribe to. But then your spirit will die and you might become ill, because you are not being true to yourself."

Akim still felt frustrated and was becoming angry with the spirit. "It's fine for you to say so and expect me to still be loyal to the world you live in. That is what I have done most of my life and look where it has brought me. Is my spirit not ill now? I really don't see what all this has to do with my problem of being unable to get closer to the girl I am in love with."

The spirit said nothing, at least not for a while. When it finally spoke it didn't really answer his question. "Are you really going to give up without a fight?" Then it pointed to Akim's heart and said, "If you believe in magic, this is where it comes from and where you will continue to find it if you remain true. But do not try to imprison the forces that shape and lead you to your destiny. Love is simply love—it needs to be free and will continue to transform you for as long as you allow it to."

"What you are saying is wise, but how do I allow it?" Akim asked.

"If you remain true to your heart's desires and keep going despite challenges you may face, you are doing what you can to let it run free and work its magic." And with that it floated its way downstream, trailing a few cloudy wisps behind it.

Akim stared at it for a while and wondered if it was worthwhile to get angry. His heart didn't feel much lighter, but he resolved to give himself a week within which he had to at least try talking to Metis. What was the worst that could happen? He could faint? He could fail? He could make a fool of himself? If he fainted then she had two options: she could run away or stay until he woke up. Either way, he probably would survive. In truth he wasn't completely confident that he would survive if she ran away, but if that would happen, then at least he had tried. That alone would make him worth the love of someone who might one day love him back. He wasn't excited about the prospect of making a fool of himself, but he could not avoid making a fool of himself somewhere along the line so he might as well get it over with.

Two days later as soon as the school let out, he walked right up to her without any idea of what he was going to say. She was with two friends who ogled him when he approached. When he started talking to Metis, they quickly lost interest and continued their own conversation.

He said hello and asked how her day had been. It was not as hard as he had expected it to be. A few exchanges followed, after which there was an awkward silence. He didn't know what to do next. His instincts told him to run away, but he had come so far, it had taken so much to get to this point. He didn't want to let the moment pass too quickly and have to go through it all a second time. Something slipped out of his mouth. It was a question and he was surprised to hear it. "Would you like to come with me?" A stunned silence followed. "There is a very beautiful place at the river that I saw the other day. I would like to show it to you. If you want to." The words came out clear and confident. Akim was surprised to find that the faintness was temporarily scared away by a boldness that he hadn't known he possessed.

"Yes, okay," she said after a few more shocked moments and smiled. They walked in silence. It wasn't even uncomfortable, but quite pleasant. He took her to the place where the magical little fish world had come alive a few days before. This time, the blue and yellow light didn't illuminate the water, but the fishes were there in all their colorful glory. The magic was there, too, and it wasn't limited to a certain spot in the river. It started there, but it emanated outwards and at the same time seemed to connect everything and to come from everywhere. It joined the water with the sky; it enshrouded the trees in a strange light that made them appear alive. It flowed in the water and hovered on the air above the water. It flowed through his heart, too. He felt possessed by this strange and wonderful energy, as if he had become it. It moved his hand to touch hers. When he looked into her eyes, he could see that her being was also immersed in this strange light.

He pulled her towards him and felt an ecstatic warmth uncurling from his pelvis and rising up through his heart. It rose slowly to a point in his forehead where it made his brain explode with a light that made him see the world in an entirely different way. He felt connected to a source much more powerful than his small self. He could see the light and the love of this force flowing through everything, connecting everything in a sacred dance of opposites that co-existed and were in conflict, but sprang from the same place. Metis' body was alight with the same sacred energy. When their eyes met, they were locked together as one, possessed by the force that pulled them closer. Their bodies became entangled in a sacred dance, speaking the language of the light vibrating in everything around them. The next few minutes played out in a mixture of shock and surprise. When it was over, Akim understood that they had visited a place where hearts are not willing to go. It was a place of unknown mysteries that could not be retold.

The next few weeks were spent quietly being in each other's presence, touching and kissing when they could and stealing every possible moment to make love in the woods. Akim was mesmerized by his new love and overwhelmed by the fascinating experience of discovering her, body and soul.

But young hearts could only know so much happiness before a lesson was learned. It was not long before trouble dawned. Metis came up to him one morning looking as if she had cried all night. She said that she had to talk to him.

"My mother doesn't want me to see you anymore," she said.

"I don't understand, Metis. Why? Are you going to listen to her?"

"She says I'm leaving school soon and I have to start thinking about who I'm going to marry. She doesn't want it to be you."

"I want to be with you. Are we not allowed to be happy?" Akim could feel the return of his despair. It looked like a lost battle. If Metis could not sort it out with her mother, then the only way would be to persuade her mother that he wanted to marry Metis, in which case he would beg for her blessing. But he didn't feel ready. To be a husband worthwhile of Metis' affections, he had to be rich and have a strong place in the community. This would also mean not only making commitments to Metis, but to her entire family. He would have to live up to certain agreements and expectations. He could not do it. If he weren't good enough just the way he was, then he couldn't spend the rest of his life trying to be. He knew that his spirit would die, just as the river spirit had warned him. He would end up being miserable and resentful of her and her entire family. In that case, he wouldn't be a good husband no matter how hard he tried.

"How do you feel about this, Metis? Are you going to let your mother rule your life? I love you and I want to be with you."

"I want to be with you, too, Akim. But she is my mother, and family is family. I don't know what to do. I'll try to reason with her."

Alas, Metis was not successful. Her mother threatened to ground her indefinitely if she found out that they were still seeing each other. If she didn't comply, then her mother would make sure all financial support was withdrawn as soon as she finished school, "... and then your boyfriend can look after you." For a little while they continued seeing each other in secret whenever they had the chance, but this couldn't go on for too long. Metis was a nervous wreck, not only afraid that she would fall pregnant, but also that they would be seen together and word would reach her mother. The emotional strain of having torn desires was showing its effects on her. Her eyes were now filled with a sad light and she had lost her joy in the small things. Akim couldn't stand watching her suffer. The feeling that he was the cause of it all was possibly even harder to bear.

It was not long before she ended it. "It feels like nothing remains of me but an empty shell," she said. "There are days when I am not even sure whether I am dead or alive. I cannot give my all to you, but I cannot move forward either. What my mother has done is not right, but she is my mother. I cannot stand lying to her, always afraid that she would see the guilt in my eyes. I love you and I want to be with you, but I also want you to be happy. As it is, I cannot make you happy much longer."

Akim felt as if his heart was being torn from his chest but he knew that she was right. It would be no use begging her to change her mind. As much as the thought of being without her terrified him, he also loved her and wanted her to be happy. He was willing to part from her if that would mean resolution for both of them. He would miss her tremendously and yet he knew that the power of their love would remain. It would sustain him during hard times, knowing that he had been true to his heart. Soon, what had been a deep, passionate love made way for acceptance. Although they still saw each other living in the same town, they became mere acquaintances to the eye of someone who couldn't see past appearances. But occasionally their eyes would meet and their souls would remember that while the flames of their romance had turned to ashes, the love they knew was eternal. Each would forever carry a fragment of the sacred flame they had shared.

Chapter 3

Time came for Akim to leave school. Whereas most other young men of his age would take a job with a wealthy merchant or join the local army, Akim wasn't interested. There was a hermit who lived on the outskirts of town manufacturing furniture. The man was considered a bit strange by most townspeople, but Akim decided to approach him. He was called Asteodor and he didn't live too far away from Akim and his mother, which suited Akim perfectly.

Akim knocked on his door and Asteodor opened, looking slightly aloof. "Can I help you?" he asked.

"I am looking for a job. If you could show me how to make furniture, I could help you with your business."

Asteodor turned around and walked back slowly to where he was sawing wood for an armchair. He continued working without saying anything. Akim didn't know what to do so he just stood in the doorway, waiting for Asteodor to speak.

"Why did you come here, son?" he asked at last. Akim started to explain again to him that he needed a job and would be interested in learning how to make furniture, but Asteodor interrupted him. "You have just left school and from what I have heard, you are a smart lad. You have the world open in front of you. Most young men your age would take the first opportunity to go and fight for their country or become rich and gain power. So why do you come to an old carpenter?"

"Because I would rather make something with my hands that people find useful than fight for no cause or make money and gain power, only to be enslaved by the laws that govern moneymaking. I want to create and I want to be free. And I want to learn."

"What do you want to learn about, young man, besides how to make furniture?"

"I want to learn about how the universe works and what my place in it is." Akim didn't know why he had said it—perhaps because he had learned that when you are in a corner it is best to speak the truth.

Asteodor stopped working for a moment and looked up, seemingly surprised at Akim's frankness. He looked at Akim intently for a few minutes, fathoming him. His focus seemed to be in another place. He finally said, "Okay, you can start next week. Please be here at nine o'clock sharp every day." They agreed a small wage to start with and commission for furniture sold by Akim.

The journey with Asteodor was a peculiar but exciting, yet sometimes tedious affair. The first thing Akim learned with Asteodor was that making furniture was hard work. It was physically taxing and required patience and perseverance, not only to complete one piece of furniture to a sufficient standard, but also to get it sold for a reasonable price.

Akim soon found out that making furniture wasn't the carpenter's only skill. He had a lot of knowledge of various things, including the properties of plants, the imprints of the stars and the planets on the lives of earthlings, and how to read omens in nature. He taught Akim how to find plants in any part of the world for specific purposes. He also taught him basic astrology and how to identify a person's cosmic imprint at birth. He taught him how to ask questions when looking for guidance on any subject, and how to find the answer in what nature presented to him.

"One of the most important things to bear in mind if you want to know how the universe works," he told Akim, "is that everything is alive. Nature always talks to you, but you have to learn how to communicate with her if you want her to assist you. The second thing that you must always remember is that life gives you back what you put into it. With that I don't mean that life is a jealous, insecure parent that is there to haunt you if you do it wrong. No, rather that life presents itself as a gift to you. You can make the most of it or deny it and hang it out to dry because you are afraid of your own power. It all depends on what you choose. Some useful advice I would give to you is remember who you are. If you start to believe what the world tells you about yourself, your power will dwindle. You will become a passive character in a play written by someone else. But if you remember that you are a light from a Source greater than yourself, you might use every opportunity to celebrate the gift of life and become the best you can be. How you project your light into the world is up to you."

Akim enjoyed the old man's teachings and his company. He was back in the world where plants talked to him and that suited him perfectly. He soon discovered that people didn't only come to Asteodor to buy furniture, but also to ask for advice on important personal matters. His instincts had been right. Asteodor had a collection of dried plants, stones and animal bones which he used, "to show him the truth and possibilities," as he put it. Many passing travelers from all over the country came to seek advice from Asteodor. Among those who looked beyond appearances, he seemed to have a strong reputation as a skilled and accurate advisor. Akim asked him to teach him the art of reading the omens.

"I will teach you," he said, "but first you have to find your guardian spirit."

"How do I do that?" Akim asked.

"I cannot tell you how to find it. The matter is between you and your guardian spirit. You have to ask it to show itself to you. You have to be open and listen. If you have expectations about the form it will take, it will interfere with communication from your guardian spirit. If you are not sure, ask it to confirm its presence. But when you know that you have received an answer, you have to trust it."

Akim didn't really know what to do with this information, but he put aside one afternoon with the firm intention of finding his guardian spirit. He decided to walk out of the village where he would not be distracted. He set out, not for the woods, but towards the rocky mountains behind the village. The sun was scorching and the path was physically testing, but Akim continued, not quite sure what to look for, but determined to keep his eyes open for the signs.

He climbed the steep side of the first mountain, following the path around it until he got to the other side where the village was out of sight. Here he found some shade. Below him was the most beautiful valley he had ever seen. The rocky terrain gradually made way for more lush plant growth. At the bottom the trees grew dense and he could hear the sound of water and birds singing. On the other side of the river the ground started rising again, forming the steep slope of the opposite mountain which he thought was probably close to a mirror image of the one he was standing on. The cliffs on the opposite side were the same blue as the color of the sky. It felt to Akim like the mountain's stillness was talking directly to his heart, opening up the same stillness inside him. He had the mountain in him. He felt completely at one with its strength, its sturdiness, its quiet endurance of centuries and centuries of raging elements, of all that changed and all that stayed the same. He wanted to move inside the mountain, to become the mountain, and know what it was like to possess that enormous strength.

He didn't feel like walking any more. He searched for a shady place where there was some shelter and he wouldn't be visible from the mountain path. He walked down the side of the mountain until he found an excavation in the rock face that was almost deep enough to be a cave. Right at the entrance there was a large flat rock on which he lay down, still entranced by the beauty of the natural surroundings. He was overcome; he felt a presence almost as strong as the day that he took Metis to the river, this time in the form of beauty and the life of everything in the environment. His entire body was in a drowsy state. It felt like he was floating in the air above him, at one with all the living things around him. He had lost track of time. Eventually, he closed his eyes and gradually crossed the threshold to the sleepy state of the subconscious, where broken parts of the self were encountered and souls roamed free to create according to whim.

He was walking in a path in the woods. It was twilight and the semi-darkness had a substantial quality, almost like there were light particles and dark particles floating in the air at the same time, clouding visibility. The trees had a faint light about them but the forest was quiet otherwise, anticipating, holding its breath. He walked and walked and had the feeling that something was watching him. All the living creatures in the forest were his audience. He walked some more until he reached a golden gate in a black steel frame. The gate had large spikes as one would imagine of an old, spooky house, which meant that he couldn't climb over it. The gate seemed to be an opening in what looked like a wall of trees. The trees were joined at the lower parts of their trunks and their top branches were moving, even though there was no wind. They looked somehow quiet but intimidating, and Akim knew that there was no other way to get past the gate than finding a way to open it.

He walked closer and saw that there was a large bolt at its handle with a keyhole in it. An image of an eagle was engraved on it. He searched his pockets trying to find a key but had no luck. He looked around to see if he could find any clues, but to no avail. He thought of walking back, but behind him the forest had now turned completely dark. The only thing he could see was little pairs of ominous lights appearing in the darkness. Though he couldn't see what was behind those lights, he got the feeling they were sad eyes, watching him with desperation and yet a glimmer of hope. He somehow understood that he didn't want to see the creatures behind the lights as it would open gates to an unknown despair. He felt that their hope depended on him. If he could open the gate successfully, they would find a way out of their entrapment.

He looked up and down the gate. He was stuck. He had no tools available, he couldn't move back and he didn't know how to unlock it in order to move forward. It felt like he had a very important task to fulfill. He had no clues and was very, very afraid that he would be trapped there forever. He shivered, looked down at his feet, looked up into a pitch black sky, and then his eyes came to rest somewhere in the middle again, on the golden engraving of the eagle in the bolt. He remembered what Asteodor had told him about all in the universe being alive. He decided to take a chance and to do what had always came naturally to him: talking to things which to the ordinary eye would seem not to have the ability to communicate. He tried to talk to the gate first, asking it to open for him, but it didn't move or make a sound and neither did he get a response. He then tried to talk to the lock, but before he started, he knew it was in vain. The lock intended to stay ever more firmly shut at any request to be opened.

He looked at the eagle on the bolt and felt something move within his heart. A pair of wings were opening inside him, establishing a line of communication between him and the engraving of the eagle.

"Please, show me the way to open these gates so these people could be free," he said with a voice coming from his heart. The eagle engraving remained static, but he could feel it starting to wake up. Akim kept the line flowing and willed the eagle to awaken, commanding it from the center of his heart through the thread of light flowing between himself and the bolt. In his imagination the eagle image was looking surprised and confused, unwilling to be woken out of its deep sleep and summoned to service. Finally, it started spinning, slowly at first, then faster and faster. Red and white sparks were flying from the bolt of the gate and Akim expected it to fly open at any second. But instead a real life eagle was pushed forth from the golden engraving. It flew out with a majestic spread of its wings, emitting a light that seemed strong enough to set the entire forest on fire. Soon the forest was engulfed by the strong light. The surroundings disappeared and it was only Akim and the eagle. The forest floor had vanished and there was no sign of the daunting gate, the desperate eyes or the intimidating wall. They were floating in what looked like a vacuum of light in the middle of nowhere.

He tried to catch hold of the eagle, afraid that it would fly away and leave him in the vacuum. He managed to grab its wings right above the point where they joined its body. As soon as he touched it, the vacuum made way for visible surroundings again. They were in the air above the mountains where he had fallen asleep, hundreds of meters above the ground. Afraid of falling, he clutched the eagle around its neck and clung for dear life. As he was riding on its back, fear soon gave way to exhilaration. He felt at one with the sky, the sun on his face, the mountains below him, and the river hundreds of meters down. He and the eagle were one. Its strength was his own strength and he was fearless. Its sharp mind was his; a mind that had the ability to focus without wavering on whatever task he set his sight on until it was accomplished. It felt as if the eagle was giving him its life blood, pouring all its qualities into Akim so that he might have a spirit akin to an eagle. Akim felt wide awake and surprised by the magic he seemed to witness and participate in at the same time.

The sky gradually became lighter and lighter until he couldn't see anything but white again. This time he could still feel the wind on his face. He was aware of them moving; the strange sensation of being in a vacuum didn't return. The eagle slowed down and Akim hit the ground. As soon as he landed, they were back at the gate where they had taken off. This time, however, the forest looked different. It was much lighter and it felt friendlier. It was alive with the sound of birdsong and insects. The trees were whispering due to a cool breeze stirring their leaves. There was no sign of the despairing eyes or the creatures they belonged to. The gate was open.

He dismounted the eagle. He went to stand in front of it so he could look into its eyes. He touched its neck and thanked it, once again talking with the voice coming from his heart. There was a pendant around the eagle's neck. Like the river spirit, it spoke to him without audible words, asking him to kneel and look down while doing so. He did as he was told and felt the beak of the eagle touching the top of his head. The pendant that was around its neck dropped down to his own chest with the chain now around his own neck. It was a golden key with an eagle's head engraved on it. Akim looked up and thanked it again. The eagle moved a few yards away and beckoned him to walk through the gate. On the other side of the gate, the forest started clearing, making way for open fields and hills with colorful flowers. Akim walked towards it. As soon as he had passed through the gate, he woke up in his place on the rock where he had fallen asleep earlier the afternoon. The sun was now setting and he had to hurry back to the village before darkness fell.

Chapter 4

Akim was eager to discuss his experience with Asteodor. Although he had succeeded in finding his guardian spirit, he didn't understand the meaning of everything that had happened in his dream. The old man had now become his mentor not only on furniture related matters, but also on things concerning life. A friendship was growing between them. Whenever Akim felt that he needed to talk about something, Asteodor was usually the second person after his mother he would turn to.

The next day while they were having tea, he told Asteodor that he had met his guardian spirit. He asked him if he could now proceed with teaching him the art of reading omens.

"Tell me what your guardian spirit is," he said.

"It's an eagle," answered Akim. Asteodor looked content with his answer. He even seemed slightly amused, as if he had known all along and was surprised that it took Akim so long to figure it out. Akim proceeded to tell him all about the dream he had had, and said that he was confused by the events in the dream. "Does it contain some sort of message that I need to understand?" he asked.

"If you want to understand the language of omens, you have to learn to interpret your dreams. But be careful—if you analyze it too much and assign the meaning of your will to it, the message will come out broken and confused. The more you assign meaning by will, the more distorted the message will be and the less helpful the counsel. If you insist on taking control, the dreams might stop speaking to you. Eventually, nothing will be left but confusion. You have to ask what the dreams mean, intend to understand, and listen. Know that dreams want to talk to you—you only have to allow their message to come through.

"The most important thing to understand is that dreams are not logical. They are disordered; untrue to the waking life that we know. They don't follow rules as far as chronological order of events is concerned. Because of this, they can seem nonsensical. But they are not irrational to the imagination because both speak the same language: the language of symbols. If you judge your dreams using your logical mind, you would fail to understand them, just as you cannot understand the meaning of a song by using a scale to measure it.

"The next thing that you need to know is that dreams give you information. They are the soul's way to express its desires and longings. It's also the way of the subconscious mind to show you where you are on the map of your life.

"Although we might not know it, we create our reality through what we imagine. Understanding the language of dreams will help you release the soul's darkest moments that you no longer wish to influence your reality. The soul will always give you feedback on what you need to heal, but it doesn't end there. Your soul is your most valuable tool to create a meaningful life. If you listen carefully, it will tell you what your highest vision is. It will show you how to be truly happy in a way that would make the world—your world—a better place. You will never get this information with your logical mind, doing the things we do every day to survive in an ordered, structured society. So learn how to listen to what your soul tells you. Be determined to let it sing its song.

"Now take a moment, be quiet and listen to your dream. Allow it to talk to you. Then you can tell me what it tells you, and I will give you my input."

Akim sat for a moment, drifting back to the events in his dream. He felt his anxiety when trapped in front of the gate with the darkness behind him, the eyes on him, the sense of desperation coming from all corners of the forest and the fear when he didn't know the way out. He stopped and focused on the moment when he started talking to the eagle. That was the moment when his predicament turned into opportunity and eventually presented itself as a gift.

"The eagle is there to help me," he said. "But it is not so much the eagle that helped me as it is the fact that I turned for help that saved me. Because I asked, I was able to use my resources to the best of my ability. The eagle is within me, a light that is always there to draw from. When I act from my heart it will give me a way out even in what seems to be the direst of situations. I had the power to help others in my dream. Because I used my gift to help them as well as myself, it transformed reality for me and others, turning a dark place into a gift. The eagle has given me a key that hangs around my neck so I may always remember how to find help when it is needed."

Asteodor smiled. "Not bad," he said. "You might not understand it now, but you have been given the power to lead others to freedom. Listen to the advice of your guardian spirit, but use this power wisely. If you use it foolishly, you will sin against your soul and thereby create your own downfall." He added, "You are now ready to learn the art of reading omens."

He taught Akim the basic principles of this skill. "Omens speak to us in dream language. If you are skilled at understanding dream language, the signs will be clear when you ask for them. You have to use your imagination to understand what the symbols tell you. Each symbol can mean many different things depending on the intent behind the question. The way in which the symbols present themselves in a group will also give you information.

"So how do you make sense of it all? No question will be the same as the last one and no combination of symbols will ever give you the same meaning. If you recite a text book response for every symbol you see when you ask a question, you will never be successful at reading omens. The key is using your intuition. Ask your guardian spirit to help you and listen to your inner voice. The first meaning that comes to mind will usually be the right one. If it is not clear, keep listening to what the omens tell you. Pay attention to the images you see and dream up the meaning."

Asteodor proceeded to teach him different systems of symbols, such as old runes and a set of magical cards dating several centuries back and handed over through tradition. He advised Akim to find his own set of symbols as these would speak to him more clearly having his own imprint on it. Akim had to find these symbols with the help of his guardian spirit and through clearly defining his intent. Other than that Asteodor couldn't give him much advice. A system of symbols created by the reader would carry the mark of the reader himself and would therefore render more accurate information. Because they were a means of communicating with the universe, the reader had to find them by consulting the universe directly. By creating the symbols, the reader poured a little bit of himself into them, thereby strengthening his purpose when asking questions.

As before when attempting to find his guardian spirit, Akim set aside a day to find his own set of symbols. He asked the eagle to help him find the best way to communicate with the universe. The eagle led him to the top of a mountain outside the village where there was a large old oak tree. Akim could feel magic at work and was entranced by it. He could see a shimmering light around the old oak. Between its leaves there were smaller, bright lights which he imagined to be fairies. He walked closer and wanted to move right up to the oak to hug its trunk, but he found that he couldn't move past a certain point. It was as if an invisible barrier was holding him back. He sat down on his knees, bending his head in front of the oak out of respect. He tried to feel if he could move past it but the barrier was still holding him back. Finally, he turned around where he sat for a while taking in the view. He didn't quite know what to do to get beyond this point.

He watched the movement of his shadow as the sun rose in the sky. He started feeling hot and wanted to get some shelter from the sun. He turned around to look at the tree. The shimmering light was now gone and it looked like a normal, very old oak. He remembered what Asteodor had said about the mind being in a dream-like state. From his dreaming mind's eye, the oak had the majestic quality of an old sage. Akim stood up and tried moving closer again. To his surprise he found that he could now move past the barrier. As soon as he had entered inside the space where the barrier hadn't allowed him to go, the air was suddenly refreshingly cool. The coolness had the quality of a liquid, similar to a substantial mass that he was plunging into. It felt incredibly energizing. Continuing from his focused dream state, he imagined talking to the oak, just like when he was a child and talking to the nature spirits. He told it about his quest to find his system of symbols that would help him to receive messages from the universe. He asked if it knew the way and if it would be kind enough to show him.

The dense air mass grew colder and the outside branches started moving slowly, as if the tree was pulling him into itself, hugging him tightly. Looking through the air, it now had the appearance of peering through water. He was relaxing, drifting away from his present surroundings while the branches were pushing him, gently nudging him closer to the trunk. It felt effortless, cool and calm, like being in a womb in the center of the earth. When he reached the trunk, he hugged it and his body stuck against it like a magnet. He felt his consciousness slowly moving through the membrane that was the outside of the tree-trunk. He was now inside the tree. There were stems of different colors moving up and down in channels of light. They were flowing, connecting the earth with the sky in a kaleidoscope of light. He decided that the purple stem was the one to go with and moved into it, letting its flow carry him like a stream. He drifted with it, moving up along the tree trunk. It felt endlessly long, reminding him of a story of a boy named Jack who had magical beans which grew up to a world in the sky. Around him the sky was filled with colors and he could make out the shapes of clouds.

The stream finally ejected him into a sky-world. He was standing on a surface of clouds. There were stars and comets and giant flowers all visible in the sky. Beyond all these things were many more objects floating into an infinite vortex. Everything had an ethereal quality of light and color. He could see different flat levels like the one he was standing on starting higher up, their edges appearing to have blunt ends. This enabled access to the point where the tree trunk joined the sky.

There was a staircase of clouds in front of him. He walked up it and saw that it was leading to the edge of the next level. On reaching it, he walked through a portal where there was a dark-haired woman waiting for him. She was dressed in elegant white robes and gave him a very friendly smile, putting her hands together in a prayer-like gesture of greeting. She took him by the arm and led him across a garden to a tree that looked very much like the one through which he had entered this world. There was a pool of water surrounding it with large orange fishes swimming in it. At the edge of the pool there was a bench. The woman gestured for him to take a seat, so he sat down and waited while she walked away.

She returned bringing a xylophone. Without a word, she told him to play the most beautiful song he could come up with. Akim wanted to protest that he didn't know how to play the xylophone, but remembering his intent, he decided to improvise and let the song come through him. He took a moment to remember the happiest moments of his life and tried to relive them, bringing them back into being through the sound of the xylophone so the dark-haired woman could understand them. He thought of his playful times as a child in the woods, of the warmth he had felt when his mother read him a bedtime story and kissed him goodnight, the day at the river with Metis. He imagined what these memories would sound like when conveyed by the sound of a xylophone. His hands started hitting the keys as if the memories were using them to express their own song. What came out was the most beautiful melody he had ever heard. It was lively, yet soft. It had a life and personality of its own and spoke of the deepest joy a human heart could imagine, but it also contained a hint of sadness at the losses encountered along the way. The song danced its little dance, took him right through to the end and announced its exit by way of a short spurt of lively notes. He could almost imagine the tune making a bow and leaving the stage.

When he had finished, the dark-haired woman clapped her hands, smiling, and took the xylophone from him. She pointed at a part of the sky that was black and starry despite the fact that it was daylight in the garden. Akim could see a tiny speck in the sky that grew in size. Soon it didn't look like a single object any more, but a cluster resembling a flock of small birds. Closer and closer they came until he could see that they were bubbles floating in their direction. They were moving as if in a bundle, seemingly chaotic yet sticking closely together. When they were only a few meters away, they lined up to form a neat row. They were probably a bit smaller than the size of Akim's head and they had tiny objects inside them.

The line stopped and only the first bubble kept moving forward until it was right in front of Akim at eye height. He could see the object inside it: it was a small, round stone with a sign painted on it. Akim looked at the sign, dreaming into it as Asteodor had taught him to. It came alive and transformed itself into a man riding a horse, creating scenes in the bubble to tell Akim a story of its own. As soon as he felt that he had grasped the meaning of the story, the scene turned itself back into a painting on a pebble. The bubble moved on and came to a halt on the other side of Akim where it waited for the other bubbles.

One by one the bubbles moved past Akim and told their story. There was a leaf floating down a river, a flower enduring an onslaught of the elements, an acorn that was the seed that could grow under the right conditions, a fairy with a magic wand, a cloud that promised a lot of rain and many others. Akim watched every story carefully and made mental notes, focusing until he felt that their meaning was etched into his consciousness. When the last bubble had finished presenting its meaning, the dark-haired woman took out a small velvet bag from her pocket. She opened it and held it out to the bubbles, commanding them with her eyes. In a flash that made the bubbles burst, the small stones gathered together and threw themselves into the bag. The woman looked satisfied. She neatly closed and folded the bag and handed it to Akim. He accepted it with grace and thanked her, upon which she took him by the arm and escorted him back to the edge where he descended the staircase of clouds.

Holding the bag tightly to his chest, he walked down the stairs until he reached the column of light that was his way back. He decided to take the green light this time and walked right into it, floating all the way down. He passed through the membrane and was back on the ground, his body leaning heavily against the tree trunk. The branches that were pulled in around the trunk retracted to their normal position. The air was losing its dense coolness as the stifling heat made its way into the shade, creeping up from his feet and spreading across his body like a plant growing up a tree. For a moment Akim expected to see the bag clutched to his chest. Since there was nothing, he knew what he had to do.

On his way home, he collected small pebbles that were closest in shape, size and color to the ones he had received inside the trunk of the tree. The eagle showed him where he could find useful stones along the way, directing his attention to the pebbles that contained the strongest magic. Back at home, he found an old can of dark green paint formerly used to paint the chair on the porch of their home. He sat and recalled the story of each sign while carefully painting it on the pebble, all the time working from a dream-like state. He poured life into the pebbles, infusing them with the meaning of each story. In that way they would be the doorway to get information from the world of the unseen.

When he had finished painting, he put the pebbles outside in the sun in a place where they wouldn't be seen by anyone. He asked the sun to bless the stones with its light and left the pebbles to dry. When night came, he asked the moon to share its energy with the little stones so they may have within them a guiding light in the darkness. The following morning the pebbles were ready; all he now needed to do was prepare a bag.

He found an old piece of velvet among the materials his mother used to make clothes and washed it in a stream coming from the mountains. When it was dry, he held the cloth in the smoke of burning herbs. He then borrowed needle and thread from his mother and carefully sewed a bag that would be just the right size to contain all the pebbles. He blessed the bag with the help of the eagle and asked it to keep his symbols safe. His tools were now ready and all he needed to do was get used to working with them.

He started by asking them simple questions on inconsequential matters and listening for feedback, sometimes applying it in the real world and testing the outcome. It didn't take long before he was very skilled at reading omens. Even Asteodor was impressed when he asked him to do a reading. On occasions when Asteodor was not available to see people who came to ask him for advice, he referred them to Akim. Akim soon had a reasonable reputation as a reader among those who believed in it, although many people still didn't take him seriously because of his young age.

One day while they were busy making furniture, a woman came into the workshop and said that she urgently needed help. Asteodor was busy working on a table for a client and didn't seem to be in a mood to deal with people anyway, so he told the woman to speak to Akim. The woman's face was mostly covered by a cloth, but by the expression in her eyes he could see that she was distressed. She told him that her five year old daughter was very, very ill. The local doctor had diagnosed her with flu and didn't seem to think that it was anything serious. He had simply prescribed some rest and said that she would be up and running again in a few days. But her mother's instinct told her that something needed to be done. If they didn't act quickly, her daughter's life could be in danger.

Akim consulted his symbols and the woman was right; the prospects didn't look good. Akim didn't quite know what to do. He asked the woman where she lived and said that he would come to see what could be done for her daughter. He then told her to go home and wait for him while he prepared. He went outside, deeply troubled by the images he saw in the symbols and the woman's anguish. He sat on a rock facing the mountain and prayed. He asked the eagle to assist him. He asked the mountain for its strength and then asked the sun, moon and stars for their healing light. He asked the woman he had encountered in the sky world to guide him. Then he set off to find herbs that would heal the girl.

When he had found the right plants, he went to the woman's house. Upon entering the room where the girl lay, he could feel that something wasn't right. She was pale as death with red blotches in her neck. She was sweating and crying and her eyes looked feverish. She looked at him begging for help. He could see that she was in a lot of pain.

He asked the mother to bring him a dish of cold water and a jug of hot water. He prepared an herb mixture in the cold water and added other plants to the hot water. He soaked a cloth in the first mixture and wiped the girl's face and body with it. He then asked her to drink the second mixture. She resisted at first, but he lifted her to a sitting position and held the cup to her lips. He gently put his arm around her shoulders and asked her quietly to try her best to drink it all up. She seemed too tired to resist and proceeded to drink the contents of the cup. A few minutes passed while he waited to see if she would show a reaction. He held his hands a few inches above her body, all the time praying and sending healing light into her body through his hands. He could sense that there was some sort of obstruction in her abdomen, right below her ribcage. To the eye of his intuition it looked like a large, hairy spider.

Asking the eagle for protection, he caught the spider by its hairy body and pulled it out. He threw it to the mountain and asked the mountain to take care of it. He placed some fresh herbs on her body at the spot where he had pulled out the spider. He prayed some more for her healing. In his mind's eye he watched while a shimmering light filled the spot that was left empty by the spider. He let his hands pass over her body in the air one more time until he felt that her energy was restored. When he felt that he had done enough and that the girl would recover well, he slipped back to normal consciousness from his dream-like state. He was exhausted.

He looked at the little girl. She had fallen asleep and now looked peaceful. He touched her forehead with his hand; her temperature felt normal. He thanked the eagle and all the other entities that have helped him. After sprinkling the remaining herbs on the floor, he asked the mother to burn a candle in the room every evening, praying for the girl's healing and protection. The woman still looked drained with worry, but she thanked him and he could see some hope in her eyes.

Akim was distraught for a few days. He knew that he had done what he could and tried his best, but he also felt that he had had no idea what he was doing. So far he hadn't had any news of the girl. Her begging eyes and the mother's agony still haunted him. He felt that he wouldn't be able to relax until he knew that she was all right. A few days later while he was working on an armchair, he found relief for his troubled state of mind. The woman appeared in the doorway and she was smiling. In her arms she was carrying a basket. She knocked and entered without waiting for an invitation to come in. She put down the basket and threw her arms around Akim in a big hug.

"I don't know how to thank you," she said. "My daughter is well again and it's all thanks to you. After your visit, she needed a few days to rest where she slept quietly without any crying or pain. She is now well again and has almost forgotten about her illness. Can you believe it?" She let out a laugh. "I have brought you a gift from myself, my husband and my daughter. Although it doesn't come close to representing the gratitude that I feel, I hope that we can repay you some day." She handed over the basket. It contained a bunch of shiny, red, delicious looking apples. He accepted it with gratitude while he felt his spirits lifting. He was almost as excited about the news as the woman looked happy. She left and for the rest of the day Akim felt a sense of purpose. The experience had confirmed that he was on the right track.

What Akim didn't know was that the woman's husband was the king's messenger and that they were very good friends. The woman had covered most of her face when coming to visit because she was afraid the women of the town would see her and gossip—it wasn't customary for a woman of her standing to consult witchdoctors. However, on returning she didn't care and neither did her husband. He knew that the king, although sometimes stubborn, was fairly open-minded and didn't have anything to pretend, being a king. He also knew that the king would consider any means to achieve the best results and generally didn't base his judgment on preconceived notions, but rather on merit. He spoke to the king about the possibility of getting advice from unconventional sources. He thought that this might help the king when making complex decisions in the same way that it had helped his family. He also reasoned that if the king decided to use Akim's services, it might be a very good opportunity for Akim as the king would probably offer good compensation. This turn of events marked the start of a new chapter in Akim's life.

Chapter 5

A traveler on a horse came by the two carpenters' working hut one day. He asked if he could speak to Akim and gave him a letter. He said that the king wanted to see him. The letter was a personal invitation from the king himself. It contained the following message:

Dear Akim

I believe that you possess the power of prophecy and are a skilled reader of omens. Although at this stage I still have a neutral disposition towards the value of the skill, I could do with advice on some matters, especially as far as strategy is concerned. I hereby invite you to come and see me at your earliest convenience to discuss the possibility of putting your talents to use in the King's service.

Regards,
The King

Akim wasn't sure whether it was an order or a request, but he told the messenger that he would be able to see the king in the next ten days and asked if transport could be arranged. The man said that he would be picked up five days later and with that he left.

Akim went to share the news with his mother, who was both excited and surprised. She hugged him and wished him the best of luck. She also said that if the king did anything to harm her son or make him unhappy, she would personally see to his downfall—she didn't care whether he was the king or not.

A horse carriage arrived on the appointed day and Akim got in, taking a small bag that contained what was needed for a few days as well as his bag of symbols. He was nervous; he didn't quite know what to expect. He resolved to keep an open mind and if the king asked anything that he wasn't willing to agree to, he would refuse as politely as possible. The omens looked fairly positive—they showed new and fresh possibilities, but also a warning. Akim didn't get too much information on the warning, but he intuitively understood that he had to be very careful to remain true to himself and honest to others if he wanted to avoid falling into the trap of people pleasing. The king was, after all, just a ruler who probably also had his frustrations and secret yearnings. That was his role in the greater scheme of things just like Akim had his own place and a destiny that was unfolding every day. He would treat the king with the respect he deserved, but would also remember that he was a person like himself.

The journey was monotonous as Akim wasn't used to sitting still for so long. He shared the carriage with the man who had originally come to deliver the message. The man didn't talk much, which suited Akim because he wasn't in the mood for small talk, either. However, the silence was uncomfortable at times and he wished he had had a companion who was also his friend. He was seeing many new parts of the country that were unfamiliar to him and it would have been nice to have someone to share the experience with.

They stayed over at an inn where the inn-keepers had the same temperament as his fellow traveler. His companion informed him that they were only about three hours away from the palace. They set out early the next morning when the sky was an orange pink color but the sun had not shown its face yet. The landscape was changing. Instead of dense forests and rocky mountains, they were now seeing rolling green hills with occasional clusters of woods. The houses were becoming more frequent and soon they were in the city. They took a few turns until they were on a road leading up to the palace gates. Akim could see that this was where the rich lived. The streets were wide and clean and the houses tall and imposing. There were gardens with fountains and the shop windows displayed the finest quality merchandise. The palace gates were large and shiny. Inside the grounds were the most beautiful gardens he had ever seen.

His companion gave the palace guards a signal, upon which the gates were opened and they could enter. The road continued through the gardens until they reached the palace. There were two massive doors flanked by guards on each side. They recognized Akim's companion and opened the door for them. They entered a courtyard, after which they went through another door and walked through another courtyard. On the opposite side of the second courtyard there was a smaller door in the middle with another guard at its side. The guard opened for them and Akim's companion led them inside. Akim had expected to see some great hall, but the room was fairly small and looked very official, even boring. There was a single table in the middle with a few simple chairs around it. That was all. Akim's fellow traveler asked him to wait until he received further instructions. Akim expected him to be away for a few minutes, but only after what felt like hours did he return with the king by his side.

The king welcomed him with a smile and a handshake before Akim could even ponder whether he had to bow down or greet him with some other formal gesture. To his surprise he didn't find the king intimidating at all. He was fairly friendly and appeared agitated, like a nervous person who was afraid he might drop the ball somewhere. He looked like he didn't have a lot of time. He gestured for Akim's travel companion to leave the room.

He asked Akim to tell him more about himself. So Akim told him where he came from, that he had a mother and no other family that he was aware of and that he was a carpenter who loved nature. He didn't know what else to say. The king asked him a few more questions on his political views. Akim answered as best he could, although he didn't really have an answer in most instances. He made it fairly clear that he was not interested in any sort of military activities and that he didn't really have an opinion otherwise, as long as the country prospered and the people were happy. He also indicated that as far as matters of reigning were concerned, he held one strong belief: peace was important above all and only in exceptionally dire circumstances should there be a resort to war. These circumstances would be of such a nature that war was absolutely the only way to return to and maintain peace. The king seemed satisfied by his answers and Akim understood that he wasn't a man of war. Although there were occasional military excursions, mostly on the defensive side, he generally reigned in peace.

The king then told him about the matter that he needed advice on. There was a dispute about a river that flowed through a canyon, forming the border between their country and a neighboring one. There was a general agreement between countries that river borders were treated with respect from both sides. Although people were free to use them for purposes of travelling by boat or swimming, most rulers discouraged any sort of activity that directed too much traffic to these rivers. This was for two reasons: the first being that it would become a nightmare to monitor who crossed the border and the second being the question of who made decisions on any river activity that might require regulation, such as commercial fishing. The monarch in question wanted to turn the river into a sporting terrain for his people. The king wasn't in favor of this as the canyon was a source of rich wildlife that would be disturbed by too much activity. It was also the home of a tribe that were the unofficial guardians of this area. They fulfilled an important role in the protection of the country's natural heritage and the king wished to pay them due respect. He also knew that the canyon was sacred to them and saw it as part of his regal duties to protect their rights.

Neither ruler was interested in taking up arms, but both wanted to have their way. Since the dispute fell outside the boundaries of normal rules and regulations, they had to find an alternative means to solve it. They had agreed to have a contest and the ruler who would walk out the winner would have the final say in what happened to the river. After much deliberation, it had been decided that they would play a game of chess. The other ruler was a very good chess player so he was keen to bargain in this way. The king himself wasn't too confident but was hoping that with proper preparation and the right mind-set he might stand a very good chance. What he wanted to know from Akim was what the best way to approach the match would be to give him the optimum chance of winning.

Akim carefully laid out his symbols in the right configuration and asked them to reveal their wisdom. The first thing they showed him was that the king's intention was sincere. Next they gave him information about the tribe: they were courageous people who worshipped the land. The canyon was as much part of them as their own bodies. Their souls were rooted in its soil and the river could have been their life blood. To defile it in any way would be akin to poisoning them or cutting off a limb. He could also see that while the king might not be aware of this, they played an important part in the maintenance of peace and the well-being of the country's people. Their will to protect what was sacred to them created a positive energy that lifted many people's spirits. Akim had no doubt that it was important that the king won this contest, not only to the king himself, but also for the greater good.

The symbols started telling him about the nature of the other ruler: he was capricious, fiery and in a way deadly. Not that he was specifically dangerous, but when he set his mind to something he normally went for the kill. It didn't mean that what he set his mind to had to be anything of particular importance. It could be based on whim and the desire to make his mark. He did have a weakness, though. He tended to place excessive value on self-importance and was unnerved easily when faced with uncertainty. The symbols told Akim that the best way to handle this ruler was to surprise him in some way and when he became unnerved, to play conservatively and let him fight to regain control. In this way his killer instinct would be maneuvered and he would steer towards impulsiveness.

The king looked satisfied that Akim had correctly detected the nature of the other ruler. He then asked Akim how he could surprise the man. Akim consulted his stones again and advised the king to act in a way that wasn't normal for him. He had to dress in unusual clothes and think of a role that was completely different from his normal persona. He had to imagine himself to be that character, pretending so hard that he believed himself to be another person. He needed to lose his inhibitions and be so focused that he would fail to notice his servants' reactions to his strange behavior. Playing the role was even more important than hoodwinking his opponent through the game of chess itself. This would imply playing chess like the assumed persona would play, thinking with the unfamiliar character's mind. All the time he had to wait carefully for an opportunity to present itself. When it did, he had to move in and win fast before the other ruler could regain his composure.

The king thanked him and asked him to be a witness at the match which would take place three days later. Each side could allow up to five witnesses so Akim accepted, grateful for the opportunity. He was eager to see the outcome. The king then discussed with him payment for the consultation and the trip to the palace. It was more than Akim had hoped for. He took Akim to a room on the left flank of the palace; it would be his room for the duration of his stay. The room was simple yet elegant. He could see that it was intended for the use of the king's guests, albeit not the most important ones. Although he missed his room at home that contained all the special objects he collected, he felt at ease in the allocated room. It had large windows that looked out on the beautiful gardens. A lot of sunlight and fresh air flowed in.

Akim didn't know what to do with himself for the next two days. Although he felt comfortable in the room the king had given him, he didn't know the ins and the outs of the palace. He would have liked to walk around to explore the building, but he couldn't quite shake the fear of walking into someone who would ask him what he was doing, in which case he would have no answer. He was afraid that someone would think he was prying and tell the king that his guest was up to no good. In short, he still felt like an intruder in the palace whenever he was outside his designated room. Since he started feeling claustrophobic when spending too much time indoors, he resorted to the palace gardens. They were exquisite and it was an adventure to explore them. He imagined that he could see the characters of old fairy tales lurking in the shadows. The trees were wise and strong. They told him about all they had seen in the palace gardens and he was mesmerized by their stories.

In the evening he had dinner with the king and other palace guests. During dinner he tried to act invisible while observing what was going on around the table. The king's family was not present and it seemed that most of the people around the table were official guests or assistants to the king. Since Akim didn't know what to expect, he was very nervous during these dinners. However, he soon realized that the king and his entourage acted much like normal people, only they were very business-like. They seemed distracted most of the time, as if their minds were in another place with the hordes of things they were worried about. They talked mostly about matters that needed attention. Akim was surprised to find that they had no particular air of self-importance. They were simply formal and concise with the crisp efficiency of people wanting to get things done.

The king's guests, on the other hand, were a mixed bunch. Some of them were really quiet and reserved like himself; they were mainly the ones who didn't look rich or important. A few others behaved in the same way as the king and his assistants. There were also guests who Akim thought acted very strangely. Some of them were dressed in elaborate clothes. The women's faces were heavily painted, making it hard to discern their natural features. These guests were talking loudly, evidently in competition for being the king's most important visitor. Most of the things they said sounded like an effort to appear distinguished. Akim didn't know who these people were, but his guess was that they were rich people whose dealings involved the consent of the king in some way or another.

There was one boy who appeared uninvolved and very bored. He looked about ten years old and wasn't accompanied by an adult. He was very skinny with large brown eyes and brown hair. He wore a white shirt, brown trousers, shoes and an old brown jacket. Akim watched, amused, as he ate his food without paying the slightest attention to anyone else. The boy looked like an adult in the company of children. When one of the guests asked him something, he politely answered the question and returned to eating. Akim could almost see him inwardly rolling his eyes. The boy seemed to become aware that someone was watching him. He looked up and caught Akim's eyes. Akim didn't look away. He expected to be greeted by the same reaction of ennui, but the boy held his gaze for a moment and Akim thought he could see a flicker of interest in his eyes. Then he felt that the boy was talking to him through his eyes without moving his lips.

"What are you doing here?" the boy asked. Since Akim received the question in his mind, he answered it in the same way, his eyes still connected to the boy's.

"I am here to advise the king. How about you?" he asked in return.

"I have given the king some lessons," he answered.

Akim smiled and for the first time he could see traces of a facial expression other than boredom in the boy's face. He smiled back.

"Lessons in what?" Akim asked.

"The king wanted to know how to play chess," he answered.

"I think our duties are very similar," Akim said. "Will you be a witness at the match?"

"Yes," the boy answered. "But I am under strict instructions to stay very still and not make eye contact with the king, in case I give him some sort of sign. Who are you?" The boy asked.

"My name is Akim. And you?"

"Samuel. I have seen you walking around in the gardens today. If you want to we can meet sometime tomorrow? If you look for the fountains I am sure you will be able to find me."

Akim was glad for the prospect of some company. He told the boy that he would be out in the gardens in the morning and that he would try to find him. Dinner came to an end and the guests and the king all scattered as fast as lightning. Akim didn't know what else to do so he retired to his room where he sat watching the stars and the garden in moonlight. A few shooting stars caught his attention and he wondered if it would be worthwhile to make a wish. He looked at the city lights and imagined the people behind them. In his head they were all warm and comfortable, fulfilling their citizen's duties and participating in the structure of this great city. The women enjoyed taking care of the children and the men loved their competitive jobs where they had the opportunity to make their mark. They rejoiced in the security of their homes and the protection the government offered. They lived in a prosperous country and for them that was enough, as long as they could go through each phase of life without too much disruption. "Why can't I be like them?" Akim wondered. "Why does the 'real world' make me feel trapped? I don't understand why I feel so drained when going through the motions that most others willingly embrace. Why isn't being comfortable enough for me?"

He sighed. Normal sounded flat and lifeless. The mere resonance of the word made him want to yawn first and then run away to a faraway world where magic prevailed and where he was free to create and try new things until he hit the mark. He didn't actually care if he failed a million times or about what the end product would look like. He cared about having the freedom to apply his efforts as he chose to, because that was when his spirit felt most alive. He didn't even want to be free to do nothing. Doing nothing would just generate the same quality of emptiness that would result if he forgot everything he cared about in favor of falling in line, doing what was necessary to make society function well. He didn't need to always be happy in the sense of the absence of things going wrong. He didn't care that much if things went wrong a million times along the way. What he cared about was maintaining his resilience, remaining spirited despite the odds. Even if he had suffered so much that he would lose all his faith, even if his body were battered and bruised, he wanted to come back with a vengeance and claim the joy that he believed in. Light was stronger when it kept shining despite having known the depths of darkness. It wasn't about preserving himself. He wanted to know the light of joy that was beyond the reach of suffering that could extinguish it.

"Who am I?" He asked the stars.

"You are one of a kind," they answered.

"That is no answer," he thought. But since he had seen shooting stars he might as well express a wish. So he asked to be led to a magical place where he could find out who he was and where he came from. What or where the magical place was he couldn't say. The stars would have cast their eye on it at some point or another so they would have to show him the way. He imagined a pair of giant eyes blinking at him from the sky. Then he drew his curtains and went to bed.

Chapter 6

The next day was the day he would meet the curious boy, Samuel, in the garden. He found him at one of the fountains, sitting in the sun with his head hunched over a book. He was dressed almost entirely in brown again, with a neat white shirt showing from underneath his jacket. His hair was combed neatly to one side and he was wearing glasses while reading. He looked up from his book, seemingly without the need to squint in the sun. Akim tried to see what he was reading. The page he was on contained drawings of what looked like celestial bodies with diagrams around them. A few strange creatures appeared here and there. Samuel didn't seem to mind Akim seeing the pictures, but he politely closed his book and put it aside.

"I'm glad you came," he said. His eyes showed interest and were completely different from the expression of boredom that he wore the previous night. Akim sat down next to him, unsure of what to say. They sat in silence for a little while, watching the fishes in the pond around the fountain. The sound of birds eased the initial lack of conversation. Soon Akim felt very relaxed, with the sun gently stroking his hair and the birdsong lifting his spirits. There were a few gardeners working and most of them looked very happy tending to the plants.

Samuel didn't seem inclined to make small talk. When he did speak, he gave the impression of not wanting to waste energy on unnecessary conversation.

"You are the first person I have ever met that I can talk to without using my voice or mouth," he said.

Akim explained that he didn't have the habit of talking or listening to people through their eyes. It was the first time it had happened to him, at least as far as people were concerned. Samuel asked if he could talk to spirits. Akim said that he could, but it happened in a different way, not through his head like the conversation they had had the previous night, but through his heart.

Samuel said that he had tried talking to spirits before, but he had never been successful. With people it was a different matter. He could hear what was going on in their heads, more so when they were focused. Most of the time they were so scattered, though, that he only heard rambling. Akim asked if that was why he was so good at playing chess. He answered that it had been the reason initially and that listening to his opponent's thoughts had helped him to learn really fast. However, he could switch off from tuning into people's minds and that was how he preferred to play chess, not only because it was fair, but also because it was a greater challenge. He said it was good to meet someone else who was also one of a kind. Although he would love to learn how to talk to spirits, it wasn't part and package of his gift. He doubted that he would ever be successful.

Samuel asked Akim where he was from, and Akim responded that he lived in Silvidere. Samuel then said that he was talking about his home in the stars. He wanted to know whether Akim originally came from another constellation. Akim said that if he did, he wasn't aware of it. He didn't know what the boy was talking about, but he thought of how much he loved the earth and nature. He didn't quite feel at home on it, but he felt very much connected to it.

Sometimes he imagined that he had been called to awaken the sacred in a time that earthlings were profoundly disconnected from their planet. They saw it as a dead mass of rock and soil with some hot liquid inside that occasionally exploded here and there. It was an object that had randomly been spewed out from space. Although millions of organisms could live on it, because it happened to be the right temperature and contained water, it served no other purpose than to provide a solid platform under people's feet. In the view of most earthlings, the primary reason for their existence was to procreate, ensuring the survival of the species. The earth was there for them to take advantage of its resources. Since humans were the most intelligent species alive, they were naturally placed at the apex of the pyramid, not creation, because creation would imply something sacred, a Source. This fact put them in the privileged and rightful position of knowing how to extirpate the planet, taking what they could to enrich themselves. Why else would they have faculties that no other species alive on earth had? It was their right by birth. Akim shook his head. No, he didn't feel at home among the earth dwellers. Nonetheless, he cared more about the planet than its other inhabitants of his kind who apparently did feel at home.

Samuel looked almost disappointed. Then he told Akim that although he had been born as a human child almost eleven years earlier, his real home was far, far away. He was old and could remember a lot about where he came from, but he didn't really know why he was on earth. It was as if he had to learn or remember something in order to find his way back. He felt alienated and lonely on earth. Although he had read about a few like himself who came to earth, but wasn't from the earth, they were few and far between. He was a mystery even to his own parents who loved him very much but didn't know how to cope with his peculiarity. Akim felt a surge of compassion for this old soul in the alien body of a young boy. Even though Samuel's body language spoke of resignation to his fate, his eyes were filled with despair.

"I sometimes wonder if I am making it all up to justify the fact that I don't fit in," he said. "But I remember. I do! I see the same purple-green ocean in my dreams that doesn't look anything like the ocean here, the same people who I know are not human, the same volcanic mountain that I know has the answer to my destiny and entrapment. But there is a certain point that I never get past. It always ends where I stare at the mountain from the beach, knowing there is something inside that can reveal the secrets I need to know. I never find out what it is. I always wake up when I am about to remember." His eyes were now on the ground in front of him. Although his facial expression was calm, Akim knew that there was a storm raging inside him. He wanted to comfort Samuel, but he didn't know how.

"You're not making it up," he said, and he knew it to be true. Somewhere deep within him he was sure that this place existed. There was a reason why Samuel was there, even though it might not be known to him yet. "But you don't have to worry, you will get back there eventually."

"How do you know?" Samuel asked.

"My guardian spirit has given me the information," Akim answered, for lack of a better explanation. It didn't look like the information had lifted Samuel's spirits.

"Can you help me to find my way back?" he asked.

"I cannot," Akim answered. "You will have to find your own way back. But I might be able to find some information that could make your journey easier. I will ask. If the spirits want me to pass this information on to you, it will be revealed to me. If not, I will just give you a blessing. I will meet you again tomorrow to tell you about my progress, or lack thereof."

Samuel looked a little bit lighter. He was reassured by the fact that someone acknowledged his experience as real. He thanked Akim and returned to his reading, to which Akim left and resumed his stroll in the garden.

Akim walked down the flank of the palace where his room was and past the part of the garden that he could see from his window. He walked in the same direction until he reached a hedge which prevented him from walking further. He turned away from the palace and walked along the hedge, lost in thought. He didn't notice where he was going, but at some point the hedge had an opening to a path that was bordered by more thick hedges, resembling the entrance to a maze. He stepped on the path, still not paying attention to where he was going. The path continued for quite some time before it finally ejected him into a new section of the garden. Looking back, he couldn't see the palace at all, only thick hedges and blue skies. He wasn't sure why that could be. It was probably because he had strolled too far off, or maybe the hedges were just too high.

In front of him was a giant tree with large, bright red fruit. The rest of the garden was beautiful, but these fruits fascinated him. He walked closer until he was standing under the tree. Was it an apple tree? He couldn't really tell. The fruits looked similar to apples but they were larger and their color was a much deeper red. The skin of the fruit had an undertone of gold that shone through the red in the sunlight. He put his hand out to pluck one, but stopped in mid-air. Something told him not to. He slowly dropped his hand. He stared at the fruit, still mesmerized by its color and shine. He yearned to remove one from the tree and take a bite. But he felt that if he did that, he would be violating something sacred. It came to his attention that there was something in the tree. He wasn't alone after all.

He looked at the trunk of the tree. It was a rich golden color with pale green patches. The bark started moving, spiraling up as it appeared to be a cylinder form curled around the trunk like a spring. The movement was strong yet smooth. It wasn't the bark after all, but a gigantic serpent. It unfurled itself, moving up the tree to the branches. It pushed its massive body along one of the branches that was closest to him. It came closer, seemingly curious, scrutinizing him to find out who he was and what he wanted. Although everything about the snake was imposing and magnificent, Akim was awed rather than afraid. He felt that he needed to show deferential respect rather than flee. The snake seemed to have found out what it wanted to know so it dropped its head to Akim's level, then a bit lower before it started rising again, following the loop with the rest of its body to form a coil. Its head dropped again and gently nudged Akim forward into the coil so he was in a sitting position. The serpent pulled him up until he was in the tree, still holding onto its body. It wrapped itself around him loosely once or twice so he would sit comfortably without being afraid of falling. Its head was right in front of Akim; it was watching him.

He felt that the snake was gentle. She was assessing him softly, not only with her eyes, but she was using her entire body to probe into his heart, feeling his vibration through her skin. He imagined that she wanted to know that his spirit was sincere before teaching him about the secrets of the tree. If he didn't pass the test, he had no doubt that she would expel him violently from the garden, but without hurting him. She finally seemed satisfied as she spoke to him in a melodious voice that he could hear in his mind as clearly as if detected by his ears.

"What brings you here, young warrior?" she asked.

"A friend of mine is looking for help. I would like to bring him a gift that would ease his suffering," he answered.

"Your request will be granted," she said. She lowered him to the ground and ordered him to repeat his message to the tree. He had to stay there and wait until the doors were opened. He didn't know where the doors were, but he remembered his experience on the mountain on the day he found his symbols. He imagined the columns of light flowing through this tree as it had flowed through the old oak. He knew that the tree was intelligent, so he spoke to its source: the energy flowing through the trunk into the branches, giving life to those beautiful fruit. He thought of Samuel and the despair in his eyes. Turning his attention back to the tree, he asked it to give him what was needed to help Samuel on his journey. He could sense a golden sliver of the tree's essence moving from the trunk along the branch to the closest hanging fruit right above him. When the sliver reached the fruit, it was cut loose from the tree and landed in the soft ground right in front of Akim. He knew better than to touch it immediately, so he asked the tree how it could be used. The tree answered that the fruit was now on its own and that it had been ordained the task of helping him find what he needed. He had to speak to the fruit itself and allow it to guide him.

Akim sat down next to the apple, still not touching it. He looked at its shiny hue that was now more golden than deep red. It became like a mirror that he could see into, showing him images in the reflection of the light on its skin. The images became larger, turning into a reflective mirage looming above the fruit. They were becoming more real than his physical surroundings, until eventually he was pulled into what he was seeing. He felt a strong wind on his face and everything in front of his eyes was blurring for a few seconds. Next he hit the ground hard as he entered another world, one that was completely different from the one he lived in.

Chapter 7

The first thing he noticed was the arid ground. It was completely parched with cracks, yet it looked clay-like, as if it had been wet the day before. He was on a colossal plain that stretched out for miles on end. Looming far in the distance he could make out the shape of mountains on all sides almost blending with the sky. The plain was largely devoid of vegetation; the vast emptiness was only interrupted close to the mountains where he could see some covering of a dark greenish blue color. The mountains in the direction he was facing were closer than those on any other side. Above them there was a round yellow orb hanging in the sky. It was larger, brighter, and yellower than the moon he was used to and yet it was far milder than the sun he knew. Around it the sky spread out in a reddish brown color. It had a peculiar quality, almost as if it had texture.

Where the brownish textured glow around the orb began to dim into the thick greyness of the rest of the sky, there were little sparks that looked like stars, except they were of the same color and intensity as the orb. It was twilight, not quite day and not quite night. The yellow orb didn't cast a defined shadow behind him, either. The atmosphere of the place was entirely unknown. He felt a strange sensation that it was cold and windy, yet he didn't feel wind blowing. Temperature was almost absent, if slightly cool. The air had a heavy quality, yet not completely dense and liquid like the day he was in the space of the oak tree. Rather, he imagined that if he would speak, the sound of his voice would be loud and echoing and it would take some time to reach a recipient who didn't stand too far away. His feet also felt a lot heavier on the ground than on the earth he knew.

Again he looked up at the orb and the curious circle around it. There was a dust-colored trickle coming from the highest of the mountains below the orb. He guessed that that was what caused the texture in the sky. Was it the volcanic mountain that Samuel had told him about? He wanted to go closer, to find out the secret that was inside that could help Samuel. The mere thought of wanting to know propelled him forward again through a wind tunnel. He was vaguely aware of his surroundings rushing past but it was all blurred. He could only see the mountain with the orb hanging above it. When he stopped, he was right at the foot of the mountain. The twilight quality of the air was deeper, the color browner. The most notable difference between where he was standing now and his former location was the amount of life around him. He was now standing at the edge of a forest. The trees mostly wore leaves of a bluish green color with a purple one here and there. Their barks were silver and bronze rather than brown. He could hear strange sounds of birdsong coming from the trees. It sounded loud and echoing, almost artificial.

The mountain rose up in front of him. Where the flat surface of the ground he was on started slanting, the forest stopped abruptly. The mountainside looked naked; the soil as parched as the ground on the plain. He walked a short distance in the direction of the mountain until he reached a clearing covered with grass and a few small shrubs. The forest was behind him and only two trees on the other side of the clearing were between him and the foot of the mountain. The trees were very tall, very upright; their tops stood out among the smaller surrounding trees. Their leaves were massive and had pink patches on the bluish green leaves. What was even more peculiar about them was the fact that they looked symmetrical. At the bottom, right between the two trees, was a large, rectangular object which looked like something that was built.

He walked closer. The object was built of stones and cemented into the ground. It was about knee-height and in the length it was a bit shorter than the length of his body, with the width about half the length. On top of it was a raised edge of stones that surrounded a marble slab with engravings that he didn't understand. At the top there was text that looked like runes, seemingly forming a few short words. The rest of the slab had drawings on it very similar to the one he had seen in Samuel's book. There was a sun-like figure with a broken slanting line coming out of it and two solid, perpendicular, straight lines forming angles with the slanting line and the sun. Was it some sort of map? The sun was in the top right hand corner. Outside the shape of the line construction were different figures, some of which looked peaceful and others that looked aggressive. Akim didn't understand at all; the only thing he knew was that this held the answer to why Samuel was no longer part of this world. He tried to read the symbols the way he normally read them back on earth, but to no avail. They didn't transform to life in order to give him information. Instead, they remained flat, meaningless markings on a piece of stone.

He knew instinctively that Samuel would be able to understand this language, but the doors wouldn't open to him no matter how hard he tried, in the same way that Samuel couldn't talk to spirits, although he could listen to people's minds. There had to be a way, he thought. Their gifts connected somewhere, which was why he could talk to Samuel across a table with many other people using only his eyes. His gift of being able to communicate with spirits was also what brought him here, in search of help for Samuel. He looked at the altar thing again.

Although he couldn't bring the engravings to represent meaning by imagining them to be alive, he might as well try talking to the altar itself. He gently put his hand on the stone edge on top. He then looked at the engravings and looked past them, deeper, into the body of the altar. He imagined that there was an essence inside, slumbering, waiting for him to wake it up. He softly told it why he was there and asked it to awaken and tell him how he could help Samuel. He continued repeating his request softly, like a mantra, all the time willing the essence to wake up and speak to him. Eventually he got tired and was about to give up when he heard a rumbling inside the mountain. It was a deep, thunderous growling, halfway between anger and sorrow.

The writing on the altar came alive. It was burning, flaming yellow with an intense, liquid light. A cloud of smoke exploded from the top of the mountain, making the sky even browner. The script was now dancing with life and the meaning came to him:

"You are now on the sacred ground of Montana, protector of this holy land.

Be careful how you treat her and pay her due respect.

If you allow her, she will protect you and look after you.

She might even bestow the gift of heavens onto you.

But disregard her, and she will expel you from the body of this land, which is her own body.

Her power is yours if you find it within and value without.

But destroy within and disdain without,

And you will unleash the wrath of Montana

Who treats all as one and whose body is your own."

The rumbling became louder and louder until Akim's ears were buzzing. The earth started trembling and the altar quivered, culminating into an explosion with rocks flying everywhere. A bright figure arose from the altar, surrounded by different colors of light that were flashing in every direction. The rumbling was now at its deepest and most intense. Gradually, the light diffused and retracted to within the figure. The sound eventually also died down until Akim could only hear the ringing of his ears. The light was now a soft halo around the figure. It was a female and yet not quite a woman. She was tall and impressive. Her body was completely silver, as were her eyes and her hair. She was slender and naked, but it looked like she was covered entirely in quicksilver. Behind her were large silver wings that were almost the same size as her body. She looked wrathful, and yet she was soft and sensitive. She turned to face Akim. Her eyes were flaming and intense.

"Are you the one who woke me up," she asked in her own language, which Akim understood in the same way that he had understood Samuel's mind-speak.

"I am," Akim answered in her language.

"You must be a warrior," she said, "for only true warriors wake up the irate Montana. Do you know that there are only three reasons to wake me up?"

"I didn't know, and I don't know if I am a warrior, either," Akim answered, "but if you tell me what they are I would be able to tell you if my reason is valid."

"One: if the land is in danger. Two: if my help is needed to change the destiny of one which would change the destiny of all. Three: to bring tidings of the deepest remorse for a sin committed and ask for my forgiveness."

"I'm not sure which one it is," Akim said. "I actually came to ask for information but by the sound of it, I'm guessing it could be the third. I'm hoping that you might be able to tell me what needs to be done for such remorse to pay its debt in full."

Montana looked at him fiercely and walked a few steps closer, presumably to be able to look into his eyes from up close. It felt like she was scanning his insides through his eyes to see what was going on within him. She relaxed and looked away, like a cat that had been ready to leap when faced with danger but no longer felt threatened.

"Is it the fallen ruler?" she asked, her voice soft. She sounded sad rather than angry. "He was prosperous, a great ruler. The people were happy and the land thrived. Then he brought it all down. Now there is nothing left, nothing. Just Montana's old lair and the sacred forest. The rest is all gone. The plants, the city, the people—nothing left. He destroyed it all." Then she looked up into his eyes again. "Was he unhappy with what I had given him? Was he bored with affluence and success? Couldn't he handle being an impressive leader?" She looked away again, forlorn despite her fierceness. She walked back to what was left of the altar, searching it as if the stones could provide an answer.

Akim walked closer to her. He told her about Samuel and how much he suffered being in a place and body that was not familiar to him. He said that he wasn't sure if Samuel was the ruler she was talking about, but if she could provide information that would help ease Samuel's suffering or help him find a way home, he would be most grateful to be of assistance to his friend. He also said that he wasn't sure if he could help her in any way, but if she wanted him to do anything in return, he would gladly do what he could.

She asked him to sit down and listen while she told her story. She had been asleep for so long and missed having contact with people, whichever form they took. If he could listen to her while she talked, it would aid the healing process of her broken heart. That was all she wanted from him. If he did that for her, hopefully he would also be able to find the answer that he was looking for. And so her story started.

"I am very old, much older than you can imagine. I am part of the land; I came with it out of the very oven where it was forged and was assigned as its guardian body. I grew with it; I lived on it through all its seasons and changes. I saw it evolve and I steered it through space until I found a place where it was comfortable and where life would grow on it. I loved it and cherished it. I watched all the marvels of space on it and was amazed at being alive. I watched the heavenly bodies and learned how to read their messages, how to talk to the universe. I was happy and excited to be alive for a very, very long time. But then I became lonely. Although I could talk to the universe, it wasn't quite the same as having other creatures I could see and touch. I told that to the One where I came from. I said that I was happy to be alive but that I needed some company, something similar to myself to share it with. For a long time I sat on my rock talking to the universe, praying to it to send me others to look after and share with. My wish was granted.

"First the plants came, the stationary living things. Next came the animals, the fishes and the birds: the living things that moved. They all came from my body, the land, each following on the other. Then the last species came, the analytical ones. I was warned that they could cause trouble in paradise because each of them had a will of their own. Yes, I was told that it would be a risk, but it was one that I was willing to take. What was the point of being guardian and protector of the land if there was no reason to protect it? If I had no companions to love and share the experience of living on our planet with?

"The analytical ones weren't bad at heart. Initially they had no problem understanding that all came from me and although we could share and be different, the happiness of one depended on the happiness of all and vice versa. But they forgot who they were and where they came from. I learned to understand what the warnings had meant about paradise being lost and the gates being closed. That was when I started to retreat into my lair more often. It wasn't that I didn't take my responsibility as protector of the land seriously. I would do what I could to protect it, but I had asked for them to be there. Since they had wills of their own, I couldn't interfere with it and force my will onto them—that wasn't part of the agreement. Besides, if I did, I would only move back to what I had known before and be lonely in my bliss. I didn't want to learn the same lesson all over again, so I had to find a way to fulfill my duties without interfering with the will of those that had sprung forth from me. I had to accept that we were no longer one, and we wouldn't be unless they remembered. I withdrew further and further, still answering to the needs of those who called me, but sadly I was called upon less and less often. I hadn't forgotten who I was, though, and resolved to look after those who looked after my body, the land. Although I never intended to unleash my wrath on those who mistreated me, it turned out that that was what I needed to do to protect myself. I could stand only so much abuse, and when my body had had enough, I lashed back in pain.

"I was saddened to the depths of my being. I kept hoping that there would be one who wanted to make a difference, who could change their hearts and lead the race to a place of enlightenment. He did come, and he was exceptionally gifted. He was aware of me like none of his race had ever been. He listened to me. He took my teachings to heart and shared them with the people. He showed them what a different world could look like if all lived as one and everything on the land was treated with respect. He stood out amongst all the others since he was very young of age. They listened to him—he was charismatic. His enemies were few and far between, he was much loved, but all great men have enemies, and he was no exception. However, his followers were more plentiful. As they grew in numbers, my spirit returned to strength. I looked after them and because they had my power on their side, his enemies created their own downfall. Naturally, he became the leader of the race and governed for a golden era. All was well in the land and although everyone knew what evil was, or rather stupidity, they chose to live as wise beings. This went on for many years until things changed.

"I don't know why it happened. I am not sure if he had become tired of governing or prosperity or if he thought that life always had to be rosy and that people could live forever. He was quite old, even for beings of his kind, who tend to live very long compared to those of your race. His wife passed away. She didn't suffer and was ready to go. She told me that she had learned what she had come here to learn and that she had had enough. She wanted to move on. Maybe come back, forget who she had been before, face new challenges, but for now, she was ready to move on. So I took her back and her body became one with my body again and her spirit was free to roam wherever it wanted to. She was happy to go even though she still loved him. She gave him her best wishes on her death and afterwards. Even though she was in a different dimension, her spirit kept blessing him, giving him the strength to persevere with his task until it was time for him to go, too. I supported him through his hours of darkness, continually providing what he needed to get through it and become stronger. But he stopped listening to me and he didn't seem to mind his wife's blessings, either. His spirit faded and he didn't care. He didn't try to fight the urge to lie down and fade away, despite the fact that life was still with him. He didn't have the will to return to his strength, to remain who he was and do his best despite adversity. He was bitter and wanted to stop existing even though, unlike his wife, he was not ready to go.

"He grew angry at me. 'Why have you taken my wife away?' he would shout at me in the middle of his sleepless nights. 'You know I need her, so why did you stop looking after me?' he wept. I told him that I was still looking after him, that he could go on without his wife and that we were both still there to support him if he would only allow us. But he didn't care and he didn't listen. I think he wanted revenge.

"As the leader changed, so things in the land started to change. People were becoming greedy and selfish again. Nobody cared what his neighbor was up to as long as each could get what he wanted and get it fast. There were brawls, unfairness, and soon chaos reigned. People were killing their neighbors without really blinking an eye. The golden era was falling apart faster than a rock falling from a cliff. All the time the leader had the power to change things, but he didn't. Although he never participated, his carelessness only fueled the disorder. Even though the appearance of civilization was still there, it was but the structure; the heart and soul of it had disappeared. In truth, people were acting as savages.

"The problem, perhaps more than anything else, was the fact that the structure still remained. Through the golden age this race had grown their knowledge and put it to good use for the purpose of creating a better society. Technologically they had advanced very far, but collectively their characters weren't ready to handle the implications of their knowledge. While they still had a ruler who could truly lead them and provide spiritual guidance, they were growing along safely. But without guidance, they were becoming a danger to themselves. Things were going from bad to worse even though on the outside it would seem that society was still functioning. There was no more heart; no appreciation of what was sacred. The leader did nothing to stop it. He never even looked sad and it was as if he had willfully lost all awareness of me. Whenever someone requested something he would approve it without giving thought to the consequences. He didn't try to protect them, not against each other or against themselves. In the meantime, they advanced further and further technologically while their spiritual development dwindled.

"They invented all sorts of strange things, some of them more useful than others. They traveled into space but respect for the neighbor had become obsolete. They were becoming greedier than ever. Next they started to strip the land, my insides, for so-called riches. They were using my resources to fuel their schemes and build their society beyond anything that was necessary for or conducive to positive living. They were using it to manipulate each other and create conflict. The bad energy was literally spreading and making the air filthy, like a diseased mind. I retreated more and more into myself while my body was being abused. I didn't even try to contact the leader anymore; things were so out of control. I felt asleep most of the time, dreaming of better days to come and praying that they would see the light and change their ways. I remembered who I was, the protector of the land, but the time for action had not yet come. Also, I suppose I was still hoping that things would turn out for the better before they went too far.

"But they didn't change. The day that they went too far eventually came, a bit sooner than I had expected it. By that time they hadn't discovered all my most sacred places yet. Since they had lost touch with my essence such a long time ago, I thought that I would be safe because they wouldn't know where to find it. But fate intervened and called me to action. There was a sacred valley hidden away between many, many mountains. It had a deep canyon with a river flowing through it. It was surrounded by the oldest of trees, many different species. It was the richest source of life on my body, the land. You could find every kind of insect, bird and animal there. The river was hidden away beneath the trees. Concealed underneath the river was a bed of rocks containing a mineral that formed a substantial part of my body and was necessary for my balance. They used this mineral for building their extravagant homes, even though it wasn't necessary as there were several other perfectly suitable and less sparse substances that they could use. I had shown them how to use soil and blend it in the perfect mixture with plant material to build homes that would be strong and cozy. I had also pointed out to them where they could find the strongest rocks for buildings that needed extra fortification. But they were no longer interested. These materials didn't make buildings look spectacular enough.

"Two explorers went out in search of mineral beds where they could find an abundance of this material. The leader knew that there had been groups in search of this substance for quite some time, and he also knew why. He did nothing to stop them. These two explorers were searching every distant corner of the land, determined to find something because they knew how rich it would make them. I suppose in some way they were still adequately in touch with me to understand my essence and track the leads there. But they used their almost long forgotten ability for their own gain even if it meant that I would be harmed in the process. They didn't respect me at all. They found the canyon despite the miles of similar looking mountain ranges around it. They found the river despite the density of the forest. I have no idea how they knew that there was a mineral bed beneath the river. I guess that somewhere within them they could still remember the concept of sacred and, consequently, understood the meaning of this place. However, in their twisted minds, it translated to monetary value. Soon enough they made the connection.

"The leader was still their leader in structure, even though he had long ago stopped being a leader at heart. The explorers submitted their proposal for a mine right in the center of the sacred canyon. To make it easier to get there, they would blow up a few of the mountains. They would also build a mining village on the riverside thinking that the more people who could work on getting it out, the better. He approved it! They came with their machines and drilled right into the inner parts of my being, excavating my essence to take from me as much as they could. The pain was excruciating. I felt my strength draining away as my energy was being depleted. But something within me lashed back. I sensed a voice from the oven where I was forged asking me, 'Who are you?' I felt anger stirring from the insides of my being. Stronger than that, I felt passion. It was indeed rage, but the love was more potent. I cherished these beings despite the harm they did to me. I knew that if the leader didn't stop them, I had to. The love for what had been given to me—the sacred forest, the river, the animals—was overwhelming and I wanted so badly to keep it safe. I could also no longer deny it; I needed to preserve my own well-being. The voice kept nudging me gently, 'Who are you? Who are you?'

"I stood up. I gathered all my strength and asked the sacred voice from the oven to help me. I remembered the day I was born. I owed it to my Creator to be true to myself, and I would give my all to protect the gifts I had received unconditionally. It took some time for my strength to accumulate. They didn't even notice that something was going on. Despite all the movement in the land, the different quality in the air and the noises coming from my lair, they were still ignorant in their greedy bliss. When I was ready, I exploded.

"I am the protector, I roared. I am Montana of the sacred land! You, my offspring, have sinned against yourselves as much as you have sinned against me. I shall no longer tolerate it. You will face oblivion until you are ready to try again and do better. I love you as I love the land and all that has been given to me. I will no longer support you in your self-destruction. Let those who can live in harmony on me, continue to do so, and let those who disturb the concord be destroyed. It took a long time for my rage to be depleted. When it was over, I was drained and exhausted. I felt empty but reassured by the fact that I had remained true to my destiny. I also felt lighter in a way now that the blockage had been removed. It would take time for something new to grow, but it would eventually happen.

"Since I wasn't sure what the consequences of my outburst were, I came out of my lair to assess the damage. I was flabbergasted. Smoke and steam were coming out of the scorched earth. Although parts of the land were unaffected, nothing was left of the places where the analytical ones had lived. Where their city used to be, there was nothing left but a flat, arid plain, like a hole in the land. It was empty, quiet, deserted. Even the forest was quiet as if in shock, although it had not been touched. A few lost souls were still hanging around, confused by what had happened, unaware of the fact that they were dead. But they soon received help and moved on. Only one remained, not in body, but in ghost form, still haunting the plain. It was the leader himself. I didn't want to talk to him. I had made my point clear enough and there was nothing left to be said. I am not even sure why he was still hanging around—whether he thought he could find a way to reverse what had happened or if he wanted to stay until he was forgiven, I did not know. As far as I was concerned, it was a matter between him and the hand that had created him; he was no longer my business. Eventually he also left and it was only me with the forests and a few of the animals.

"I was so tired that I went into a deep sleep to allow my body to recover from the abuse and the outburst. I knew that I would only be woken up when tidings of new things would come. It seems that you, dear traveler, are the harbinger of change."

She now looked at him with expectation. Akim didn't know what to do. He came to her looking for an answer to Samuel's dilemma and here she was, expecting him to bring her important news. Although he had an inkling of how it all fit together, he had no idea what needed to be done to create a favorable outcome for everyone. He also wasn't quite sure whether Montana had guessed what he suspected.

"Do you think your leader could be my friend Samuel, now on earth in a different body, on a planet and amongst a race where he feels he doesn't belong?" he asked her.

She narrowed her eyes for a moment. He could see a hint of longing on her face, which she shrugged off after a few seconds. Her expression was once again stern, but her voice was soft, giving her away. "Yes ... yes, it's him," she said, "My Lemusa, now Samuel on another planet." She looked at him sideways, the grief now visible. "Do you think he is sorry?" she asked. "Do you think he regrets what he did to me and to himself? To his people? His Creator?"

Akim explained that Samuel didn't consciously know what had happened, that he only knew that he came from a different place and that he didn't know why he was where he was. He reassured her that

Samuel would do anything to return to where he came from, but that he didn't know the way back. He asked Montana if she could give him any information that Samuel needed to find his way back, or whether the information she had given him already was sufficient.

Montana stared at him for a few moments. She turned around to face the mountain and the yellow orb. She put her hands together as if in prayer and stood for a while, chanting under her breath. He could feel the vibration of the surroundings changing, as if everything had been set alight in reverence. A halo appeared around Montana. A thread of light went out from the halo towards the orb in the sky, connecting one light to the other. She stood a while. Her chanting became more intense and the halo around her grew brighter. Then it died down again as the ray returned and the light withdrew into her body. She turned around. She looked energized although her eyes were distant, like one who had seen paradise and had to return to the real world. She still seemed entranced, in touch with the place that the light in the sky had shown her. When she spoke, her voice was clear.

"Lemusa will return eventually. We will be reunited and I will regain a part of myself that I have lost. But when he returns, things will not be the same as before. He will have gained a lot of wisdom, maturity, and endurance. Next time he will not be as gifted, but he will have gained enough understanding to make the most of what has been given to him. It will be his perseverance, rather than his gifts, that will enable him to be the best he can be. Things will not come as easy, but because of the price he has paid and the willingness he has shown to learn, he will have greater potential to succeed in his life task."

She looked dreamy, but there was still a light in her eyes.

"What he needs to know is not what had happened or why he had left, although you are free to tell him if you wish. He needs to know that if he wants to return, he has to make the most of what he has now. He has to serve others despite his suffering and he has to accept and willingly endure his fate. He must not try to find a way out, but instead be determined to be happy and use his gifts wisely. Perseverance will win the battle, no matter how long it takes. If he remembers this, he will find his way back home in the right time. *But*, he must also know that he has to forget about ever returning. He must heed the message and do it for the sake of it, because he wants to. Then things will fall into place whether he comes back here, which I am sure he will, or not. He must let go of his old home and embrace the new one."

Montana walked closer to him, her eyes still bright and dreamy. She put her hands on his shoulders. Through the fabric of his shirt he could feel that they were cold and soft. She looked him in the eyes, her face coming closer. She stopped a few inches from his face, her eyes still trapping his, before she spoke.

"Thank you for the tidings you brought," she said, her voice clear and melodious. She embraced him, her body tight against his. He could feel the curves of her breasts against his chest, her thigh against his. She pulled back to face him and kissed him. Her lips were smooth and icy and her kiss tasted sweet. He desired her. She was beautiful and fierce beyond measure. Her eyes were holding his and through them he could see a world of paradise, no doubt the place where she had just been when connected to the orb.

He wanted to go through her eyes, move into that place of light. His body was taken over by the desire to go there. He surrendered to the pull and as their bodies joined, he merged with the place on the other side of her eyes. He forgot about being with her, he was one with all that was and the deepest joys of being were all his. The pleasure became more intense and he never wanted it to stop. All he felt was an indescribable happiness, so complete that he never needed to know anything else.

He eventually returned, becoming himself again in a strange place that he didn't know. The feeling of being fulfilled beyond measure lingered. Montana was cold and soft against him, the light of paradise still in her eyes. He wanted to stay there forever, at one with the place he had entered through her. She let him hold her for a little while more, lying next to him in the sacred forest. Then she gently pulled away and said, "It is time for you to go back." She put her right hand to his forehead, still holding his gaze. The place in her eyes gradually faded out as he started spinning and everything became a blur. He wanted to hold on, but queasiness took over as the movement accelerated. He didn't know where he was going or in which direction.

When he came to he was at the bottom of the tree with the large red fruit, the snake curled around his body. His first instinct was to panic, but then he remembered that the snake had helped him. He asked it gently to let him go. The snake told him that he had been away for a long time. Although she trusted the fruit on the tree, she had to keep a hold on his body because she didn't know where he was or what he might encounter. He thanked her, the tree and the fruit and got up to make his way back to the palace. He was eager to share his findings with Samuel. It was good to feel some solid earth below his feet, yet at the same time he was reluctant to return to the world of dull reality.

Chapter 8

Akim was excited to see Samuel at the dinner table that evening. Samuel's, and all the other guests' behavior, was very much the same as it had been the night before. Akim tried to make eye contact since Samuel was sitting quite far away from him. However, Samuel either didn't notice or he was avoiding him. He guessed that Samuel was a bit distracted after the conversation they had had earlier the day. Either he was afraid that Akim might have no news, or he felt exposed after sharing so much about himself. He was, after all, just a boy. At last he looked in Akim's direction. It was as Akim had guessed; Samuel looked terrified, yet hopeful. Akim told him, through his mind, that he had been able to find information. He asked Samuel if he would like to meet him outside the main palace door after dinner. Samuel politely accepted. but Akim could tell that he wanted to jump out of his skin with excitement. Since he didn't want to disappoint the boy, he gently reminded him that although he had information that would be useful, he couldn't get Samuel back to where he came from. Samuel was put down, but he still looked grateful.

Akim was afraid of making a bad move. He hadn't even decided what he was going to tell Samuel and what he would leave out. Nevertheless, he didn't want Samuel to suffer much longer in anticipation so he intended to break the news at the earliest opportunity. When Samuel met him, he was wide-eyed with excitement. Akim instinctively knew that Samuel would be very disappointed that he couldn't give him an easy way back, despite the fact that he had warned him that it would be the case. However, he also knew that the news would greatly reduce Samuel's burden once he had processed it.

He broke the ice with the bad news, informing Samuel that there was no fast route to return. The boy's disappointment was heart-breaking, so he put an arm around his shoulders. He gave him a few moments to recover and dry his tears. He told Samuel that there would be a way to reduce his suffering, but it had to come from Samuel himself. If he was determined to implement this advice, then the outcome would be favorable. However, he should have no expectations of going back to the place he loved the most. He also had to know that things would never be as they had been before, but that didn't mean that he couldn't be happy. The reason why they had fallen apart in the first place had to be a crack in the foundations of that happiness. It was up to him to build the base for a deeper joy until he was ready for the next adventure.

Samuel was sobbing uncontrollably again despite having dried his tears a few minutes ago. Akim simply comforted him; these tears were part of the process that would set Samuel free to build a new life. They belonged to the ghost that had haunted the plains with no body to feel the pain necessary for healing and they needed to be cried. They were also eleven years' worth of tears of a boy who didn't feel comfortable in his own body and an alien among his people. He held the boy and asked the eagle to guide him to healing, to a place where he would be willing to start something new and accept his surroundings.

In his mind's eye Akim saw a phoenix arriving. It was large with a golden body and brightly colored wings and tail. It wrapped its wings around Samuel and did a fiery dance surrounded by a circle of flames. The flames moved in and closer until the bird itself was on fire. The dance continued, then the bird self-destructed into a heap of ash. When it rose from the ashes, its body was white and its wings and tail brighter than before. From its mouth it spit out an object. It was a golden ring with engravings on it which Akim didn't understand, but knew were in the same language as the runes he had seen on Montana's altar. Akim thanked the phoenix, took the ring and put it on Samuel's finger. The bird breathed on the ring to secure its energetic imprint onto Samuel. It told Akim that it would enable him to release himself from the hold of the past. It also told him that it would look after Samuel, whether he was aware of it or not. Akim thanked the bird again for the information and for its presence before he turned his attention back to Samuel. The boy was now quiet and, Akim guessed, feeling empty.

"Don't worry," Akim told him, "everything will be all right." It felt like such a mundane thing to say, but he knew it to be true. He told Samuel that his parents loved him and that love could perform miracles if we allowed it to. Samuel had to focus on that love and appreciate it. A little bit of love was sometimes all that was needed to transform a destiny. When we heeded the tiniest bit of love, we invited it to enter our lives and work its magic. When the gates were opened, the wave might not always be smooth. We might fall hard several times while the things we no longer needed were being destroyed. But we had to persevere with an open heart if we wanted to become more whole and occasionally experience a glimpse of paradise within ourselves. It would be very hard to trust love. But sometimes when we doubted its power, all we needed to do was think back to the moments when we had experienced love in its purest form. Even if our minds rejected the memories as meaningless, our souls would remember that these moments were real, and would continue their quest for fulfillment.

Akim hugged Samuel again and when the boy looked up, Akim could see a light in his eyes. He knew that the boy was thinking of the love of his parents. Perhaps he was also remembering a distant life where he had known a woman whom he loved, and perhaps this woman was sending her love to him at that moment. Maybe he was feeling the love of a being that he had worked with to create prosperity in a faraway land. Maybe he knew that although he had betrayed this goddess, her love for him couldn't be destroyed, and forgiveness was possible.

Akim sat with Samuel for a while longer until the boy got tired and said that he wanted to go to bed. The day after was the day of the king's great chess match. Although neither had been overly thrilled at the prospect of attending, both now felt that they were very much looking forward to it. So they said good night and went to their rooms.

Chapter 9

The day of the match had arrived. The other ruler, called Hassan, alighted with a great display. There were many white horses pulling the meagre carriage. Behind it were dozens of men walking. They were extravagantly dressed in official clothing. All of them wore black trousers and shiny jackets with golden dragons printed on them; some with a blue background, others in red. Their hats were large and black with a golden tussle hanging from them. In front of the horses there were a few more men leading the procession. Some of them were playing trumpets and others were playing drums. The music wasn't extremely loud but was lively and almost aggressive; it sounded a bit like a war tune. The men playing the instruments wore blank facial expressions. Akim suspected that they were supposed to look angry but they were enjoying playing their instruments too much, so they settled for neutral. Those at the back were scowling, as if they angrily wanted to get this over and done with. Akim was sitting with Samuel outside the palace, watching the whole procession. To his relief, Samuel looked much better than the night before. For the first time since Akim had met him, he appeared to take an interest in his surroundings. He looked lighter, even though Akim knew that his journey to acceptance would be tedious.

The procession finally came to a halt in front of the palace doors where the king and his advisors were waiting. The parade had the desired effect as Akim found himself waiting in anticipation for Hassan to get out. He wanted to see what the ruler with such a gaudy entourage looked like. The ruler, helped by his men, dismounted from the carriage. He was dark-skinned with long, pitch black hair. He looked more serious and cranky than all his men together. His eyes were fixed on some invisible point ahead of him, as if he were staring into a dark dream world. His outfit was a stark contradiction to those of his men. He was wearing cream colored linen with no accessories, not even shoes. The trousers were wide and calf-length and he had no shirt, only a plain waistcoat in the same color. The waistcoat wasn't buttoned up, exposing his strong brown chest. His movements were stiff as he walked up the palace stairs to greet the king. The king smiled and Akim thought that there was a hint of amusement behind the friendliness. For the first time since Akim had met him he seemed relaxed. Akim liked this face of the king. Hassan didn't seem to notice the king's light-hearted mood. With a grave expression, he turned his eyes to the ground as both governors bowed down in greeting. The king took both

Hassan's hands in his and smiled, looking Hassan in the eye. Then he pulled Hassan closer in a quick embrace. He put his hands on Hassan's shoulders and said a few words which Akim guessed were words of welcome. They disappeared into the palace, the entourage staying behind.

Akim and Samuel followed to the room where the match was to take place. Akim was delighted to see that Samuel was enjoying the display. He even sensed a bit of excitement on Samuel's part. The boy was, after all, the chess master. It should be no surprise that he would be interested in how his pupil fared. As for Akim being the king's advisor, he was fairly detached from the outcome. While he hoped that things would go in the king's favor, he trusted his craft and wasn't nervous about losing the king's goodwill. As far as he understood, this was an experiment. If the king wasn't happy with his service, he would go home and forget about it. If the king was satisfied, then he might consult Akim again. Whatever the outcome, Akim could live with it.

They entered the hallway where the game would be played. Unlike the room where Akim had had his first meeting with the king, this one was spectacular. There was a giant chess board in the middle with massive pieces. The floor was made of green marble and there were paintings on the ceiling. The curtains were heavy and of a deep red color with golden trimming. There were many other paintings in lavish frames on the walls and pillars nicely decorated with frills. The figures in the paintings reminded Akim of mythological characters: there were naked men with long white hair, their nudity covered by blankets that seemed to randomly float past. These men wore angry expressions and often had tridents or similar accessories in their hands. They sometimes appeared to chase women who were fully clothed and looked afraid, yet sensual at the same time. There were lightning bolts, waves, clouds and mountains. Akim felt as if these figures were alive and about to view the match with as much interest as they were. However, he imagined them to be much more light-hearted than they were portrayed. These personas were a cover that would allow them to eavesdrop on activities in the room which they might discuss later with amused concern. Akim was about to greet them when he remembered that he would make a fool of himself in front of all the people.

Akim and Samuel were led to one side of the giant chess board with three of the king's men. On the other side were four of the ruler's soldiers with one man in different clothing—Akim assumed him to be Hassan's right hand man. Two referees walked in and took their place next to the board on both sides. Akim wasn't sure whether they were independent referees, or if each ruler could appoint one. Both rulers disappeared for a few minutes. Hassan's soldiers were dead quiet while they waited. Akim and Samuel were making light conversation and the king's men were talking about serious matters as usual. When the rulers returned, they were both dressed differently, apparently wearing their match outfits.

The king was dressed in peculiar clothes that made him look like a wizard. He wore a skew blue hat made of satin. It had prints of stars and moons on it. His coat was a matching blue and was lined with gold around the edges. Beneath the coat he wore a golden shirt of textured fabric and black trousers. His shoes were black and pointy with little bells secured to the tips, like those of an elf. The bells were jingling audibly while he walked. It was his belt that made the outfit, though. It was very wide and dark green with large golden stars on it. The buckle was a massive golden heart shape. This was almost too much for Akim as he struggled to restrain the laughter that was bubbling up inside him. It didn't help that he knew intuitively that Samuel was also fighting to contain his giggles. The king, however, wasn't laughing but smiling; he was acting loud and gaudy as he came over to hug all his supporters, talking incessantly about how excited he was. Akim was happy to see that the king had taken his advice to heart. He was so immersed in his role that he didn't notice his men's surprise or Akim's and Samuel's disguised hilarity. Even his gait was heavy and bouncy in contrast to his normally focused movements. When he took in his spot, he was scowling deeply, like a fool trying to be serious.

Akim was so taken by the king's performance that he had hardly noticed the other ruler. Hassan was wearing exactly the same style outfit as his cream colored suit, but this one was bright orange satin with a golden shimmer. He also wore a turban of the same color, covering his black hair. His demeanor spoke of someone who was about to participate in a contest of martial arts. His exaggerated seriousness would have been almost as comical as the king's act if it weren't for the fact that it appeared to be a matter of life or death for him. Akim was watching him closely. Although he looked as alert and focused as a tiger ready to leap on its prey, Akim sensed a hint of uncertainty, perhaps more noticeable by his exaggerated confidence. When he turned in their direction, his eyes gave away a shadow of uncertainty which probably only Akim and Samuel could see.

The two referees had drawn the lots and the match was ready to start. The king was white and had to make the first move. He was deep in thought for a few seconds, then he trotted over briskly to the pawn on the opposite side where Hassan's supporters were standing. He stood still, watching it intently for about a second before he quickly lifted it and moved it two spaces forward. Akim thought that the chess pieces were probably light, but the king lifted it like it took a lot of effort.

Akim stifled a snigger when he saw the king smirking, looking very impressed with himself.

It was Hassan's turn. He moved over to one of his middle pawns with precise, fighter-style movements. He moved it two spaces forward in the same way that he would have thrown a missile if he had had one. He stared at the king defiantly with narrowed eyes. The king smiled at him, then hummed a silly tune as he waddled over to the pawn on the other side, moving it two spaces forward. He turned to smile at his supporters, after which he scowled again as he stood next to his pawn, staring into nowhere. Hassan made another fast and calculated move. Akim thought that he was moving a bit too quickly, as one who wanted to prove that he knew exactly what he was doing. His left knight jumped out, one space to the right. He went to stand in front of it, staring at the king as if inviting him to show his fighting skills. His legs were two shoulder widths apart and slightly bent. His lower arms were lifted and his hands were straight in the air in front of him as if ready to block a blow from his opponent. Akim was hoping that his hunch was right about Hassan being unnerved and that it wasn't simply his style of playing chess. The two rulers really were acting comically.

The king took ages to make his next move. He stared at Hassan first, then he walked over to another side of the board where the knight was in plain sight. He stared at the chess piece as if waiting for it to come alive. His face bore an expression of focused attention, as one would look while listening to someone talking about their problems. He stayed in the same position for a few minutes. Hassan became uncomfortable or tired, Akim wasn't sure which. He relaxed his fighting position and moved away from his knight, probably wanting to get away from the king's intense staring. The referees signed to one another and then one of them prompted the king politely to please go ahead. The king started, as if coming out of a reverie. He looked moody as he moved another of his pawns forward, closer to Hassan's knight.

Hassan looked more careful when he made his next move. The king mimicked him for the next few moves in body language, but also in some of his moves. Hassan noticed this and now was becoming angry. His movements on the board remained clear-cut, but Akim could feel waves of irritation coming from him. The king seemed oblivious as he continued to make move after nonchalant move. By now he was playing defensively.

Hassan's moves were becoming increasingly aggressive. Each move was made faster than the previous. The king, on the other hand, continued to take his time, although he didn't push the acceptable timeframe as much as earlier. Hassan was outside of himself by now. He appeared to be following a routine he was used to, relying on ingrained practice rather than thinking every action through. Akim and Samuel were both holding their breaths as Hassan looked ready to jump his opponent in a full on physical fight. His face was turning red in anger. Akim thought he probably had to stifle a cry of annoyance each time the king took his time to make his move, only to make a very defensive one. He imagined that Hassan wanted the king to either succumb to the pressure and make a mistake, or play with the same fiery disposition as himself. He was aggravated more and more by the fact that the king wasn't playing his game.

Akim couldn't believe his eyes when Hassan made a very bad move that would eventually put the king's queen in danger, but exposed his own king to a very obvious check mate if the king could keep his wits about him. Hassan was so focused on moving in for the kill that he had temporarily forgotten about the most important aspect of the match—keeping his king safe. Akim prayed silently that the king would remain calm and take the opportunity to end the match. It was obvious that it was the moment the king had been waiting for as he almost dropped his act and didn't even take that long to make his move. When he did, Hassan realized his mistake. He cried out in rage. The next move would very obviously be check mate, so he knocked his king over as if giving it a slap. He stormed out, shouting something in his own language at his men without even turning around to face them. They looked embarrassed and fearful at the same time and quickly followed to placate him.

When Hassan had left, the king seemed to take a moment or two to adapt from the persona he had been playing in order to become his normal self again. He looked like someone who had just woken up: tired and sleepy with not much memory of the dreams of last night. He appeared relieved to be able to drop the act. Akim thought that he would probably have been embarrassed at his behavior if he hadn't been so absorbed in the role.

He walked straight up to Akim and Samuel, now back to his normal, occupied self. Content with the outcome, he smiled and sincerely thanked them. Akim was so relieved that he forgot to act formal in the king's presence. He giggled spontaneously and hugged the king, telling him what a good performance he had given. The king was surprised. Samuel followed suit and congratulated the king. He seemed to have been as engrossed in the game as the king himself. Akim smiled inwardly. He was glad to see Samuel showing such great capacity to participate in what was happening around him. Their light-hearted mood was contagious and for a few more moments the king stood chatting and joking with them. He resumed his occupied manner when he walked over to his men.

Now that the match was over, Samuel was on his way home. Akim accompanied him to the garden to bid him farewell. Samuel's mother was waiting for him outside the main palace door. She had already collected his things, which he had packed before the match. She was delighted to see Samuel. She beamed and smiled from ear to ear as she hugged him tightly. It was time for Samuel to say goodbye, so he hugged his new friend and thanked Akim for all the help and support he had provided. He told Akim where he lived and asked him to come and visit when in the vicinity. Akim pressed his hand reassuringly one last time before they departed.

Akim spent a few more hours in the garden, somewhat lonely after all the excitement had gone. He was supposed to go home the following day. Home felt like eons away after all the strange things he had witnessed over the last few days. He missed home, and yet it felt like an era passed. Now that he had experienced a different setting for the first time in his life, he felt a desire to explore the world and expand his horizons to more unfamiliar places. He loved home and it was part of him, but he also wanted to know what not-home felt like. He was surprised to find himself feeling a bit reluctant to return. He didn't want to stay at the palace forever—it wasn't his world and he didn't want it to be. But the novelty hadn't worn off, and he felt that there were many more things to be discovered.

He sighed and slipped into a dream-like state as he looked around at the beautiful garden. He was sitting next to a large pool with a statue of a little boy functioning as a fountain in the middle of it. He looked into the pool and could see the reflection of two magpies flying closely next to one another, one a little bit ahead of the other. He looked up at the magpies in the sky. One cawed once, after which the other cawed three times in answer. They circled and returned, showing their reflection in the pool once again. The one that had been ahead was now behind and their calls were also reversed. Akim looked down into the pool again and noticed that its surface was smooth despite the bubbling fountain. In it he could see the reflection of clouds and the blue sky. When he used his imagination, the shape of the clouds turned into a city with thick walls around it. The shapes shifted and took on the form of two large birds. Oddly, the reflection of the statue was clearly visible even with the water flowing around it. In the water the statue didn't look like a boy at all, but rather resembled a young, very handsome man. Could the pool be magical, too? Akim was too tired to give it much more thought, so he got up and went back to his room, where he patiently packed all his things as far as he could and lay on the large bed to rest for a while.

Chapter 10

He had fallen asleep without noticing. When he woke up a few hours later, it was already dusk. It took him a few seconds to remember where he was. Next thing he noticed was a woman in his room. Her knocking must have woken him up. She was now standing in the doorway with only her face visible in the light of the lantern she was carrying. The door was semi-closed with the largest part of her body hidden behind it. She looked apologetic to disturb him; he realized that she had been sent there. She was young and dark and looked very shy, probably because of embarrassment at having woken him up. She pulled herself together and said, "The king requests your presence." She turned around and quickly closed the door behind her, softly but firmly. Akim rushed out after her.

"Wait," he called. She was already halfway down the corridor. She turned around, her evident discomfort now under control. He walked up to her in brisk strides to avoid raising his voice in the palace.

"Where should I meet him?" he asked.

"In the same room where you met him on the day that you arrived." She looked at him with dark eyes, then turned around and hurried away. Akim stood in the corridor for a few more moments, still a bit sleepy. He walked back to his room in a haze, after which he tidied himself to be ready for the king's council. The light-hearted morning he had had with Samuel was now forgotten. He was back to normal—just the peasant Akim who was out of place in the king's palace, feeling uncomfortable and unsure of himself. The prospect of home now seemed far more attractive than earlier when he had felt like an adventurer. He just wanted to be back with Asteodor and his mother, making furniture and talking to the nature spirits. Nothing would feel quite as good as sitting at home next to the fireplace, drinking home-made tea out of his own, massive teacup. Suddenly he was very, very homesick, not so much because he missed his home intensely, but because he felt so lonely where he was. Despite the magic in the garden, the palace wasn't his world.

The king sat waiting for him in the designated room. He wasn't quite as cheerful as he had been after the match, but he looked more relaxed than normal and even smiled as Akim entered. He welcomed Akim and asked him to sit down. For a while he talked about the ins and the outs of the palace and some of the problems he was dealing with at the moment. Akim was puzzled by the conversation. The girl who had woken him up came in to bring tea. She was bashful as she served them but when she walked away, she held her head high. Akim was confused—she didn't look like a servant and the king looked very familiar with her when he thanked her. His mind was clouded after she left. He had to fight to remain focused on the king's speech.

"...what I am in fact saying is that I am offering you a job as the king's advisor. You can stay in the palace in the same room where you are now. We will arrange for you to be taken home for a few days every month. Your duties will include convening with the king every day to advise on current matters. You will sometimes be requested to accompany the king on expeditions to be of strategic assistance. Although you are not obliged to come with me on every single trip, I would recommend that you do not accept this offer if you are not willing to escort me at least occasionally. So, what do you think?"

Akim was wide-eyed with surprise. He stared at the king, uncertain what to say. The king took this as a sign of reluctance so he went on to discuss compensation. The wage he offered was in the range of that of an average middle class citizen or a first-rate palace servant. To Akim it was colossal. He had always been happy just to have enough to live from, as long as he could have direct access to nature. The king kept talking, although Akim didn't really hear him. He was interested in the opportunity, mainly because of the experience. But he didn't want to become a slave to the king's money. He was afraid of falling into the same trap as most people, thinking that he had to work hard for someone else if he wanted to survive. His thoughts turned to the proud girl who became so shy in his presence. It crossed his mind that it might, after all, be useful to have money to send home to his mother. Not that he owed her financial assistance, but she might be able to apply it to a cause that she saw fit. He interrupted the king without listening further.

"I'll do it," he said, looking the king straight in the eye. The king was surprised. "But I have a few conditions. I will accompany you on excursions, but not if it interferes with the time I am supposed to go home. I reserve the right to say no if my integrity is at stake. My talent has been given to me to assist me with objectives that are my own and yet go beyond the person that you see in front of you. I do not wish to compromise them. If I do, I will pay a very dear price and my symbols will no longer be of any use. The symbols tell the truth. When you seek council from them, the truth will be shown. It is your choice whether you want to heed it or not."

The king looked taken aback. For a moment Akim thought he could see a hint of rage in the king's eyes. He was used to ruling, not being overruled. The moment lasted for a second or two, then the king relaxed as reason took over. He agreed to the terms and sincerely welcomed

Akim to the palace and his entourage. He said that he hoped and believed that Akim would be happy and gain valuable experience.

Akim stood up and bowed before the king. The king smiled and as soon as Akim rose again, he put his hand on his shoulder.

"You are a valuable asset to my kingdom, and I hope that I can learn from the wisdom you are given," he said. Although he didn't look comfortable with the scenario, he said it like he was talking to an equal, not a servant. The king knew deep down that although Akim was his servant in the traditional hierarchy of power, this young man had a power that was unlike his own but by no means inferior. He was wise enough to recognize it and use it to his benefit, regardless of whether he felt at ease with it or not. Beyond reasons of strategic benefit, he liked and respected Akim as a person. In some way he also wanted to be worthy of Akim's respect, perhaps more so than the average middle class citizen living in the city. Although no more words on the matter were spoken between them, their eyes were talking. They made a silent agreement to work together for the greater good.

The king thanked him for his time and said that he would be taken home the next day to be picked up again a week later. This would give him enough time to greet his mother and Asteodor and tie all the loose ends at home. Akim felt excited and in a way numb as he left for his room, pondering the way his life had changed dramatically in such a short time. He could only hope that there would be time and room for magic in the king's service.

Chapter 11

The next few days back at home were spent preparing for the months ahead, talking to his mother and visiting all the places he loved. Asteodor accepted his resignation without a fuss—he didn't look surprised. Akim wondered if he was happy to have the place to himself again, but he knew that behind the man's grumpy facade he had grown fond of Akim. He suspected that Asteodor might know more about his future than he pretended to. In any case, Akim knew that he and Asteodor would be friends across time and space and that Asteodor was detached because of that. He invited Akim to take a walk with him in the woods for old time's sake before leaving.

He took Akim to a part of the forest that he didn't know very well. It was on the other side of the town in a valley between two mountains. They walked deep into the forest until it was quite dark and Akim couldn't see much in front of him, reminding him a bit of the dream he had had when making contact with his guardian spirit. They descended further until Akim thought they would have a hard time making their way back up again. He could hear the sound of water. They made a turn left against the steep slope of the mountain. They had reached the end of the one side of the mountain and was now moving around it. They climbed a bit and the sound of water became louder. The trees were less thick above them and it became lighter; he could even see patches of sunlight on the ground. The sound of water was by now drowning the other noises in the forest. They ascended more and reached a spot where the sunlight came through the forest roof clearly. Akim was relieved, although he loved the forest and the trees, the denseness had made him feel a bit claustrophobic. He knew that Asteodor could be trusted, but a fearful part of him had been worried that they were lost.

The light coming from the same direction as the sound of the water was almost blinding to one whose eyes were used to darkness. They climbed over rocks and between trees until they reached a waterfall with a pool at the bottom. The spray made clouds around the pool and soon they were rather wet. When he looked up, only a bit of blue sky was visible. The pool was interesting. It was clear on the surface with a turquoise and dark color swirling in it a few inches deeper. The dark color looked like water plants; he wasn't sure what the turquoise color was. It had a glimmering quality, as if containing tiny particles of silver that reflected back the sunlight. He put out his hand to touch the pool, but Asteodor held him back.

"Don't," he said. His stern expression told Akim that he had to listen and be quiet. Asteodor looked up at the heavens as if in prayer. When he came out of his trance, he looked satisfied that he had received the information he had asked for. He gestured to Akim to look into the pool again. "What do you see?" he asked.

At first he saw a large, dark colored fish. But then his attention was drawn to the turquoise color with the shiny particles. It was showing him something.

"I see an owl," he said.

"Tell me about the owl. What does it say to you?" Asteodor asked.

Akim looked again and let the owl show itself. It was larger than any owl he had ever seen in the physical world. It was a horned owl of a brownish color with spotted plumage. Its chest was largely silver-white and its face contained specks of black. It looked caring and wise, but he couldn't discern much else. The owl was talking about some important mission that he had to carry out. It told him not to lose hope, even when he would get discouraged. When feeling tired, the owl would be there to support him. But he mustn't give up, no matter how unlikely the prospect of success. Akim listened, absorbing the owl's care and gaining strength from it. He knew that he had to accept whatever power was given to him then because he might need it later. He thanked the owl and let its blessing flow to him from the pool until he was filled to capacity. The owl disappeared and Akim closed his eyes and relaxed, waiting a moment for it all to settle. When he opened them again, he could see a section of a rainbow in the spray. For a moment he thought he could see a trace of wings in the light. He blinked and then it was gone. He looked back at Asteodor, who looked satisfied.

"Good," he said. Akim wanted to ask him what it all meant, any information he could get about the mission the owl was talking about. However, he didn't feel like talking much, still half in a reverie. He also knew better than expecting to get much out of Asteodor, so he decided to leave it there. While they walked back in silence, his head was still in a world where there was a massive, caring owl looking out for him. When they arrived home, it was almost time for him to start packing his things to get ready for the trip back.

The last day or two was spent talking to his mother and contemplating the fact that things would soon be very different. He was apprehensive after the encounter with the owl, but was as prepared as he could be. It was time to move on. If he had stayed where he was for much longer he would have stagnated and become resentful of things always staying the same. So he thanked the stars and the heavens for a new opportunity and prayed for grace to help him along the way. The time came when the carriage arrived. He said his final goodbyes and took the things he would need, knowing that although he would return soon, he was officially leaving home.

Chapter 12

The months that followed were very different from the life Akim was used to. He was in the king's company often and had to become familiar with the ways of his entourage. There was constant pressure and worry about decisions made. The things that had been a large part of his life before were invisible to the king's men. If it weren't for the fact that this invisible world was what defined his relationship with the king, it wouldn't have existed at all as far as they were concerned. He often felt that they regarded him as a bit of a nuisance because of his different perspective. However, the king respected his understanding of things and he treated Akim with kindness and esteem. Akim sometimes found it hard to stay centered in a world fraught with worry, and he had to be careful not to internalize hierarchical values. When he felt himself swaying from his internal compass, he prayed to the eagle to guide him back to his center.

Although he loved the palace garden with all its magical passage ways, he missed the wildness of the forest and mountains. The gardens were not his own, and although he could talk to its inhabiting spirits, he would probably always feel like an outsider there. The room had become his home. Yet, he still felt uncomfortable in all other places inside the palace. The feeling that he had to be careful in case someone asked him what he was doing persisted. On the positive side, he was becoming more comfortable in his role as the king's advisor.

Only now and then did he have the chance to escape from the bustle of palace life. He would go out to the hill outside the city, on the other side of which was largely no-mans-land. There he would sit, hoping to connect to the universe. The spirits were fairly quiet, which made him slightly impatient. He wanted to know more about the important mission that the owl was talking about. But no matter how hard he tried, he couldn't find a clue of what it was or what he needed to do about it. When he consulted his symbols, he kept getting the same message: he had to remain true to himself.

Occasionally he would become angry and frustrated. He believed in his mission, but with the company he was surrounded by, it was sometimes hard not to see his gift as make believe, regardless of his success. At times he couldn't help seeing himself through the eyes of the king's men, according to which he was just a young man with a grand sense of destiny, but whose world was spectral. In terms of the "real" world he had no tangible power or position. From this perspective, he was clinging to things that didn't matter to make himself feel secure.

Akim would alternate between shrugging off these thoughts and confronting his insecurities, observing them without losing his sense of knowing. It wasn't easy.

There was a man among the king's other advisors, called Waddan, that he didn't trust. Waddan had a county to look after, one that bordered a neighboring country. Half of his time was spent at the palace to liaise with the king. The other half was spent in his region looking after affairs. He largely managed relations with the neighboring country. While the king was responsible for giving direction, Waddan was the person who implemented agreements and managed potentially problematic situations. The king leaned strongly on him as his right hand man.

Akim understood that the king had a strategic mind-set. In those terms it was probably the right choice to place Waddan at the head of this important section. He was a strong leader and he seemed to be loyal to the king. He was intelligent and diplomatic; an ideal combination for dealing with foreign affairs. But the king didn't have Akim's intuition, and Akim's instinct was telling him that something wasn't right. This man was perhaps just a bit too strategic and Akim thought that the king might do well by having a second, independent eye in the same region. The king never asked his opinion about it and he was sure of his choice in Waddan. If Akim had known more about what was going on in that county, he could have offered a voice of reason, which would have been better than an inkling. He didn't get the feeling that the king wanted to withhold information from him in that respect; rather that Waddan always found a way of making sure that discussions about possibly contentious subjects were held in private, away from Akim's ears.

Akim mulled this over while sitting on the hilltop outside the city. He was at a loss for how to handle the situation. He didn't know whether it would be best to bring his concerns to the king's attention or just sit back and wait. He asked his guiding spirits and the message was clear: keep a low profile, don't act too soon. He accepted the message but was still unsatisfied because he couldn't put his finger on Waddan's agenda. Although he felt that the king had to be warned, he was afraid that the king wouldn't listen and would dismiss him. As much as he valued Akim's input, he wouldn't appreciate that sort of advice when uncalled for, especially when he had no real grounds. Akim sighed and resolved to keep his agreement with the king, speaking up only when he was asked. He would bide his time and if it happened that the king would get a hunch, he would give his opinion when consulted. With that thought he got up and made his way back to the palace.

The opportunity to express his view came sooner than expected. When the undercurrent that the king had been unaware of came to light, it was almost too late for damage control. They were in the middle of a meeting with all the king's immediate subordinates when a messenger knocked on the door. The porter opened it a little and spoke to the person outside. He closed the door again and addressed the king.

"There is an urgent message for you, your Majesty," he said.

The king looked annoyed. "Not now," he said.

"It's urgent, your majesty," the porter said.

"All right, bring in the messenger," the king conceded, still looking irritated.

The person that entered was very young, almost a boy. He wore a blue and silver uniform, the same colors as the flag of the country that bordered on the region where Waddan was in charge. He walked until right in front of the king as if taking center stage before making an announcement. Then he took on a dramatic posture and spoke with a booming voice.

"The King of Extar wants to thank your majesty for your support in his enterprises. He is delighted to work closely with your majesty and share common ground. But ...," he paused dramatically for effect and waved his finger in the air, "he wasn't happy at all to hear about the disrespect with which one of his men had been treated when tending to his affairs in this country. He wishes your majesty to take note of the report which I shall now present, signed by four witnesses, two of which are citizens of your country and two of which are his. He demands a public apology for the way in which he was offended. He also wants to increase the security of his officials. If such requests are not complied with, the peaceful agreements in this relationship will no longer be valid. In that case, your Majesty should no longer consider Extar a friend of this country!" His oration ended with an exclamation and a frown while he stood like a soldier, staring into the distance. Looking belligerent, he marched over to the king and handed him a piece of paper. His frown remained as he turned around with exaggerated movements and stomped out.

The king couldn't decide whether he was astonished or bored. Surprise took over as he read through the letter. When he looked up, he was not only shocked, but very angry. He stood up and turned straight to Waddan.

"What is this?" he asked. "Business interests in my county that you look after? Arms to protect his men against the aggression of our citizens? His men in charge of my towns because apparently my towns revolve around his business? I request that you explain yourself, Waddan." By the end of his speech the king's tone was lethally soft. He looked both livid and disappointed.

Waddan didn't look perturbed. In fact, he was prepared with a comeback. "We have discussed this, Your Majesty," he said smoothly. "You agreed that it is in our interest to use their resources to assist with the processing of grain until we have built up our own industry. You put me in charge of the project and I managed it to best serve the kingdom, as I knew it would please your majesty. I am now sorry to hear that our citizens have treated his men with disrespect. It looks like there is not enough law enforcement to protect outsiders—something that I suggest your majesty sees to immediately. In the meantime we have to appease him if we want to ensure that grain production continues to a sufficient extent to feed the people of this country."

The king looked astounded. "Have you read this?" he exclaimed, waving the piece of paper in the air. Realizing that Waddan probably hadn't, he continued, "His men are not only in charge of enterprises, but they own an entire town! How did this happen without my approval? His representative acted towards our citizens in a way that might be acceptable behavior towards an inferior in Extar, but not here. But that is beside the point; the man wasn't supposed to be in that position to start with." He stared at Waddan, who was now starting to cower behind his confident facade. He hadn't expected such a strong reaction. Akim thought that Waddan could have been under the impression that the king dealt with power in the same way that he did: using it for personal gain. It looked like he hadn't considered that the king might genuinely care about his people. The king continued, "I am really, really disappointed in you, Waddan. I thought you were one of my strongest men." He turned away and paced the room once after which he returned to his seat and sat with his shoulders hanging, looking very sad indeed.

Waddan still looked taken aback, but recovered his composure while talking. "This is not bad, Your Majesty," he said, looking like he almost believed himself. "I didn't run it by you because it's a small town consisting of a union of farming villages. According to the last valid statute, this falls under the supervision of the head of county and appointing a chief doesn't necessarily need the approval of the king. It's in our own best interests. The town has grown and more people are fed. Our profits have grown in the last year. This surely is a sign that the economy is growing ...?" He wavered a bit, looking anxiously at the king as if begging him to concede.

But the king was still outraged. "That statute doesn't apply to foreigners being appointed, you fool." His voice boomed as he hit hard on the table with his hands. "What are you talking about feeding the people? They were well fed already." Akim had never seen the king so angry. All the other men were sitting like quiet school children in the face of an angry teacher, too afraid to move. The king slowly lifted his hands again and brought them back next to his body as his voice dropped. He was back in disappointment mode. "What happened to the flower fields?" he asked softly. "They were the pride and joy not only of the county, but of the entire country. They were the heart of the people who cultivated them and they attracted benevolent visitors from all corners of the world. The people knew how to look after themselves because they had such a good relationship with the land. What has been done to their land?"

Waddan looked down as he spoke. "The flower fields didn't serve much of a purpose any more, your majesty, so we removed some of them to make way for crops. It's more profitable, Your Majesty." Akim hadn't thought it possible, but Waddan looked ashamed and even a bit guilty. The king put his hands on the table again and leaned forward, his head down. He looked incredibly dejected.

"I said that the grain industry could be grown within limitations, mainly for the purpose of providing food to more barren parts of the country. I said that exporting grain was something we *could* look into in future. I said that you always had to act in the best interests of the country." His voice rose in a crescendo and he boomed out the last sentence. It took him a little while to grasp the implication of his words. "That is where we have misunderstood each other, isn't it? Our view on what is in the best interest of this country. Haven't I made it clear that the people living here are the country?" he asked in disbelief.

"Your Majesty, it is also in the interest of the people if the country obtains greater wealth. It would mean more food, better services—"

"And being reduced to slaves in the process! No more land to live from though it has always looked after them. Instead they will be forced to work for someone who doesn't even care about them for the sake of having more bread on the table?" The incredulous expression on his face gave way to something close to sorrow. "This is my fault," he said. "I shouldn't have given away so much authority. I should have kept a closer eye on what was going on." It took a little while for him to regain his composure. When he spoke, he was clearly assessing the situation in order to decide how best to salvage it. "This meeting will be adjourned for now. I shall let you know when we will convene again. Akim, please meet me in my main office in thirty minutes."

With that he stormed out and left the rest of them in an awkward silence. None of them knew how to handle themselves. Waddan looked uncomfortable as well, almost apologetic, but his demeanor was by far the most relaxed of everyone in the room. He was the first to walk out, his gait suggesting excited determination. As soon as he had left the room, the distress lifted slightly. After him, each man exited in his own time, deep in thought about the ramifications of the conflict.

Akim felt that he had failed the king by keeping silent about his suspicions. He made his way to the king's office. He wasn't sure how he would handle the situation and was hoping the king would simply expect him to do what he normally did—provide information when asked.

He felt lonely as he stood in front of the door after knocking, waiting for the king to call him inside. He missed home. He missed living on the outskirts of a small village, only concerned with what was going on in his own life and how it related to the spiritual world that he loved so much. He missed spending his time making furniture and assisting people. For a moment it seemed completely bizarre that he found himself in the company of the king, dealing with betrayal on a level that was so far removed from the world that he knew. The responsibility felt too heavy to bear, despite the fact that he was a relative nobody in the king's entourage.

He was finally called to enter. The king looked more composed now, but still abrupt when he asked Akim to sit down and take out his set of symbols.

"You know that I love this country, don't you?" he asked. Akim nodded. "Do you know that I love the people and that I would do my utmost to be the best king I can be?" He didn't wait for an answer before he continued. "I am not even sure whether I am a true king or not. I came to this position because destiny led me here through a combination of being born in the right family and luck, although I am not convinced that luck is the right term any more. Common law doesn't dictate that the throne should be passed on by lineage, although that is the way it happens most of the time. The king has the right to choose his successor. But he has to consult his assistants and take their wishes into consideration. My uncle was a good king and he chose me. He had sons of his own and they weren't bad men—they didn't even bear me ill will when their father bestowed the unexpected honor on me. I hadn't expected it. I had had no idea. I don't even think I ever really hoped for it, although I had a dream for this country: to see the people well fed and happy.

"And now I'm here, thirty years later. There have been good times and bad times. I haven't always felt worthy of my position, despite the fact that the people have known a fair amount of prosperity. I have had difficult decisions to make and I have felt fear of failure. But since the day that I was inaugurated as king, I haven't felt as undeserving as today.

"When I look at other kings, I see what the heart of a king is mostly made of: the ambition to make history, to be remembered as the strongest and most important of them all, the one whose empire extended to all corners of the earth. All kings want their countries to prosper and want to be successful in their own right. In that respect I am no different to any other king. But when I look around and see the lengths most rulers would go to in order to achieve their ambitions, I wonder at myself. What makes me different is that I don't measure the prosperity of my country in financial terms only. I don't measure my own success by how much I have grown my empire, nor even by how much I am loved. I feel that if I always have the best interests of those living here at heart and act accordingly, I am ruling to the best of my ability. It doesn't mean that I will not make mistakes. Do you understand that, Akim?"

Akim nodded that he did. He wasn't sure what the king was on about. He was waiting for the king to express his disappointment because he had let him down in his hour of deepest need. But the king looked satisfied and said, "Good, now let's get to work."

He asked Akim what the best move would be under the circumstances. Akim looked at the symbols. They were not showing drastic changes, so he told the king to hang back and be defensive. The king asked if there was danger. In answer, the symbols showed fire and upheaval. As much as he didn't want to be the bearer of bad news, he had to tell the king that danger was imminent. He advised the king to act carefully or be prepared for cataclysm. The king then asked if there was a way that catastrophe could be prevented. The symbols showed courage and the eagle. They also showed him the bends of a flowing river and the phoenix. Akim told the king that only through acts of bravery could its effects be minimized. In that case catastrophe would be transformed to revolution. The country would adapt well to changes and find a new, more beneficial way of being.

The king was worried. He thanked him and asked if there was anything else from Akim's side. Akim gathered all his courage, forgot his position for a moment and blurted out, "Yes, Your Majesty, but it comes from me, not from the signs. I don't think Waddan acted the way he did because he is a fool. I also don't think he is simply ambitious and wanted to take advantage of his position just because he was enjoying the power. I think he has an agenda, although I have no idea what it is. I don't think he can be trusted. I cannot tell you what to do about it; I just have to tell you what I suspect." He kept his eyes locked with the king's. It was hard not to look away, overpowered by the king's superiority. The king narrowed his eyes and Akim could feel that his statement had perturbed him. Could he really be surprised? He couldn't imagine that the king didn't have his own suspicions.

The king eventually nodded and just said, "Thank you." He started scribbling on a piece of paper as a way of trying to work things out for himself. He continued, "I had reasons for having trusted Waddan, but I take your opinion into consideration. You may now go." Akim let out a sigh of relief when he saw that the king's eyes were still friendly. He greeted the king and left.

Chapter 13

For the rest of the afternoon he wandered around in the garden, mulling over the implications of all that he had witnessed that day. He resented himself for fretting over the king's matters the way the king himself and the rest of his entourage did. He was there mainly for the experience and because that was where life had taken him. But this time things were looking less than rose-colored. He was distressed because of what the symbols had shown him although he knew that it wasn't the way of the signs to inspire fear, but rather to tell the truth and assist. If they had shown him trouble, it meant either that it could be prevented or they were giving information to help them prepare. He had a feeling that it wasn't the former. If it was the case that nothing could be done, he was concerned that peace could be threatened. The king was a good king and they generally lived in a good country, regardless of whether or not he felt normal. At least he had the freedom to practice his own way of making sense of the world, and that in the company of the king, too. What would he do if the king would lose his sovereignty? What if they had to take up arms in order to protect the country? He tried to shake off the worry, but he couldn't quite get rid of a sense of doom after the events of the morning.

He came to rest at the fountain where he had met Samuel the first time, the same one where he had seen the reflection of the two birds flying side by side. Daylight was turning to dusk. The setting sun cast a fiery red ambience to the sky. Akim imagined that at the end of the world there was a dragon's lair. The dragon was now having fun catching the sun and blowing fire in all directions. The thought made him feel lighter. He missed Samuel; it had been nice to have someone to talk to at the palace for a few days. He missed his mother and Asteodor and he even missed Metis. The stars were coming out. It was new moon and soon the velvet sky was speckled with tiny sparks. The lights against the black sky made him think of a wizard's cape. Looking at the stars at night always stimulated his imagination. The universe was communicating with him. He asked to be shown the way for his life, but the thought struck him that life itself was the way. If he kept looking for guidance, he would end up confused. However, if he recognized each moment as one filled with potential, all he needed to do was to be the moment. The doors would open automatically and it didn't matter where he went.

A woman's voice came from the dark, startling him. "Can I join you?" At first he didn't know where it had come from, then he saw a movement to the left on one side of the fountain. An orange glow accompanied the movement; she was dressed in elegant clothes.

He blurted out, "Who are you?"

"Just someone," the woman said and came to sit next to him. She sounded amused but also slightly annoyed. He was afraid to look at her because she was so close—he didn't want to create the impression of staring. He could hear her breathing but she didn't say anything else. He wasn't sure if she expected him to talk. He wanted to turn his attention back to the sky but was afraid of appearing foolish, so he kept his eyes on the fountain. A swan swam by in the pool, looking like it was joined by the stomach to another one swimming upside down. The surface of the water was placid again despite the ripple of water from the fountain. The swan's plumage was visibly bright, as if it shone with a special light. It disappeared behind the fountain, leaving them in the darkness. The silence continued.

Akim wondered what time it was. He had probably missed dinner, but on this day he didn't care much. He was relaxed, almost sleepy. It was awkward sitting so close to a stranger and yet his drowsiness intensified. Soon his eyes started drooping. At the moment of falling asleep, he felt himself walking out of his body, wide awake in a world that was ethereal. He could see very clearly, but the world was much less dense and more malleable. Everything had a life of its own and could change and transform in an instant.

They were still next to the pool, but it was now as light as in daytime. On their side of the fountain he could see the palace and garden in the same arrangement as normal. Everything was in its right place but it looked different in quality and color. Most objects emitted light, especially the plants. The palace had a few patches on it that weren't normally visible. On the other side of the fountain, however, there was a vast desert with no sign of the normal surroundings. The fountain marked a boundary between two worlds, one that resembled the normal view of things and the other which belonged to a different dimension.

He looked around and realized that the woman had come with him. He turned to face her directly. Her clothes, which looked the same otherwise, were now blue, not orange. She looked at him with large, playful eyes. She was vibrant and didn't look afraid. She said, "You did know that the fountain was enchanted, didn't you?" She laughed at his surprise. "You didn't? Please tell me that you recognize me."

He didn't know what to say. He wasn't that astonished by the fountain opening the door to another realm, but by the fact that someone had come with him. He scanned his mind for mental images of the person in front of him but couldn't find any, which made him more bewildered.

Wait, Akim thought. Those dark eyes, the long, dark hair. It was because her expression was so different that she was almost unrecognizable. Could this lively woman really be, "The girl who woke me up that afternoon to tell me the king wanted to see me?" She nodded and giggled.

"Were you fooled by my shyness, my apparent pride?" She walked closer to him, smiling seductively. She stopped when she was very close, then giggled as she turned away. "Don't worry, you weren't fooled, I am that woman. But here I am not confined by the anxiety that goes with being in my body. I am free to express a lighter and bolder aspect of myself." She jiggled a bit with joy and excitement. Then she calmed down and continued to stare at everything around her, experiencing the quality of this different world. Akim was feeling a bit uncomfortable. He hadn't intended to cross the boundary and wasn't sure what he was doing there. The woman, however, didn't look concerned at all.

"What are we doing here?" he asked her.

"You don't know the legend of the fountain," she remarked. "I don't blame you, not many people do. Most of those who have heard about it think it's just folklore dating from a time when people still believed in magic. Many centuries ago, the spirit world existed by default consensus. Nowadays, if someone has a magical experience, the world thinks they're insane. But the stories that have survived through the ages are the ones of legend. That is the way of the spirits to stay with us.

"We all have memory of the spirit world in our subconscious minds; most people just don't believe that it's real. But even the unbelievers can't escape the world of the imagination. It stays with them in some way or another, mostly through the stories they tell their children. They enjoy dressing up like the Tooth Fairy, but because it doesn't help paying the bills, it's considered unimportant.

"Because people love their children, they allow them to live in their own worlds when they are very young. They want to protect them against the harsh truths of reality for as long as possible. But they never stop to consider that perhaps if grown-ups related better to the world of the imagination, the world maybe wouldn't be a place where children needed protection. People nowadays might believe that someone is insane if they believe in magic. But the fact that the folklore has survived means that there were a lot of insane people around many centuries ago. Still, not many people know the power of the fountain anymore.

"A long time ago the king was just the face of the country. Everyone knew that the real power was behind the scenes. In those days the goddess was still celebrated and people were more connected to Mother Earth. Since it was very important to look to her for survival, the women leaders were revered. Their subtle power didn't operate with grand displays of dominance. But because there was balance, people knew that these energies had to be esteemed if they wanted to build constructive lives. The gift of the female divinity would seem to have gone lost or underground. Yet it has not disappeared, it's just not visible to those who don't wish to see it.

"Although the palace has always been dominated by male rule, there was an agreement in olden days that the gardens would bear the mark of the priestess. They served as protection for the palace because of their spiritual nature. Its purpose was to fend off all bad vibrations before they had the chance to materialize. If malicious intent couldn't be fended off by magical means, the garden would at least provide a warning. This ensured that the king's rule would have enough time to prepare for danger before it was too late.

"The magic here is so strong that it would continue to be present despite any attempts to suppress it. The mystery in the garden has been woven in such a way that it would always be a gateway for true seekers. The enchanted pool will take those who want to go with it, even though most don't sense its mystery."

"I still don't understand why I have come here," Akim said. "I have crossed boundaries to the spirit world many times, but this time I haven't intended to do so. Did the fountain simply sweep us up and drag us along with her spell?"

"It would seem so," the girl said. "She must like you. Not only that, but she also must have something to show you. Shall we cross over to the desert?"

He nodded and took a step in her direction. She took his hand and they walked over the water in the direction of the fountain. They walked through it and dropped into the desert. Looking back, they could no longer see the fountain, only a very faint glimmer in the air which threatened to disappear. Her eyes told him not to worry.

There were only dunes around them. Akim followed the girl as she started walking across the yellow sands away from the portal, her hand still in his. She was caught in a reverie and he wondered what she was seeing. The sands around them were gathering as if in a whirlwind, moving in every direction. He could feel no wind. He recalled seeing a cactus here and there but otherwise nothing, apart from two or three large crows flying across the sky. He looked down, disturbed by the vastness of the sands and the brightness of the heavens. The girl kept walking as if hypnotized. He noticed that his shadow was jiggling about as if the sun were a massive torch rather than a stationary heavenly body. Before he could think twice about it, he looked up in the direction of the bright light. He couldn't stare at the sun directly, but his eyes came to rest close to it. There was a shimmer of movement that looked like a chariot of light. He only caught a glimpse of two dragon-like figures at the head before it disappeared. Further along there was a hint of the movement again, but the quality was too ethereal for him to distinguish the object in full sight.

He turned his eyes back to the ground as he kept walking next to the girl. The lightness of the sand with its brownish color and fine texture was a focal point that became more interesting as he went along. The color and the light of it was all that existed in the vast emptiness. The details gradually faded. First the crows vanished, then the cacti they encountered, then the blueness of the sky, the girl next to him, although he was still holding her hand. It wasn't that she wasn't there, she just wasn't a separate entity beside him anymore. She was part of him, part of his awareness that encountered the very special quality of the sand, its lightness. Gradually the sun, having absorbed the sky first, was also absorbed into the sand. His awareness and the sand were the only two variables. His awareness was grasping the sand being itself while the essence of the sand was communicating with him simply by being its light quality. There were only the observer and the observed. The observed was aware of itself being appreciated and shining all the more brightly because of it. At some point, the observer merged with the observed, having been fascinated by it enough to forget its own existence. He became the sand, which was so excited about being itself that it exploded with joy. He became one with the moment when the sand had come into existence. In that instant, he knew that within the creation of a tiny grain of sand, the entire universe was contained and all things were happening at the same time. All things were joyful for the sake of being themselves and also everything else.

Then the goddess showed herself to him, if that were possible. She assumed the form of the woman he had been walking next to a short while, which seemed like a thousand years before. She was the image of that woman projected in the sky, but more than that. She was a far older woman who simultaneously looked young and innocent. She was an angel with wings but also the snake he had encountered in the tree on his mission to find out about Samuel's past. She was saintly and pure but wrathful, too. She was an eagle and a mermaid, a virgin and a witch. She was the one who inspired through her chastity but also held men captive through desire for her, bringing them under her spell by giving all or little of herself but refusing to be imprisoned. She left men always wanting for more because her freedom of being was so spellbinding. She was everything Akim imagined a goddess would be and yet she was nothing close to anything he could imagine. She was completely indescribable. She was mother earth, giver and sustainer of life; she was the moon and the stars and her energy flowed through all that was. He understood that a little bit of her was inside him, but more so in his female companion.

The image dissolved and all that was left was a black sky filled with the most amazing heavenly bodies he had ever seen. There were stars, colors, milky ways, comets, and extra-terrestrial beings, each containing a life of its own and moving with the flow of the universe, incredibly content just to be itself. He stood wondering at this glorious canvas until at some stage he again became aware of the desert around him. It was alive with the light that was the same essence that flowed through all the marvels in the sky. The sands were showing a different aspect of themselves underneath the pitch black sky. They contained the same light of the sun as in daytime, but day and night communicated their essence in different ways even though they were the same.

Now that the desert had come back into his awareness, he realized that the woman was still with him. He looked in her direction and saw that she, too, was becoming aware of the person next to her. In her eyes he recognized the same sense of wonderment that he had felt, and he knew that she could observe it in him, too. The sky gradually changed back to blue and the scorching sun returned to its place. The character of the desert resumed its subtlety. The woman smiled at him and through her eyes he was back in the world the goddess had shown him. She squeezed his hand. When he looked up, there was a portal of light in the air, similar to the one they had entered the desert through. Looking back, he saw that the sky was a hybrid of the magical night sky and the blue sky of day. One was a layer over the other and he could see beyond the veil of one into the depths of the other. The woman nudged him and he turned back to the portal. She took his hand and led him through it.

For a few moments he didn't know where he was. He could see only black and felt dizzy. The world around him came back into his sight, but everything was blurring. When his focus returned to normal, he had a splitting headache. He was back at the fountain and it looked like daylight, but he realized that it was still night time, maybe close to dawn. The fog was thick and the palace garden quiet. He looked around him; the woman he had shared the adventure with was nowhere to be seen. The birds started singing again as the garden let go of its breath.

It was a shock to be back to reality after all he had seen and felt. He needed to find the woman who had been with him. He wanted her to explain to him what had happened so he wouldn't feel so alone and deprived back in the material world. He wanted someone to soothe his pain, not only because he had a headache, but because he was painfully aware of the fact that he was human and he didn't know what to do about it. Through all he had seen, the world had become too large for him to handle. He missed the days when he had been a child and his mother was always there to make everything right. He missed being too young to ask questions about who he was and precisely for that reason not having any responsibility.

He eventually got tired of looking for the woman and thought that he was lost in the palace gardens. Maybe they were just tricking him again and planned to swallow him whole at some stage. At that point he would almost have welcomed it. He stopped for a drink of water from the canal. When he had satisfied his thirst, he found the closest tree and sat down with his back to it, resolving not to think or care about anything until he felt recovered. He sat for a while, his mind completely devoid of everything except the need to rest. The atmosphere changed as it turned to daytime. His spirits were lifted by the birdsongs.

When he opened his eyes, she was there, lying asleep at his feet. She looked peaceful and was elegant even when sleeping. He curled up next to her and put his arm around her, drawing comfort from the warmth of her body. Morning turned to afternoon while Akim was in a deep, dreamless sleep. When he woke up, she was still there, her face close to his. There was a half-smile around the corners of her mouth. Neither of them spoke for some time while they looked into each other's eyes. He didn't feel ready to return to the world of the palace and all its problems. The world they had left behind felt unreal and too far away, and yet he couldn't be concerned about the things he normally dealt with after everything he had seen. The rush to get things done seemed more senseless than ever before.

As his senses and body were returning to normal, his awareness that the woman next to him was a stranger returned. Awkwardness ensued and he felt it was time to talk to her about what they had experienced.

"What was that all about?" he asked her. "I've been to other worlds before, but never with another person and never without intent. I don't know what it means." He looked at her questioningly.

"You sound so sure that it means something," she said as she got up and brushed the twigs and leaves from her clothes. "But maybe you don't have to know now. Maybe it will all be revealed to you in due course." She didn't look at him as she said it, which made him wonder if she had understood more than him. Suddenly, she was self-conscious again and in a hurry. The shy girl he had encountered on that fateful first day was back and she was fretting in his presence. "I have to go," she said, looking away and fidgeting with her hands. "Maybe I'll see you around the palace somewhere or bump into you again in a different world." She half-smiled again as she said it and a remnant of the intimacy they had shared was reflected in her face, but the nervousness returned and she hurried away.

"Wait!" he called after her. "I still don't understand anything."

She only half turned around as she called back, "Neither do I. I just know I have to go now." She was almost running as she said it.

"And I want to see you again," Akim said, more to himself than to her as she was now out of earshot. He watched her hurrying away, turning a few corners towards the direction of the palace until she wasn't visible anymore. He was disappointed and angry. All he wanted to do was to ask to see her again and have a proper conversation. Why did she have to hurry away? Although he had moved on from the pain of losing Metis, the hurt of unrequited love came bubbling up afresh as if the wound was recent. He didn't feel ready to fall for someone so hard again. If meeting the goddess would only bring him pain, then he wasn't sure if he was interested.

He thought of Montana—a real and specific goddess. Making love to her was easier because it was impersonal. She couldn't belong to him, and hence he didn't feel any loss for not being with her. And yet, an actual goddess couldn't lie next to him and provide warmth, nor be the person that he talked to every day. She couldn't be the one to love him more than anything else, for that reason alone making him feel that he deserved a place on earth because he made one person happy.

He resolved to forget about the woman whose name he didn't even know. If she cared about him, she could come and find him, and by the time she did, he might not be available anymore. He walked back to the palace, hoping the king hadn't looked for him. He had missed almost an entire day. The heaviness of the everyday existence, that he had by now gotten used to, soon returned. He willfully ignored the dull ache in his chest and pushed on, trying to focus on the normal happenings in the king's world.

Chapter 14

A few months passed without significant incidents. There was an underlying tension mounting in the palace, but most citizens still weren't aware of the menace. The king looked weighed down most of the time, and Akim felt sorry for him. Although the atmosphere in the palace was far from pleasant, he decided to stay to support the king. The relationship between the king and Waddan had become strained, although the latter had managed to keep his position. Akim was surprised that the king didn't treat Waddan with the kind of mistrust he would have expected. However, he felt at peace having spoken his mind—the king could take his advice or leave it.

Slowly but surely, Waddan's county was infiltrated by the men of Extar. Akim had a suspicion that the king was still in denial about what was happening. Little by little, the spaces of the natural countryside were making way for crop fields. The king didn't visit that region too often and when he did, he always found ways to justify the situation.

Akim didn't understand why the king didn't dismiss Waddan, but he appreciated that it might not be a solution. Waddan was bound to have considered this possibility and have a backup plan in place. Also, an impulsive move would probably not be wise if the king wanted to avoid conflict. While Waddan was still in his position, he had to at least pretend to serve the country. When communication with him was maintained, they had a better chance of picking up inconsistencies in his reports. If he had to disappear, they would have no way of knowing what he was up to. The best the king could do was to prepare for the worst and keep reigning to the best of his ability. Akim felt sad for him—it certainly wasn't what he deserved.

Even in the garden the magic was hiding. The spirits were reluctant to make contact with humans when circumstances weren't favorable. They felt at home when there was joy, love and freedom, but when these qualities were inhibited, they moved deeper into their own world.

He saw the woman he had shared the journey through the fountain with once or twice. When he did, she was friendly enough but didn't come close to being as personal as he would have liked. He treated her with aloofness and decided to pretend that nothing had happened. He still felt hurt by the way she had treated him and he wasn't going to beg her for attention. Her eyes always laughed when she saw him, though. He didn't understand her friendliness. He feared that it was a consolation prize because he couldn't have her even though he wanted her.

What confused him more was the way he always got the feeling that she was hiding something. He resolved not to care. On the few occasions that they spoke, she mostly talked to him about something official or made small talk. He wasn't interested in either. For all he cared she might as well stay away until she was willing to talk to him as someone whose hand she had held in another world.

He had a dream about her one night. She was standing at a balcony at one of the palace windows. She was dressed in light blue and had a lovely jewel strapped to her forehead. She looked as if she was yearning for something which she didn't have access to because she was trapped. The longing made her miserable and happy at the same time. She was happy with the thought of what she was longing for, but sad because it wasn't a reality. Although she appeared shut in, she didn't resemble a caged animal because she willingly chose to confine herself. It distressed her, but she tolerated it for the sake of an ideal that she served. The sacrifice was far from easy.

He approached her from inside the room that led out to the balcony. When she saw him, her eyes widened with surprise. But then she looked expectant, as if she had been waiting for him to come and tell her something without quite knowing it.

"Why are you here?" he asked her.

"Because I have to be," she said. "It is my duty. It is who I am." She looked away as she said it, out over the city. The light in her eyes was dim and he got the impression that she didn't understand her own choice to confine herself. She knew that it was necessary, but hadn't expected her light to burn lower because of it.

"It is who you are because that is what you choose," he then said, not trying to persuade her but as a matter of fact. "If you want to choose differently, that is all you have to do—choose differently. You can and will remain yourself if you choose what you are now as well as choose who you want to be and where you want to go from here." He turned around and walked away, not hoping or expecting that she would change her mind.

He woke up flustered because the dream had been so vivid. He immediately dismissed it because he didn't want to give her any importance. She obviously wasn't keen on returning his affection. If his subconscious mind persisted in telling him how much he wanted her, he would overrule it. However, he had trouble falling asleep again because thoughts of her kept haunting him; his heart was protesting against his will. His heart was telling him that he shouldn't give up without having really tried. But his mind rebelled against the possibility of the pain of rejection. He willfully put mind over matter, but it didn't quite work because his body was on his heart's side. Although he tried to push away thoughts of her, her image kept returning in his mind's eye and his body responded. He stood up and walked to the window for fresh air, thinking that he couldn't allow desire for her to have the final say. At long last fatigue took over and he went back to sleep.

When he saw her again, something in the way she reacted was different. There was a defiant light in her eyes, but she was blushing awkwardly, unsure of how to act around him. Although he didn't want to give in to his desire for her, he was secretly pleased with her changed reaction. His heart was hoping that the dream might have been a turning point, although he didn't really want to acknowledge this secret hope. Her new attitude didn't help to subdue his desire for her. His body would respond ever more feverishly when he saw or thought of her. The tension was mounting to a point where he thought the air would explode with the electricity between them.

The dreams about her didn't go away. However, they weren't as calm and collected as before. She was different. Instead of lonely and resigned, there was a wildness in her which she unleashed when alone with him. Whereas he was the one who had opened the door for her to walk out of her self-imposed prison in the first dream, she was now the one taking the lead in their physical encounters. In his dreams, she was like a wild cat, taking pleasure in the physical in an unrestrained way. She steered him towards what she wanted without subtlety and he was the pawn who had to play along. When she had had enough, she would push him away and go, leaving him with the knowledge that there would be more to come, but that she would decide when and where it would happen. He always woke up after these dreams feeling slightly drunk. When seeing her in real life shortly after, the memory would make him smile, and he would forget about being awkward or angry while she was blushing away. He hoped that if the dreams were telling him something, she would come and find him when she felt ready. All he needed to do was wait patiently.

Chapter 15

The night came when she made her first move. It was the king's birthday and he was holding an informal party for everyone who worked for him, including the palace servants. People from outside the palace were hired to serve dinner for the evening. Akim had a few interesting conversations with some of the servants that he didn't know well, but felt bored otherwise. After dinner some of the guests were becoming drunk and obnoxious, especially some of the king's closest men. He guessed that that was what happened when they dropped their facade of importance. Akim excused himself from the company and went outside to sit in the garden and look at the stars.

He stood on the porch at the main palace doors for a moment. With the moon a thin crescent, the garden was fairly dark and the stars were quite bright. He decided to venture deeper into the garden to find a spot where he could lie on his back and watch the sky for shooting stars. He walked into the darkness on the paths that he knew, then he side-tracked to walk into the places where the trees were denser. It became darker and quieter as he walked further away from the palace. The garden was tranquil, apart from a few crickets and the rustling of leaves as the wind blew through the trees.

He found a clearing which was the perfect spot to watch the sky. It reminded him a bit of the place on Samuel's old planet where he had found Montana's altar. The trees formed almost a perfect circle and the ground where he lay down was soft and damp without being uncomfortably wet. In the darkness the trees came alive and he could feel them watching him. The sky was also alive. If he used his imagination, he could see the colors and spirals he had seen in the desert on the other side of the fountain. He imagined the stars to be suns to other planets like the earth where there was also life and perhaps beings similar to humans.

Maybe they were more intelligent and looked after their planet better; maybe they treated each other with more respect. Maybe they were enlightened enough to guess that they weren't alone in a universe which was far too large for them to fathom. And perhaps they looked up and felt inspired by the vastness of creation to lead magical lives filled with love and courage. He didn't know, but it was a nice thought to have. He enjoyed the feeling that the night sky was talking to him. Maybe he wasn't so alone after all because everything around him was alive and made of the same substance that he was made of. He could hear the eagle's cry as if in affirmation.

How ironic was it that when he was living his "life" being busy and involved with society, he felt lonely and not particularly alive. But when he retreated to spend quiet time in nature, he felt connected and alive just by appreciating the stillness.

He was relaxed and not at all concerned about time. The routine of the palace and city life was forgotten. A twig broke not too far away from him as someone stepped on it. It took a second for him to grasp that there was another person close by. He felt slightly annoyed by the fact that his moment alone with the trees and the night sky was impinged on. He hoped that if he remained quiet, the person would walk past without noticing him.

He was disappointed when he heard the cautious footsteps coming closer. He looked in the direction of the sound. The person walked softly, as if not wanting to disturb him, if they were even aware of his presence. The footsteps came to a halt close to him. He could make out a dark silhouette between two of the trees. He kept quiet, not sure what to do. He still didn't know whether the person was by now aware of his presence or if they had, in fact, followed him there.

The figure came closer, walking carefully. As it stepped into the clearing, he saw that it was a woman. He was by now sure that she could see him since he was sitting in the clear starlight. His heart almost skipped a beat as he recognized the girl of the fountain. His instinct warned him to be defensive. He wasn't keen on having her come close to him just to be left behind again. His initial excitement at the possibility that his dreams had in fact meant something was now replaced by distrust. He decided to remain on guard and keep quiet until she told him what she wanted.

He watched her as she walked closer and sat down next to him. She looked at him and he waited for her to say something, but she didn't, and he turned away. He wasn't sure whether she was shy or waiting for him to do something. Perhaps she was just playing with him, creating an expectation for something when there would be nothing. She put her hand out and touched his arm. When he looked back at her, she came closer and wanted to kiss him, but he stopped her. She retreated and he didn't know whether she was disappointed because he hadn't immediately given in or whether she felt rejected. Still, he hoped that she would speak, but she didn't; she simply looked at him. He resumed watching the night sky.

They sat in silence for a while. He wasn't sure what she was up to while he was looking at the night sky but he managed to relax a bit. It was actually pleasant when he reminded himself that it was up to her to show him if she was really interested. His thoughts drifted into the background while he dreamed himself into the heavens, imagining all the things he had seen when they were in the desert together.

He felt her hand on his thigh where it rested for a few seconds before she explored further. He didn't pull back immediately, but also didn't look at her. He was enjoying the sensation of her touch, but he still didn't want to give in. Her hand was uncertain as it moved to his upper body. She leaned over towards him, her face not far from his. She was mysteriously beautiful in the moonlight, but he couldn't read her expression. She was acting bold, but also shy, and he found it really hard to fathom her. She put her one hand behind his neck, uncertainly, and gently pulled him closer. The message was clear: he had to either reject her outright or decide he was in and follow her lead. He waited for her kiss without pulling away, but he didn't respond fully. Her kiss was soft and her tongue tentatively felt its way to his lips and the inside of his mouth, probing gently, searching for a response. He could resist no longer, so he surrendered and kissed her back.

They made love for several hours. Through the process she transformed from an innocent girl to a goddess who knew all the secrets to enslave a man, demanding his loyalty until the end of time and giving him no choice but to concede. In the moment of fulfillment, he forgot who he was and became a speck of light on the canvas of creation. It was similar to the joys he had shared with Montana, except this time his heart was involved.

When they came out of the trance, he was surprised to see that it was turning dawn. She was holding him tightly. She let go and her hands and mouth passed slowly over his body one more time, leaving him craving for more. She got up having put her clothes back on and walked away in the direction of the palace. He didn't try to stop her, knowing that as in his dream, there would be more to come, but she would dictate when and where it happened. He could fall in with her wishes or decide not to have anything to do with her at all. There was no question as to which one he would rather live with.

He sat for a little while more, drinking in the birdsong and the trees around him, waiting for the sun to rise so he could greet it. He thanked the earth below his feet for the sustenance and stability that she provided and the sky overhead for watching over him and changing its face while remaining the same in essence. There were two small, fairly bright birds on a branch not too far away. He watched them sing their hearts out at the break of dawn. He wondered at the fact that they never got tired of singing at daybreak. They always continued to move with the same rhythms and seasons, being themselves until it was time to return to the earth. They were excited about each day in the same way that the earth welcomed the sun with open arms and a lot of beauty each morning.

There was magic in nature and all the things that had been given to us for free. How strange that humans dismissed all that was naturally good as unimportant while striving to create things that were dull and only useful for the purpose of helping them create more dullness. The earth wanted all that lived on it to be well and nature had built a mechanism into each of us to strive towards what was good for us. When and how did humans start to think that this mechanism was unnatural and that it hindered rather than helped us? Where did our mistrust of life come from? It made no sense, he thought. None of us had asked to be here, we were brought into this world as an aftermath of our parent's actions. At some point we started believing that we had to earn our right to be here.

Akim couldn't help wondering how many more people would lead happy and productive lives if they saw life as their privilege rather than an obligation. Those who became depressed with reality were actually blessed to be given the chance to rethink their priorities. Most others were just sheep being herded by forces they weren't even aware of, all the time looking at the sheep closest to them, concerned about whether the other one was better than themselves or at least playing the game of being herded better than them. Akim sighed. He wished that more people could be like little birds, considering each sunrise as an opportunity to sing their special song.

The sun came up and he made his way back to the palace where he prepared for the day ahead, determined to keep the song in his heart alive because he had been fortunate enough to witness the sunrise.

Chapter 16

The king's affairs didn't fall in place over the next few weeks or months. The underlying sense of gloom was growing in the country as more people sensed that things weren't in order. The dismal atmosphere affected Akim more than the average person. Although he continued to serve the king to the best of his ability, he did so with less than abundant enthusiasm. He went through the motions but didn't feel that he was making much of a difference.

Whenever he could, he escaped to the deepest corners of the garden or the hills outside the city. There he felt restored, but unfortunately it didn't last as long as he had hoped after his return to the city. As much as he just wanted to get away, he knew that his gifts weren't about escaping when he felt like it, but providing assistance when he was in a position to do so. That also meant that he had to know an experience first-hand to understand what others were going through. The circumstances weren't close to what he had envisioned for himself, but he resolved to endure it until the time came for him to leave or take action otherwise.

Waddan was the only person who looked content. Complaints from his section were becoming more frequent, but he was doing what he could to keep it undercover. Although Akim didn't physically visit that part of the country too often, his dreams and meditations were showing him that it was the source of misery. The people were being subdued to slaves with their livelihood having been taken from them. Feeling like a failure, Akim was finding it ever harder to trust the oracle. He took each day at a time to avoid becoming too heavy.

The danger soon took the form of armed men gathering at the border. Determining the right course of action was difficult since the forces of Extar already had a strong presence. The king still didn't understand how the ruler of Extar had managed to distort things in such a way that he himself appeared as the aggressor. He could almost believe their grounds for acting the way they did when listening to a representative of Extar. He was past the point of denial, but he couldn't decide what to do.

Akim's relationship with the girl of the fountain continued in much the same way as it had started. When they happened to meet in the palace or any other public place, she would act with a combination of cool pride and bashfulness, or pretend to ignore him when she was too uncomfortable. But on some evenings she would find him in the garden when he was outside to watch the night sky. On these evenings she hardly ever talked to him, but she took the lead and possessed him in body and soul. She knew that he couldn't resist because he wanted her so badly.

These encounters were so otherworldly that he almost couldn't make sense of the experience. Strangely, he hardly ever felt bad because she didn't talk to him too much in public, regardless of whether he understood it or not. He knew that she would always be back for more. Occasionally he hoped that the relationship would lead to something more than a secret affair. In the meantime, he would just go along without questioning it too much—it was too special to give up. It was what kept him going despite the frustration of his inability to protect the country against harm. Sharing with her was his little path to paradise even if he didn't come close to actually having her.

The day eventually came that he found out her name. She came to join him while he was walking in the garden. It was the first encounter they had that vaguely resembled a relationship other than the first day they had spent together. They were deep enough into the gardens to be fairly far from the palace. It was already out of sight, which meant that they had moved past the boundary where the magic started to unfold. Here it was no longer a predictable place that could be known by anyone, but an organism that had a will of its own and assumed whatever form it wished to promote its agenda. The best the garden dweller could do, as Akim had discovered, was to go along and trust that the garden would eventually spit him out. It was a marvelous adventure, but it could be daunting since it was impossible to orientate oneself. However, he had also learned that the garden was benevolent and usually showed the traveler what he needed to know.

Initially, he wasn't even aware that she was close to him. He was on a path where the trees weren't so frequent but were exceptionally large and old. The path was neatly paved with old stones that formed pictures like a mosaic. There were suns, moons and stars as well as snakes sliding up and down trees. There were also the waves of the ocean with dolphins and whales gliding through the water. Some of the pictures told tales of what looked like the gods of old, just like in the chess room. There were fairies and mermaids, warriors, naked people and tree spirits. It resembled the world of the subconscious that could not be accessed in normal waking life.

The most interesting thing was that it followed no particular order. The dolphins weren't far away from the heavenly bodies and the eagle was flying below the roots of a tree. He guessed that each space represented clusters of symbols belonging to a specific entity as that would account for the fact that themes weren't necessarily contained. In the same way, people could draw power from emblems belonging to different realms and they were often more versatile for doing so. There was a wolf snuggling up against a sun, for instance, with a winged horse crossing the border into the night sky on the opposite side of the path. The sun image on the pavement caught his eye and as he watched it, he became aware of the special quality of the sun in the sky. It was a bright source of light which his eyes could somehow handle. It was warm but not with the kind of scorching heat that made one feel tired.

His eye was drawn to a bed of bright yellow tulips. They were representatives of the sun that intensified its warm energy. He noticed that the garden was particularly tidy. There were lots of flowers that were clustered together according to type. There were butterflies that flew in orderly fashion, if it were indeed possible for butterflies to do so, and the hedges were cut with clean precision. The lawns were immaculate with their even surfaces and impeccable dark green color. Between the hedges the paths led to small fountains that flowed out of perfect sculptures into pools shaped in flawless circles. Even the waves that circled out from where the water dropped into the pool moved in concentric expanding rings. The surfaces were immaculate reflections of the faultless combination of tree and sky hanging over them, broken up only by the rings moving in geometric rhythm.

The caterpillars were enchanting as they conjured up images of the beautiful butterflies that they would be, concealing the fat cylindrical shapes that moved forward like waves. This garden was a fairy tale world that operated in delightful symmetry. The pictures embedded on the pavement were the only suggestion that the garden wasn't all innocent perfection, but rather a magical representation of an ideal world projected by a force that had its own plan, even if only to provide for travelers a moment of escape from the world outside. The garden was perhaps more interesting knowing this than if one were to judge it solely by what it presented other than the artwork. Akim couldn't help being curious about the story and intent behind the fairy tale representation.

He was standing quietly on the lawn admiring the garden when she walked up to him from behind and put her arms around him. When he turned around to look at her, she looked vulnerable with worry. He supposed that she felt different when the darkness wasn't around to protect her with only the moon and stars to guide her moves. Instead of being the powerful goddess that could subdue all men, she now looked soft and exposed as a woman. He wanted to ask her what was bothering her, but she just pulled him closer and buried her face in his neck. He could feel the wetness of a teardrop. When she pulled away to face him again, her emotions were under control. She kissed him, enjoying it as an innocent girl who didn't know or even want anything more than that.

She took his hand and led him to the closest tree where she pulled him to sit down next to her. She kissed him again, this time letting her usual night-self return while she took him firmly and made him her own. He enjoyed feeling the warmth of the sunlight and seeing her naked body in full as well as the light in her eyes.

Afterwards, she didn't immediately get up to walk away, but instead lay in his arms while he held her. When she faced him, he got the impression that she wanted to say something but didn't know how. The worried expression on her face was back and she looked almost timid. He watched her expectantly. She finally took a deep breath and spoke.

"My name is Matima," she said. "And you are ...?"

"Akim," he said.

"It's nice to finally meet you," she said with a shy smile. She looked affectionately in his eyes for a few seconds before continuing, looking concerned again. "I want you. I really do. But I'm not sure if I can be in a relationship with you." She tried to bring her emotions under control as she looked away. Akim's heart lurched out of his chest at the unexpected rejection, but a small voice inside him told him to be quiet and keep listening. He was hoping that his heart's protest wouldn't show on his face.

She still couldn't face him. A few times she opened her mouth as she inhaled to speak, but then she would close it again. From the angle where he was watching her he thought he could glimpse a tiny teardrop. On the other hand, it might have been wishful thinking on his part or pretense from her side, as the stubborn little voice that refused to get hurt again told him.

She finally managed to regain her composure and turned to look him square in the eye. She faltered several times. "I cannot ... This is not ... My father ...."

She gave up and started crying. The little voice was telling him again that she was just pretending to care and that she had simply used him. A part of him wanted to comfort her, but another part of him wanted to walk away, closing the door so there would be no way back. His heart finally convinced him that it could no longer take the pain of being with her occasionally, but never really having her. He got up to leave, even though it was possibly the hardest thing he had ever done. He was sure that something inside him would physically break. But with that part of him broken, he said to himself, he could not fall into the same trap again. The little voice insisted that fighting for her would be a waste of time and energy.

He hadn't walked for fifty meters when she came rushing after him and threw herself in his arms, sobbing uncontrollably. She cried, "I'm not going to let you walk away without listening to me first!" Every time he wanted to pull away, she held onto him more tightly. When her sobs were coming in slower bursts, she started talking.

"My father would kill me. This is not what I was born to do. I am already so deeply shamed because of the way I have seduced you like a woman of no values. If he had to know ...," her eyes widened with dismay as she said this. "He would be profoundly disappointed in me for letting him down. He would be shamed by my imprudence and consider me unworthy of all the privileges I have inherited. He would think that I am not serving the greater good." She sobbed some more, then her face changed and there was a defiant light in her eyes.

"And yet I couldn't resist, the pull was too strong. I could, but I didn't want to, because it felt better than anything I had ever considered important. Although my head was warning me that it was the dumbest move I could make, my body was telling me a different story. I wanted to give expression to my love for you, even if only on a physical level. I wanted to do as I please, be my own person, experience magic and ecstasy that was far beyond what the eye can see. I wanted to know what it was like to become one with the universe through merging with another person in body and soul. I wanted to speak the language that the eyes can understand but words fail to give expression to. I wanted to know the person whom my body has chosen, because without desire I cannot truly know that language, and I would rather not know it at all than experience a toned down version of it." Her eyes were on fire when she finished. A moment later she was shocked at what she had said. She blushed and continued "Oh dear ... I said that I love you?" She started rambling again about how inappropriate her actions were, but Akim interrupted her.

"You said you loved me?" he looked at her in disbelief. He was delighted. His body was tingling and yet he felt that it was too good to be true.

"Wait a minute, who is your father and what is his problem with me?" He eyed her suspiciously, feeling judged. He was well aware of the fact that some people considered him strange. However, he had a gentle disposition and he treated most people fairly. He had his reservations as far as Waddan was concerned, but other than that he didn't know of enemies. Even Waddan wouldn't consider him important enough to be a threat.

She looked confused by his question at first, then understanding dawned. She looked at him incredulously. "You don't know who my father is?" She was now irritated. "Has it ever occurred to you that the man you work for might have family even though he doesn't necessarily display them in public? Have you considered that someone of my age wouldn't hang around in the palace for no reason? Are you so wrapped up in yourself that you haven't realized what I'm doing here?"

Her words hit home as he realized that he had been making assumptions based on what he wanted to be true. Where there was a lack of information, he had been painting his own colorful picture.

"The king's daughter?" He felt as dismayed as she had been looking all along when the words came out of his mouth. She nodded. It couldn't be, and yet it was. Although he understood her position, he was stung by her suggestion that the king might not approve of him as a lover for his daughter. He knew that there was more to it than that, but still. She looked astonished that he hadn't realized the truth before. His pride got the better of him and he reacted coolly.

"What exactly would be your father's problem with me?" There was hurt behind the icy expression in his eyes. "Am I not one of his advisors that he trusts with the most important matters of the country or his career? Are we not friends despite our difference in status? Is he not a good man and don't you trust him enough to believe that he would want his daughter to be happy? Or is it just your excuse for using me to have some fun and then walking away whenever it suits you?"

"No," she protested. He softened a bit and decided to give her a chance. "He wants me to be happy. But I still have to bear in mind the best interests of the country, and that means that I have to at least consider suitors from other countries that we have a good relationship with. He wants me to be in love with the person I get married to, but he wants me to be in love with the right person. Meaning, the one with whom marriage would serve the best interests of the country. It's not that he doesn't want what is in my best interests, but in his eyes it's the same thing. I cannot escape my destiny. Especially now that things are at a point where we might lose all that is good, it is more vital than ever that I fulfill the role I was born for. Don't you understand?"

She cried out the last sentence as her internal conflict came to an outburst. "I am not free to do whatever I want to. My responsibility will haunt me until I accept it." Her shoulders were hanging in despair and she said the last part with quiet resignation. Akim didn't know what to do, so he just held her. It was no use trying to persuade her to make the choice he wanted her to make. If he did, she might resent him later. He could invite her to walk with him, but she had to determine her own way.

It didn't mean that he would give up without a fight. If he expected her to stand up for what was important to her, he had to do the same. He said without aggression, "I want to be with you because I love you. Everything you said might be right and what your father believes might also be right. But here's what I think. Sometimes we have to trust that love will show us the way. If you want to live the way you were born to live, do not try to understand your destiny. Allow what's in your heart to guide your steps. You have seen what I have seen in the desert on the other side of the fountain, maybe even more. Do you really think that you are in control and that your father knows what is best for you?" His voice was gentle as he talked to her. He didn't try to coax her; rather, he spoke directly from his heart, hoping it might wake up something within her. He didn't know where he got the strength to talk to her so openly without pushing her, but it felt as if something deeper within him had taken over for the time being. The urge to control the outcome might return later.

"There is something else you have to know," she said, looking away. "The King of Extar's son is interested in me. And if my father conceded and I agreed to get married to him, it might be the only way to salvage the situation on the border. At least then I could take charge and would have some influence over what is happening there. My father sees it as a way to maintain peace." Her hands were fiddling with a little thread that she had torn from her dress. She appeared disassociated from the information because she couldn't bear to be fully present in her body as she said it. Akim's heart sank.

"So what are you going to do?" he asked.

"I don't know," she said softly and turned back to look him in the eye. "You have to know this, I love you." She got up and left, leaving him sitting on the grass that didn't look so perfect any more, nor did the tulips look as yellow or happy as they had earlier. He didn't try to stop her. The sadness was spoiling his experience of the enchanted garden that he believed was meant for people who needed rest. The strong feeling that all would be right had left his body. He broke down in tears, fearing that he would lose the woman he loved to another man who couldn't possibly care for her as much as he did. The best he could do was to trust that love would win. He had always believed that it would eventually, but the question was when? He didn't want to deal with what would happen otherwise until it did.

Chapter 17

He didn't see her for another week or two, and he knew that she was avoiding him. He didn't know how he managed to go about his day to day duties and still be of assistance to the king. Knowing the harsh truth, it was excruciating to be unable to express his feelings. The king didn't seem to notice and luckily he didn't ask for any advice about relations with Extar. Akim was convinced that he would have lost his composure.

His depression was augmenting every day. He had never thought it would be possible for him to lose his zest for life. Up until that point he had always kept his head down and moved forward despite setbacks, believing that he would eventually emerge stronger. The problem was that the depths looked bearable from the crest of a wave. Yet the feeling that he could conquer the whole world could not last. He had to come tumbling down at some point because that was what waves did: they moved up and down. The higher he felt at the crest, the more disheartened he would normally feel at returning to a low point. He had accepted it as part of the rhythm of life, but now everything was only bleak.

When he kept busy, he felt numb and the shades of the day would be monotonous. In the dark of night, however, there was no escape from his feelings. The gloominess would multiply in his mind until it filled his entire soul. All he could feel was blackness, with the occasional fragment of silence within the storm. The despair was less flat than the grey and white in which he saw the world during the day, but it was also more unbearable. It moaned and screamed and was filled with cries for help. His pain contained the suffering of everyone else that had ever been on earth, concentrating itself in his soul. At times he thought that his body could no longer bear the pain, at which point he would get up and busy himself with something just to keep his mind occupied. Dawn would arrive and he would get ready for the day ahead, the numbness intensified by lack of sleep.

If Akim still had much feeling left inside him, he would have been surprised at his own reaction because he had always believed that love couldn't be contained. People only disempowered themselves if they believed that things had to work out in a specific way or that they needed another person in order to be happy. These thoughts still seemed absurd; however, it was much easier to believe in his own ability to make himself happy regardless of what was happening around him when life was flowing. Now he didn't know or care where his internal spark had gone. He didn't even know whether it had to do specifically with Matima. He felt that life was pulling a spiteful trick on him.

He was angry at life, because hadn't he given his best? Hadn't he loved truly and deeply from the heart and whatever other places inside him that he hadn't even been aware existed until he loved someone with all that he had? He couldn't accept that his love had gone to waste, and he no longer wanted to believe in it. If life and love were one and the same and it couldn't be controlled, then it had to find a way of earning back his trust. He wouldn't chase after it if the only reward was a slap in the face.

Akim would sit in the garden and in his mind shout out at the skies and the universe, asking if it was still looking after him. The feeling that everything would be all right had all but left him. It only showed up vaguely from time to time as an old friend that wasn't welcome any more.

When he eventually saw her again, it felt like eternity had passed. As much as seeing her provided relief, it was also a shock to his system that intensified the pain. She had followed him into the garden and approached him while he was busy ranting internally. He felt hope budding, but he was so angry at hope that he didn't want it to interfere with his self-pity. A part of him wanted to run away, but he was glued to the spot.

There were dark circles under her eyes and she was pale. The voice in his head insisted that it was all an act. However, the thought struck him that if it were possible, she looked a little bit worse than him. She struggled with herself for a moment before running closer and throwing her arms around him. His wall of defense tumbled down in a mixture of conflicting emotions. He couldn't push her away. It might be the last chance to hold her.

"I missed you," she said into his shirt. "I am so glad to see you." He didn't know what to say. It wasn't good enough; what he wanted to hear was that she wouldn't let anything come between them. She had to put her money where her mouth was, otherwise it meant nothing. He couldn't go through losing someone he loved again because they would rather succumb to other people's wishes.

"Can we sit down and talk?" she asked. His mouth was too dry to speak so he simply nodded. She took his hand and led him deeper into the garden. They sat down in the shade of a massive tree with star-shaped, pointy leaves. The sound of birdsong calmed him. For a moment he forgot his anger and despair and the urge to be close to her returned. He felt lazy and dreamy and wondered if he was being enchanted by the garden. She was uplifted, too. He suspected that it wasn't what she had planned, but under the spell of the garden she seduced him. When they emerged, they felt light enough to talk, strangely detached from their problems.

"You know, I came here today to tell you that we should stop seeing each other," she said. "Not because I don't want you, but because the situation had become unbearable for me as I am sure it had become for you. I felt that I couldn't hurt you any longer. I couldn't see a way for us to be together. Now I know that I was too afraid to risk losing everything that I thought made me who I was. I understand now that my being would be poisoned if I don't stand up for myself. I would end up living a life of resentment if I fall in with what others dictate for me. I wouldn't pretend not to care about anything I might lose, but if that has to happen in order for me to be my own person, then so be it. I shall not break off my relationship with you.

"As soon as I feel ready, I will talk to my father and express my wish to be with you. I believe that if we do what is best for us, it would also be in the best interests of everyone else, regardless of whether or not they would see it. Our love is what is most important now. Imagine what the world would be like if everyone insisted on being free to act according to their heart's desires. Do you think that there would be less conflict and hatred?" She started giggling as she said it. It was contagious and both of them laughed, partly because it was so obvious and yet nobody noticed, and partly because they were relieved with being back together. Akim knew that the road ahead would not be easy, but he was ready for it. He wanted to walk next to her, shining the light of their love into the world. He didn't care what darkness might befall them. With her by his side he was strong enough to handle it.

They made their way back to the palace, hand in hand, without caring much about whether someone saw them or not. Closer to the palace Matima let go of his hand, saying that she needed time to adjust. However, she wouldn't pretend to be unfamiliar with him anymore. If word reached her father's ears, then she would deal with it.

Now that Akim was feeling better himself, it was far more obvious to him that almost everyone else was in bad spirits. He also now realized why the king hadn't notice how depressed he had been—his mood hadn't been in stark contrast to the general feeling of dis-ease that was floating around. It felt good to be back in a position where he could provide assistance to others. Although he had conflicting emotions toward the king, he had to remind himself that the king was unaware of his feelings for his daughter. Also, he was still Matima's father and Akim knew that she loved him dearly.

At night Matima would sneak into his room and wake him up to lie next to him. She would sometimes stay until right before dawn, at which point she would return to her own room. They saw more of each other during the day in the palace. Although they didn't make their relationship obvious, he would be very surprised if people weren't noticing. It was only a matter of time before rumor reached the king.

They were riding the wave without planning too far ahead, but Akim was concerned since Matima hadn't discussed her decision with her father yet. Whenever he asked her about it, she shrugged it away. He didn't want to push her too much. It would come out sooner or later and when it happened, things would be hard enough to handle. It was best to savor being carefree while they still had the chance.

Chapter 18

While Akim was still enjoying the calm before the storm, he was getting nervous because the storm didn't come as soon as he had expected. Something was simmering underneath the surface. He wondered why the king hadn't yet confronted Matima when things between them were as serious as they were. Still, he hoped that the plan to marry her to someone else had been discarded.

But somewhere at the back of his mind, the suspicion persisted that the king had just been too quiet lately. An invisible hand would come out of the darkness during those nights when sleep evaded him. It would make its way towards his throat where it would close around his neck like a claw, preventing him from breathing freely. When he managed to fall asleep, his dreams were troubled. He would see Matima walking away from him in bridal attire, looking despondent. He would wake up in a sweat and tell himself that he needn't worry because they couldn't force her.

When disaster struck, he wasn't ready for it at all and neither was Matima, but in a way he felt relieved that things were out in the open. Matima found him in the palace garden, crying so much that she could hardly talk.

"I had a huge fight with my father," she said. "He knows about us. He wants me to stop it because the king of Extar has made an offer. It would solve most of our problems, but it involves me getting married to his son. My father says he is a good man, less aggressive and ambitious than his father, but I don't care. I told him that I want to be with you but he thinks he can persuade me to change my mind. He believes I will realize that you and I are just a silly infatuation and that real love is serving your country.

"He doesn't want to listen to me. He thinks he is the king and I will follow orders. But to me he is my father, not the king. He says that he didn't know about us. I want to believe him but I don't. He has ears and eyes everywhere; I am sure someone would have mentioned something to him. I think he willfully chose to ignore it. Doesn't he care about me?"

She took a few deep breaths. He was afraid to ask what the outcome of the conversation was. She continued.

"He told me that he had already agreed terms with the king of Extar, although he had made it clear that he would talk to me first. He made it sound like a pretense of consent. He had thought he would tell me what to do and I would fall in because he is the king. Then he would tell himself that he hadn't forced me to do anything. He looked desperate, but he doesn't understand. In the end he said they had to start the wedding arrangements while he gave me some time to think about it. He trusted that I would make the right decision. Really?" She was furious. "I have already told him that I don't want to. If he wants to pretend I said something else then I don't take responsibility!"

"So what are you going to do?" Akim asked with a knot in his stomach. As the words came out of his mouth he knew that he should have kept quiet.

"What do you mean what am I going to do? Are you mad? How many times do I have to tell you I want to be with you? You're just like my father; you don't listen to anything I say." She got up and started to walk away, but he ran after her. He asked her not to leave because he wanted to spend a few more minutes with her. She softened and he held her, trying to comfort her in spite of his own distress.

After she had left, he sat in the garden for a little while longer. Only then did the full implications of what had happened hit him. He was very angry at the king for being so willfully ignorant, but having Matima on his side made it easier for him to be empathetic. The best he could do was to trust that they would find a way at the right time. In the meantime, he would take one day at a time.

Akim didn't attend dinner that evening as he didn't want to see the king. Early the next morning he received a message from the king requesting his presence. He wasn't excited at the prospect of confrontation, but he wanted to get it over with. As he approached the king's meeting room, he was filled with trepidation.

When he entered the room, the king's usual seat was empty. It felt strange not to see the friendly yet serious face in its usual place. The king was standing at the window with his back to the door. Akim was concerned that he had not heard him enter, but when he had taken his place at the table, the king turned around. He had gotten used to the king looking worried, but this morning it looked like he had aged by ten years.

"Good morning, Akim," he said sternly.

"Good morning, your majesty," Akim answered, trying to keep his voice even. The king took his seat in his usual place. He remained quiet for a while and Akim wondered if it was as hard for him as it was for himself. Being faced with the king, Akim could imagine how difficult it must have been for Matima. He had no doubt that she was the one who suffered most. For a moment the king's outward appearance dissolved and Akim saw him in a different light—a concerned father whose objectives clashed with his official persona as a king. He fidgeted with his hands before he started talking.

"You have been almost like a son to me, Akim," he said without looking up. Have been? Apart from the past tense which bothered him a little bit, Akim thought that the metaphor was a bit strong. He remained quiet and waited for the king to continue. When he did, he was slightly incoherent. "You know that I do my best to be a good king. What you don't know is how much I love my daughter and how hard I try to be a good father. You are a good man and I love you as a friend. There is something I have to ask you." He looked very serious. "Do you love Matima?"

"Yes, your majesty, I do," he said.

"Good," the king said, almost too fast. "Now if you love her, do you want what is best for her?"

Akim thought that he was getting a hint of where this conversation was going, but he wasn't going to play the king's game. "I don't need to, your Majesty," he said. "I love her and that is all there is to it." The king looked at him questioningly, so he said, "I do not have authority to decide what is best for her. She decides. I don't *want* her to be happy because that would imply that she cannot make herself happy. I see her as perfectly capable of knowing what is good for her." He could hardly believe the words coming out of his mouth.

All the worry and the anger of the last few weeks had built up somewhere and were now coming out in controlled verbal expression, steering itself exactly in the direction where he wanted it to go. It might not work in his favor, but he wasn't interested in maintaining pretenses. He wanted to defy the king and demonstrate to him that what he was doing wasn't right, regardless of whether he found a way to justify his actions or not. He didn't care whether the king would listen. He needed to say what he was feeling. The king looked taken aback at the unexpected reaction.

"You say you love her?" he asked with one eyebrow raised, his voice calm but icy. His sarcastic tone made Akim want to grab him by his robes to shake him awake. Akim knew that he was probably the one to witness the straw that broke the camel's back.

The king continued. "Do you know what love is, young man? I don't even want to imagine in what capacity you know my daughter, but you don't know her in the way I do. You were not present when she was born. You haven't raised her and taught her what life is about. You don't want what is best for my daughter, you want what is best for yourself. She is the daughter of a king. Do you honestly believe yourself worthy of a princess? Do you think you have what it takes to lead by her side? Do you think you can escape the hand of fate? You might think so, young man, but I am the king and that means I am the one to decide. You are dismissed from your job. Whatever your services have meant to me, I don't need them anymore. You shall leave the palace and return to where you came from to be the person you were destined to be. You shall leave my daughter alone and no longer compromise her chance to fulfill her destiny. Do you have any questions?" He looked at Akim coldly. Although his voice had raised somewhat during his speech, he ended in the same cool, calm tone he had started with.

Akim was so stunned that he forgot to be upset. Now that he thought about it, it all made perfect sense. He didn't understand why he hadn't expected this. He prayed silently that the king wouldn't be forceful about it. He did a quick math and figured that his best chance would be to act resignedly and fearful. At least in that case he might have a chance to talk to Matima. He was also hoping that the king would want to make it look as if he had left voluntarily, in which case it would be easier to persuade Matima that he hadn't loved her that much. He decided to bargain on the king's fear that word of what happened would eventually reach Matima if he were to be thrown out of the palace. He cast his eyes to the ground and muttered, "I don't have any questions, your majesty, I understand." He waited for the king's next order.

The king said, "Go and pack your things as fast as you can. A representative will be sent to escort you to the carriage that will take you home. Do not even try to go looking for her. I am sure you wouldn't want to make it harder for her. If you respect her, you will leave without looking back and find someone of your own caliber. You will remember her as a fond memory, knowing she is happy in the capacity she was born to fulfill." He was quiet for a few seconds, then he said, his voice now softer, "Akim, thanks for all your assistance over the last two years. You might not believe it now, but some day you will be able to see that I have acted in your best interests, too. You have been a dear friend to me and I did love you almost like one would love a son." There was a hint of tenderness on his face, then the hard expression returned as he turned away. Akim imagined that it was too uncomfortable for the king to keep talking to him, so he took it as his queue to leave.

Chapter 19

Akim didn't know how he got through the next thirty minutes. Instinct took over as soon as he had left the room. All he needed to do was take the right gaps. He stood for a minute or two concentrating on what he had to do—find Matima. He called to the eagle, owl and the universe, asking them to present him with a plan. He imagined that the eagle was entering his body, applying its focus through his eyes. The owl told him to make himself invisible, as a bird of prey in the night.

He didn't quite know what happened next. He had a vague memory of acting nonchalantly while turning a few corners in the palace. He remembered walking fast at times and having a picture of her in his mind's eye sitting in what looked like a small courtyard. It didn't look familiar, but his subconscious mind guided him there. He prayed that she would be alone.

When he found her there was a girl with her that could have been a servant. Judging by the way in which they were talking, the girl appeared to be her friend. He hoped that she could be trusted. Matima's eyes widened with surprise when she saw him. She immediately looked anxious as his mere presence in that part of the palace was a sure sign that something was wrong. She asked the other girl to give them a moment of privacy.

He buried his face in her neck for a few seconds. He took her hands in his and talked to her in an urgent yet muted voice. He looked at her with pleading eyes so she would understand the severity of the situation.

"I have to go," he said. "I cannot stay in the palace any longer. I do not want to leave you. Will you be able to meet me outside the palace tonight?" he asked, his hands tense around hers. She was caught off guard, but she understood the importance.

"I will find a way," she said. "Just tell me where I have to meet you." Akim hadn't had the chance to think about it, so he gave her the first place that came to mind.

"We can go to the hills on the western side of the city. Meet me at the bottom of the footpath where the city ends and the hills begin." She agreed and he relaxed, knowing she was familiar with the place. "I'll try to be there early, but I'll wait for you until you come." He gave her a quick hug and she held him tightly for a second or two. He pulled away and left without looking back. He made his way out of what now felt like a labyrinth, walking in the direction where he thought his room was. He tried to keep his movements casual despite the fact that his heart was pounding in his chest. It was getting ever harder to resist the urge to run, not only away from the area where he wasn't supposed to be, but also from the palace. If he were to be escorted home it would be incredibly hard to escape unnoticed. He wanted to avoid forceful treatment for as long as possible.

He could hardly believe that he now had to hide from the king he had tried so hard to support and whom he had loved, even though he wouldn't go so far as to say that he had loved him like a father. He still wanted to give the king the benefit of the doubt. He couldn't imagine the king would take any extreme actions. However, he also couldn't underestimate the king's power. It wouldn't be hard at all to make sure that he and Matima would never be able to see each other again.

He finally reached his room and collapsed on the bed that was no longer his. He took a few deep breaths to calm down before he frantically started packing. He had already lost time and didn't want whoever would escort him to think that there was any reason to mistrust him. He had to co-operate but not to such an extent that it would raise suspicion. He resolved to act as low-key as possible; if he managed to be boring enough then he was sure their attention would drift elsewhere.

The guard arrived about two seconds after he had finished packing. It was the same one who had come to pick him up from his home the first day. He didn't look threatening, which was a good sign. After all, he wasn't a prisoner and he hadn't done anything wrong. Now he had to deal with the trickiest part: finding a way to stay in or close to the city until the following morning.

Since he had no solutions, he continued to pray silently. While walking to the carriage, he tried to slow them down without being obvious. Luckily the guard wasn't in a hurry. The eagle flew past overhead in a southern direction. He looked at it questioningly for a moment, trying to understand what it was telling him. He watched its silhouette against the mountains on the horizon which rose up against a pinkish purple and orange sky. The moon wasn't too far above and the eagle stayed between them, balancing its graceful body between sky and earth. It reminded him of a place he had seen in a different dimension. He understood then: the eagle was flying in the direction of Samuel's home. He tried to recall Samuel's address and it came to mind.

He waited until they had mounted the carriage, trying to gauge the guard's mood. He was very relaxed, almost sluggish. Akim now noticed that his face was slightly red and his eyes were droopy. An idea came to mind. It wasn't flawless but it could work. Since it was possible, although not desirable, to sleep in the carriage, it wouldn't matter if they didn't reach their destination by the time night fell. He was afraid that the guard might have fallen asleep and didn't want to wake him. Fortunately, a porter who knew the guard walked past. He was in an exuberant mood. He stuck his head into the carriage and greeted the guard loudly, asking where they were off to and telling him to enjoy the journey. The porter walked away and the guard was awake, albeit grumpy.

It was now his chance. "Sir," he addressed the guard in what he hoped to be exactly the right tone of voice: not too soft, not too loud, not too friendly or grumpy, not too insistent but neither too uncertain, just as neutral as possible, yet subtly persuasive. "Would you mind if we made a stop at Downing Street in the southern part of the city? I have a very dear friend living there whom I might not see in a long time. I have a present I would like to give him and I also just want to say goodbye. Unless you are in a hurry of course." He doubted whether the guard would be in a hurry since the mission wasn't likely to be well planned. The king was bound to have picked a guard who had some time on his hands. The guard grunted that he wasn't in a rush. He instructed the coachman to stop at the address Akim gave him.

He didn't know what he would do once they arrived there. On the way he tried to come up with something but his mind was blank, so he merely observed all the objects, houses and people on the way. They went through the main street in the area. He knew they were now not too far from the place where Samuel lived with his parents. The street was fairly narrow and had lots of shops, restaurants and inns. There was even a brothel or two as indicated by the women in scanty costumes standing beside the entrance. It was the part of the city where tourists would find a place to stay and where people on business trips from foreign countries would feel at home. If he remembered correctly, then Samuel's father had a shop in the street, which explained why they lived nearby. It was perfect, whether Samuel and his family were at home or not.

They turned out of the street and moved a block up, then turned down a street parallel to the one with the shops. They continued for about five hundred meters before stopping in front of the house. It looked quiet. Akim dismounted the carriage while considering all his options. He fiddled in his travel bag—at least this part wasn't pretense as he had in fact something that he wanted to give Samuel. He entered the yard through the little gate and walked up the path to the front door. Samuel's mother opened when he knocked. She said that although Samuel wasn't there, he would be home in about an hour. Akim and his companions were welcome for a cup of tea while waiting.

He walked back to the carriage and explained to the guard that he had to wait for his friend for a little while and that he would go in for a cup of tea. He asked if they would mind and whether they would like to join or do something else while waiting. He was careful to make the cup of tea sound extremely boring just by imagining it to be very, very dull. When he mentioned doing "something else," he thought with excitement of the bustling main road where they would be sure to get distracted. He waited for them to make up their minds, pretending that he didn't care either way.

The guard looked as thoughtful as his hangover allowed. Then a light went on in his mind. He consulted with the coachman for a minute or two. Turning back to Akim, he said that they would be in the main street having a drink while waiting. He mentioned the name of the place they planned to go to, then said that if Akim couldn't find the place, all he had to do was find the carriage. He wouldn't easily miss it and they were bound to go back to it eventually. The guard looked pleased at the thought of having an excuse to shirk his official responsibilities. The coachman looked slightly concerned, but he wasn't in charge. Besides, he wouldn't say no to an adventure. They left without further ado and Akim returned to the house. He let out a sigh of relief. The rest might be easier than expected; all he had to do was avoid raising suspicion. He hadn't planned further than the night, but he would deal with that later.

Back in the house he spent time talking to Samuel's mother. Akim was pleased to hear that Samuel was adapting to the world much better; he had even made a few friends. Since he was a pleasant child, Akim wasn't surprised that he was liked well when he opened up to others a little. Knowing who Samuel used to be in a different life and body, he surely would have brought some of his former charisma with him. It would no doubt come in useful once he started acknowledging it. It didn't mean that everything was now perfect—Samuel was still a loner and far from being the average child of his age. However, it was good to know that he was finding some pleasure in life. Akim was also pleased to hear that he was still a master chess player, teaching more people besides the king. Most of his pupils were adults, which was helpful to provide him with the company of individuals that were closer to his intellectual level.

When Samuel arrived, Akim could see the difference in him. He told Akim about the people he had met through teaching chess and some of the valuable lessons he had learned. He had also started receiving information about where he came from through his dreams. It sounded like he was remembering some of what had happened and starting to understand why he was on earth. Akim thought that he was being guided by Montana as to how to make the most of his earth life. Akim now wanted to give Samuel the gift he had brought: some herbs from the palace garden. He told Samuel that the plant wanted to work with him. It was up to him to figure out how it could best be used. He said that he might be leaving the city, and instructed Samuel to burn the herbs whenever he wished for his friend to be close.

The sun was close to the horizon and the time had come for him to say goodbye. After leaving, he was careful to avoid the main street. He hoped that the guard and the coachman had become sufficiently distracted to forget about their task. It wouldn't be the end of the world if they only left the city the following morning, regardless of whether he was with them or not.

Chapter 20

He walked in the direction of the hills outside the city. Night descended and it was getting cool. He was further from the hills and the palace than he had imagined. He wasn't worried about getting tired, but rather about losing direction in the dark when he couldn't clearly see the hills. He was scared that he might miss Matima because he hadn't confirmed a time with her.

He had to stop to get his bearings a few times, but otherwise the journey was smooth. Occasionally he encountered a suspicious figure in a dark cloak and he would become tense, but then relax as he reminded himself that he really was a nobody. Eventually, his surroundings started looking familiar and he could see the palace in the distance.

He had no idea what the time was when he finally arrived at the place where he was supposed to meet her. There was a cloaked figure but it didn't look like Matima in the moonlight. He hesitantly walked closer, wondering if the person was just someone who happened to be there on the same night, possibly waiting for someone else just like he was. It was a bit strange, though. The hills weren't frequently visited at night, especially not by people on their own. He approached cautiously, unsure of whether the person had seen him. He couldn't avoid the figure as it was standing in more or less the spot where he was supposed to meet Matima. If he had to stay in the shadows where the person couldn't see him, then Matima would not be able to see him.

His mind was telling him that there was no reason to believe that the person meant him harm. However, the darkness wreaked havoc on his imagination, making the person appear ominous. As he came closer, he saw that the person was nervous. It was a woman. He didn't want to scare her, so he proceeded with caution. She started at the sound of twigs breaking under his feet. Although she was tense, she didn't run away. He was now only a few meters away, close enough hear her talking without raising her voice.

"Are you ... are you Akim?" the girl asked, her voice trembling.

"Yes, I am. Are you looking for me?" She didn't answer his question until he reached her. She visibly relaxed knowing that she had company that was expected.

"I am supposed to be waiting for you. Come closer." It was the girl that he had seen with Matima that afternoon. "I have a message from the princess. She might not be able to make it outside the palace grounds as her father is watching her carefully. He held an entire banquet at the palace because her suitor had arrived. She wants you to see if you can come into the palace gardens." It didn't sound like good news, but he didn't want to lose hope. The girl continued. "She has asked me to give you this in case she doesn't see you tonight." She handed him what looked like a small booklet. "You must read it together with the letter that she wrote. It contains everything you need to know of where you must meet her next."

"What if I cannot make it inside the palace gardens?" He asked her.

"I will guide you there. I have very good knowledge of how the watch system works. It will be difficult, but we have a good chance." Akim was puzzled, but there wasn't time for asking questions. "My name is Landa. Stay with me," she said.

Keeping to the shadows, they walked back to the palace on a different path than the one he knew. They were on the western side of the palace, a few hundred meters away from the main entrance. She told him to wait there, after which she continued. She was inconspicuous; he had to watch her carefully to see her moving between the trees along the palace wall. She disappeared behind a small building that was connected to the wall. A little while later she was back. She instructed him to follow her, but keep a few meters behind her. She told him that he must not be overly careful as that would attract attention.

He walked behind her through the trees, crossing a road until they were next to the palace wall. He stayed along the side, taking care to remain in the shadows as far as possible without leaving the path. He felt afraid in the last stretch before he reached the small building as he suspected that it was a guarded entrance to the palace. He relaxed somewhat when he reached Landa behind the building, knowing that he was now mostly out of sight. However, looking at her body language he realized that he shouldn't drop his guard—she looked tenser than before. She signed to him to keep quiet.

She entered through a doorway around the corner and he was surprised to see she didn't open a door to go through. When he arrived there he realized why: there were two guards positioned close to the entrance. The one that was guarding the doorway they had entered was fast asleep. The other one was sitting a few meters away at the front entrance to the building. His back was turned to them and he was busy with something that took all his attention. They walked past without making a sound.

Landa led him through another portal and then a door which was thankfully also open. They descended a small staircase which narrowed on the way down. At the bottom they were in a tunnel. The roof was low and it was extremely dark. She took his hand when they were a few meters in as it soon became impossible to see her in the thick darkness.

Walking without knowing where he was going made the distance seem endless and the time drag by. He wanted to breathe more freely, but each time he made a slight noise, she nudged him. Finally, she stopped him and he heard her fiddling in her bag. A few moments later she lit a torch. Akim's eyes hurt at the bright light. She signaled to him to remain silent while they continued.

It was easier to walk now that they had light, but he still couldn't see far ahead. Soon they reached an opening on the left side of the tunnel. She turned to go in; it was a narrow spiral staircase. They ascended it and reached a door. Landa searched her bag again. He suspected that the door was not guarded but she still took care to be quiet. When she had unlocked it, she signaled for him to stay put. She put out the torch and opened the door carefully. She disappeared outside the door for a minute or two, then returned and led him outside.

They were inside the palace grounds and had left a small building similar to the one on the outside. She led him down a few stairs onto a path. He followed her and they soon entered a cluster of trees. The path turned a few more times until they were in a dense part of the garden. She took his hand as visibility was again low. They now left the path as she led him deeper into the trees. He didn't know this part of the garden well. At last she stopped and pushed her hand firmly to his shoulder to indicate that he had to stay there. She disappeared between the trees. She returned after a few minutes, this time making a lot more noise than before. He was relieved as he assumed that they were now safe from being observed.

But it wasn't Landa who had returned, it was Matima. He was overwhelmed with both joy and concern when he saw her. She embraced him but had to remind him to keep his voice down. She said that they were safe and that Landa was keeping watch in case someone came. However, Landa could only cover for them on one side and they had to be careful to listen for her signal. She fondled him, but when she wanted to explore further, he stopped her and said that they had to talk. He asked her what she planned to do. He didn't want to pressure her but he knew that if her father was having parties for her suitor, it was the time for her to be firm. If she didn't do it soon, things would become messy for her and the king. She answered fervently, "I'm not marrying him and I have already told you so, as I have told my father. It's not my problem that he doesn't want to listen to me."

Akim said, "I understand, Matima, but it is your problem. Are you going to wait until your wedding day and just refuse to show up? It would be too late then. They will find a way to coerce you."

"I will not be forced." She was upset now, but he knew that it wasn't because of him, but because of the difficult situation she was in. "I will not do anything against my will. Nobody will make me, not my father, not that silly man who thinks he is going to marry me, and not you."

Akim tried to remain calm. "I know, Matima. But I want to be with you, so could you please tell me what to do now? I have evaded your father's guard and coachman, who are supposed to take me home. If I don't find them again soon then not only will I hang around in the city without a place to stay, but I will also appear suspect. If I do find them, I'll be gone tomorrow. We have to act now. I don't want to be apart from you for much longer, but I don't want to hide, either."

"I know I can't stay here," she said. "I just don't know when the best time to leave is. If I leave now, I wouldn't know where to go. My father will have the entire country searching for me, as will Extar's king and that stupid son of his who thinks I will be his bride. We would have to hide all the time. I don't think that is the right way. I will spend a few more days trying to reason with him. If he doesn't listen then I will leave. Will you be able to wait around here for a few days?"

Akim didn't know what to say. The last twenty four hours had been too much to deal with. He hadn't thought further than seeing her that night. He was tired. He didn't want to lose face, but all the tension he had been feeling overwhelmed him. He buried his face in his hands for a few seconds. Somewhere within him a voice told him to pull himself together; he was stronger than he felt. He pushed his worries aside and said, "I will wait for you here in the city. If I am not in the city I will not be too far away. If something happens and I have to leave, then I will go back to my hometown and you will have to come and find me there. Just tell me when and where I have to meet you." Matima said that she would wait no longer than five days before making her final move, after which she would meet him at the place where he had met Landa. She also told him to read the booklet that Landa had given him as it contained more information about where she wanted them to go once they managed to get away. They said goodbye, after which Landa guided him on the way out.

Chapter 21

Akim walked into the hills to watch the sunrise and think about what to do. Luckily, he had come here quite often before so he knew the place fairly well. He found the spot where he used to come and sit watching the city in the days that he still served the king. The view was so different at night with the details of the buildings replaced with little lights. The sounds of nature were more pronounced during night time. They provided comfort, but the lights of the city looked much warmer. He felt lonelier than ever—not even his mother knew what was going on in his life. The king's men would probably check on him to make sure he got home, or otherwise they would forget about him. The latter was what he would prefer, but it made him feel more isolated.

He felt lost in a world that functioned well without him. He wondered why the people who lived close to nature, the way he also preferred to live, were losing their place. It confused him and made him feel desolate, as if he was cut off from his roots. He didn't want to lose his connection with nature in order to fit in with society, but neither was he keen to lose his connection to society to maintain his way of living. He wished that there was a middle ground, a place where all things were possible and each person could be what they wanted to be without a battle to compete for scarce resources. But scarcity was a product of the mind resulting from the perception that the source of life was outside the self.

Perhaps if the spark of life within were recognized and cherished, each person would be grateful to participate. They would take only what they needed and apply it properly. Akim imagined a world where people wouldn't find meaning in life through what they could get, but rather created themselves through what they could contribute. He felt peaceful as he imagined the city he was looking over to be built on those values. He wished that he could lay down a stone in the foundation of rebuilding such a city. Knowing that he couldn't do it all alone, he was happy with the thought that his life would have meaning if he did his best to help others. He knew that it wasn't up to him to turn people's minds, it was a flow that came from a Source independent of him. He was simply one of millions of drops that formed part of the current.

These thoughts went through his mind as he looked out over the city. He didn't want to think about what was in store for him over the next few days; he had had enough of worrying. He lay down flat on his back to watch the sky. He imagined it talking to him, telling him about his life purpose. It told him that he came from the stars. The life he was living was just a dream which he had to make the most of because he would only have that particular dream once. He asked the sky where he was going. It told him that where he was going was the same as where he was and where he had been because there was only one moment. That moment was the now that was always unfolding; everything else was irrelevant. He muttered to the sky that to him it made no sense but he would accept its wisdom anyway.

The sky told him that if he always thought he had to go somewhere, then that was exactly what he would experience: always needing to get somewhere in order to feel fulfilled, but never quite getting there. He asked the sky if in that case he was fine just where he was despite the fact that he hadn't fulfilled his destiny, whatever it might be. The sky told him that he was indeed fine just where he was because the entire universe was inside him. Whatever destiny he wanted to choose was also inside him, and he could pay attention to it whenever he opted to. He listened, but a part of him was annoyed with the sky. It was oversimplifying his life, pretending that he could pick what he wanted out of thin air anytime. It felt like the sky had forgotten that he lived in a world where people didn't necessarily agree with him. He suspected that the sky wanted to tell him that perhaps it was that simple and that he would realize it in due course. However, not realizing it was part of the human experience which he didn't want to miss out on.

Instead, the sky told him that he wasn't meant to be comfortable or happy all the time. Whatever he experienced in the moment was valid, and bravery was shown when he didn't turn away from it. His conversation with the sky was making him uncomfortable, so he indicated politely that he didn't feel like talking anymore. The sky became quiet and was just a black night sky again. A second later it turned into the most beautiful grey and white wolf that he could imagine, running along with its cubs. The owl appeared for an instant, then the eagle was spread out over the sky in the second before he fell asleep.

When he woke up, he didn't know where he was. The shade of a tree was protecting his eyes from the sun and for that he was grateful, otherwise he would have been in danger of dehydration. For a moment he imagined himself to be in a pleasant fantasy world, just him with nature and enough food to survive. He felt queasy as the truth hit him. Five days? It felt like an endless stretch ahead of him.

The time alone in nature that he had so yearned for now looked less than appealing. He knew how to survive, but he was hoping that he would be able to go into the city without encountering problems. The king's guard and coachman might be annoyed with him for having disappeared, but they might not be, either. He couldn't even determine whether the king knew that he had gone "missing". Still, he would be as inconspicuous as possible and stay close to the edges.

He remembered the little booklet Landa had given him together with the letter from Matima. He hoped that it would be useful. He was grateful for having something to do over the next few days. Right then he was starving, however, so he decided to go and buy himself food. Afterwards, he would explore his surroundings to find a place to make himself at home. When he was settled in, he would examine the booklet and letter.

The trip to town passed without incidents. He found the perfect spot to stay on the other side of the hill where the rocks formed a steep cliff face. There was a cavity in one place with a large tree next to it which also had a slight hole in its trunk. Together the cliff face and the tree formed a hollow where he could sleep and store his food and the few other things he had managed to put in his knapsack. He would only be visible to someone who came really close, which suited him perfectly. When he had relaxed awhile, it was time to embark on the adventure of the booklet. He hoped that it wouldn't disappoint because he had so many hours to kill.

First he opened the letter from Matima. Judging by the scribbled handwriting, it was written in a hurry. He read:

My beloved Akim,

The little book has been passed down to me through the hands of generations of women who at some point in their life had a connection with the palace garden and its traditions of olden times. The booklet describes a place that does exist, although it is not well known. Of those who have heard about it, most dismiss it as an old wives' tale. But the legend dictates that those who search for it will find it if they persevere. It is a place of safety for the true seekers of life and happiness. I do not know the way there, but I believe it will be shown to us if we intend to find each other there in love. This country might no longer be a place that is friendly to us. Although I love it deeply, my heart calls me to a place where we can be free to love without restrictions. If we cannot see each other or communicate otherwise, I will go there and hope and pray to find you there.

Sent with love,
Matima

Akim was definitely curious, but it sounded a bit risky. He would prefer to find Matima in a defined place in the real world and live with her as a man would live with his woman. That would entail living without reasonable restrictions, though, so he was keen to find out more despite his initial reservations. He opened the little book, which was bound in black leather and about the same size as the palm of his hand. It was square-shaped, which added to making it interesting since most books he knew were in the shape of a rectangle.

The consistency of the paper was noticeable: thick, fibrous to the touch and somewhere between brittle and elastic. It contained a yellowish brown glaze which could be an indication of its age. Upon quickly flipping through it he noticed that what was written looked like poetry. Each pair of opposite pages had an image on one side and text on the other. The drawings were simple, yet masterful. They mostly consisted of defined black lines with single color fillings which made them flat but enchanting. The background to each central image was wispy, making the foreground stand out more in its bold colors. Akim was mesmerized as it made him think of old fairy tales, which it in fact was, but with the added benefit of being real, according to Matima. This made him wonder if all fairy tales weren't actually stories about real worlds and characters that had gone lost, either because they had been suppressed or because people no longer cared about them. If that were the case, he suspected that they often came out distorted in fairy tales, with a few important archetypal characteristics remaining.

When he finished admiring the drawings, he started reading it. The first few pages contained no text; there were only pictures with blank spaces on the opposite side. The first picture was of a man wearing richly colored robes and holding an open book in his hands. He didn't look down at the book, though, his one hand was turning a page while he looked up at a point that appeared to be higher than eye level. The expression on his face was interesting. At first glance he appeared to be lonely and tired of life. A deeper look, however, revealed a sparkle in his eye and inner power. The old man transformed right in front of his eyes as Akim dreamed into the picture.

His spirit emerged, making him more potent and youthful than any physically young man could be. His understanding of life shone through in the light that was around his face, and he was grateful for the wisdom given to him. His whole heart was immersed in his destiny; he was it and they were one and the same entity. As serious as he was about it, there was a paradoxical lightness in his face which revealed that he considered all matters trivial. It gave him great joy to be free from the heaviness of the word, must. Akim understood that he was the patron of bringing higher knowledge into the world, often through what people considered to be fiction. Those writers who could sense the invisible world would receive their stories from him, whether they were aware of it or not.

This guide understood that writers could be driven mad with frustration because the spirit world had such a strong presence in their lives and yet it would keep evading them. He came to the rescue of those who believed in inspiration even though they lived in a world where imagination had little significance. He was also the one to have protected this book over the centuries, making sure it fell into worthy hands. Akim was captivated by this guide. Glad that he and the little book could connect from the start, he continued to the next page.

This page had an image of an elephant. Initially it presented itself as tame, being surrounded by the kinds of artefacts that one would find in the home of a rich person. It had a man-made cloth as a covering as well as other decorations. When Akim looked deeper, he could see that there were no signs of the elephant being captive. It simply looked at home and in charge of all it possessed. His first thought was that it would be sad about being a slave to humans. But as soon as one noticed that it wasn't imprisoned, the elephant turned into a peaceful animal who knew the secret of being happy. Akim pondered what it meant to tell him: perhaps that one could be at peace without actually being in one's right home, or maybe that riches were brought forth through one's state of spirit rather than searching for it outside oneself. He was undecided, but the amiable elephant promised some fun in the little book either way. He was eager to start reading.

This little book tells of a Golden City
One that will be found by those who seek
It is found through one's heart but don't let that fool you
It resides in physical space as much as the human body
If you need to go there you will find a way
Be blessed dear traveler, this book only lands
In the hands of those who are courageous of spirit
And possess the quality of perseverance
For those who persevere will succeed
It is the law of all things hoped for
Seek the path and the path you will find
Call from your heart and the door will be opened
The road to the Golden City is elusive yet clear
It is right under your nose but can be missed
Live, dear traveler, live your heart's desires
Be faithful to the journey of your soul
Keep walking even when you are weary
Keep searching even if it feels in vain
Keep loving even if your heart has been wounded
For if you refuse to stop loving

Your heart will reclaim its true power
The mysteries will be revealed to you
The universe inside you will emerge
Never rest, dear traveler
Keep searching for the Golden City
The journey will make life worthwhile
Search for it in the crack of dawn
And in the Northern Lights
Find it in the smallest leaf of the largest tree
Find it in the flight of a rabbit, the wings of a bird
All things hoped for and all things forgotten
All things unnoticed
The Golden City is there, right in front of your eyes
It will emerge from the shadows when you walk forth from your reverie
It will keep calling those who want to sing the song of their souls

That was the heart of it: stories of people who had found the Golden City by remaining true to themselves. All the stories were written as songs rather than prose. It was impossible to determine how they had found the road, but what they had in common was an almost desperate desire to reach the Golden City. Some of them had it easier than others; some were courageous, but most of them were far from perfect. A few were rather bad, but they were redeemed through introspection and love for something or someone outside themselves. Akim was fascinated by the characters, even though some of them made him uncomfortable. He still wasn't sure if he believed in the place, living in a world that was reigned by dullness. But he could relate to it since he often imagined a place where things worked well, not because he had to put in effort to remain positive despite setbacks, or because he wanted to make a difference, but because that was the nature of the place. People lived together in harmony because access required a certain level of maturity.

The idea of the place appealed to Akim, but he also liked the world just the way it was with all its trials. Through the dark times he had always emerged on the other end feeling more confident than before. He had to remind himself that these were fine thoughts to have when he was sitting in the middle of nowhere reading a fable. When surrounded by the "real" world, he would yearn for something interesting to keep his spirit alive. He concluded that this Golden City sounded like an adventure that he wouldn't want to miss out on.

Chapter 22

Over the next few days, while retreating into nature, the idea of the Golden City as a real possibility occupied his mind. He felt that he had to see it before he died. Whereas the idea had initially sounded attractive, it now presented itself as a place filled with wonder, one where people could know themselves as they really were. Everything was alive and filled with the same Spirit in this place. It was the place where people realized that heaven was inside them. The world they built as a result flowed out naturally from their state of being.

As Akim learned to understand the values on which the Golden City was built, the world that he lived in seemed backward in comparison. In his own world, people were unaware of how their thoughts and actions had an impact on what they created. They failed to notice that their lived reality was based on deeply ingrained constructs. That didn't make it any less valid, but he felt ready for change. A more fulfilling experience could be created if people were willing to open their minds.

He only had to go into the city one more time to fill up on food stock. This time he had lost all his fear as he knew that he and Matima were destined to go to the same place. If something happened, he knew where they would meet. The more time he spent alone, the closer he came to a state of ecstasy where he didn't need anything, not even his beloved because she was in his heart. When he closed his eyes, he could see her next to him. Their souls had a bond which was stronger than time; it couldn't be destroyed by outside events. He knew that the reason he had fallen in love with her was not because they had shared their bodies, nor because they had entered a magical world together, nor because she was really beautiful and on a physical level he desired her. It was because when looking into one another's eyes, their souls remembered that they sprang from the same womb where the web of life was formed. Souls were often forgotten, but they communicated through the eyes. Even just for a tiny second, a soul would remember and recognize another soul that it had walked with before. This power could open up veils of existence to show a higher perspective.

The sad part was that when people didn't acknowledge their souls, the portal that was opened through the love between two sparks wouldn't last very long before it closed again. In that case people would dismiss their experience as temporary insanity caused by an overreaction of hormones. The love that was ignited could become destructive, as usually happened when magic landed into the hands of people who didn't understand it and either denied it or abused its power. The more people severed their connection from their own souls, the less likely it was that the portal would reopen, allowing higher consciousness to transform them. Akim also now realized how unwilling both he and Matima had been to be open to love. He was slightly ashamed when he thought about it. Why had he denied life with all its wonder? His perception was different now. The Golden City was inviting him to accept it as a place within himself from where he could live regardless of whether his outer circumstances matched the experience. If he could only lift a veil then he would be in a different place that was in fact the Golden City. But he wasn't there yet and he knew that his quest would be meaningless unless he could access the place in the physical world as much as he could sense it through the invisible.

When the time came closer for him to meet Matima, he knew what his answer was: he was prepared to share her mission. The last day was spent in anxious apprehension. He was excited, but also terrified in case she didn't reach him. His trusting attitude was harder to maintain as he had to face the possibility of embarking on an unknown mission alone. He tried to find the Golden City inside him, but it would fade the more he reached for it and instead be replaced by fears of being an outcast. He had lost his transport home. Although he could get there by foot in a few days, he would not be walking any closer to where he wanted to go. He was no longer wanted in the city where he had served the king. If the princess managed to get away, he might even be in danger among the men of Extar. Few things were more dangerous than a bruised ego, especially when positions of power were involved.

Having had little contact with people for a few days, he was feeling disconnected from the world. Worry had crept in and nestled in his mind, replacing the sensation of peace. As much as he feared the moment when he was supposed to meet Matima, he was desperate for contact with other humans. At that stage he would have almost welcomed the king himself, or Matima's suitor, even the king of Extar, who in Akim's mind was the cause of the dire situation that he found himself in.

The last few hours passed extremely slowly. He tried to keep busy to avoid being caught in the forever-ness of the time that had to elapse before he could meet her. This was problematic since there wasn't much to do. He tried to read his omens but it was difficult when his mind was clouded by fear. He felt that his readings were becoming useless because he didn't know what to ask. The omens were talking to him in riddles—he would get a variation of the same messages he had received before. At that stage he was starting to ask himself if their advice had ever been useful. It all boiled down to staying true to himself: keep walking despite adversity, there would be danger but he would be protected, believe in what is important to you, always keep hoping and have faith regardless of appearances, don't be afraid to speak your truth.

Akim was questioning how the invisible world could tell him that when he couldn't see things going his way. He had got the message by now and had faithfully followed the advice, at least mostly so. He was now wondering if he would have anything to show for it in the end and whether he wasn't just being silly and delusional. He decided that it was useless to try to think about anything important. Instead, he would continue with something else to keep the thoughts from driving him crazy.

He started by tidying his "home" of the last few days. He knew it wasn't necessary since he would be leaving it later that day. However, it served as a way of clearing his mind. He swept the dust with a broom he had made of leaves and packed the few things he had, tying them together in a cloth. He went down in the valley in search of a place in the stream where he could wash himself—he wouldn't like to be completely filthy when he met Matima. He imagined himself to be getting ready for an appointment with her. The thought was a welcome fantasy to escape from the reality of their situation, but it also made him miss civilization very much. However, it kept him going and steered him away from the darkness of despair. When he had finished, the sun was creeping towards the horizon and there was only an hour or so left before he had to meet her.

The last hour was the most difficult to live through. He was intermittently overcome by excitement to see the woman he loved. In the next moment he would experience the deepest fear of all that lay ahead. More than anything, he was scared of losing her. What guarantee did he have that their relationship would work out? She might end up resenting him for everything she had left behind to follow her love. He imagined her shriveling with misery because of what she had lost, having been dumb enough to follow a boy she loved to all the corners of the earth. He feared she might hate him because she could have had a powerful husband who matched her social standing if only he hadn't loved her and made her believe that she actually loved him, too.

The thought made his throat constrict with panic, but he reminded himself that she had taken the lead all along. The thoughts kept plaguing him so he found a sharp twig which he used to scratch patterns in the soil as a way of distracting himself. As he did so, the Golden City came back into his awareness, fringing on the borders of his mind first, and then slowly making its way to the center where it showed itself and talked to him. He was still scratching in the soil, but now the Golden City was moving through his hands, engraving its imprints in the mud. He wasn't even aware of the process because he was so carried away by what he was seeing in his mind's eye, almost as when one is dreaming without awareness that it is but a mirror of waking life. When the sun touched the horizon, however, he started as if being woken by an alarm clock. He emerged from his reverie, anxious to meet Matima. His heart wanted to jump out of his throat, now for the first time so closely confronted with the big question: what happens next? But for now the excitement of hopefully seeing her was greater. He jumped up, gathered his few things in case they wouldn't pass there again, and ran to the place where he was supposed to meet her.

When he arrived, it was dusk and there was nobody in sight. Fantastic, he thought, as he prepared himself to wait again. He wanted to shout in frustration, unable to bear the uncertainty any longer. He breathed deeply, forcing himself to relax his body as that would also relax his mind. He tried to remain present, appreciating the beauty of the night. Whatever would happen after would be revealed to him in due course. Right at that moment he was pain free and physically in good health. The temperature was agreeable and he could appreciate the quietness of being on his own and staring at an infinite sky. The stars would talk to him as always, showing him the secrets of the universe which he couldn't possibly comprehend through words.

Chapter 23

He kept focusing on his breathing, bringing himself back to the present moment every time he started wondering where Matima was. He must have concentrated really hard in his attempt to remain calm because he soon drifted into a hypnotic state. The world of the stars was pulling him in. At first there was a lion walking through grasslands. There were a few birds in the background and the lion was drinking in the light of the sun. It imagined itself to be on top of the world and it was playful, unaware of the fact that it was a dangerous animal. Its mane was a deep, golden orange color, making it blend with the grass. It smiled, to the extent that a lion can smile, when it noticed Akim. He got the impression that although it was exuberant, it was also a bit afraid. When the sun shone on its face, the lion was overcome by contentment, relaxed in the knowledge that it was the same light that also shone through the moon at night. The lion winked at him and the image passed.

Next he saw a young woman weaving something that looked like a mat. She wasn't aware of him. She got up and opened the door of the room she was sitting in and looked outside. There was the lion. She watched it as it continued walking—it didn't seem to mind her presence. Then she returned to her spinning. She was deep in concentration and looked slightly worried, as if concerned about what the final product would look like. The thought of someone appreciating what she had created inspired her to work so hard. She was shy yet ardent, which explained why she worked alone with so much vigor. She was independent enough not to be anyone's slave. She wouldn't hesitate to stand up for what was right when called to do so. She reminded him a bit of Metis. When the thought came to his mind, she blushed and looked up. He didn't know whether she had pretended not to notice him before or whether she had only noticed him then, but she smiled. She walked to the door, opened it, and invited him to go through.

When he went outside, there was a bull that looked angry, stomping its forefoot to the ground while watching something intently. Akim looked in the same direction that it was looking and saw a little bird sitting on a fence. The little bird was tweeting and flapping its wings. Akim listened carefully and it told him that someone had hurt the bull. However, it would resume its quiet disposition once it had calmed down because it had a good heart. Sure enough, the bull lost interest after snorting a few more times. It walked away, indifferent to its surroundings. Its heart was buried deep within itself and it wanted to find someone to share its deepest longings. The young woman had by now walked away. She was fetching water from a nearby well, apparently not able to sit still for long without busying herself with work.

The little bird had taken over Akim's visit to the sky world. It beckoned to him to follow as it flew, stopping to sit down every now and again. It was singing its little heart out about all the creatures of the world up there. Akim was astounded that such a little body could produce such a loud noise. He enjoyed the little bird's company; it certainly was comical if nothing else. He followed it to the edge of what looked like a forest. As they entered the canopy of trees, a path in the woods could be seen. It didn't go on for long before they found a circular clearing. At its center was a pedestal with large brass scales on it. The little blue bird flew to it and hovered over it for an instance, singing and chirping. It went to sit at its base. Akim walked closer and noticed an inscription at the bottom of the pedestal:

"I weigh the air in equal measures
If you tip me I might lose my balance
But find it I sure will, because that is what I am."

Akim thought it was a nonsensical rhyme and the bird thought so, too. But it told Akim that it was very serious because these scales were necessary for maintaining justice in the world. Akim sat puzzled, wondering how on earth that made sense. Before he could figure it out, two young men arrived. They looked the same but their temperaments were different. Both were lean and lanky but one looked lost in thought, almost dreamy, while the other looked vibrant and displayed a keen interest in his surroundings. It was the latter who approached Akim first and started talking to him.

"Could you help us, friend?" he asked. "My brother and I are looking for a lost city that was written of in the works of the great philosophers. We think we used to live there and were involved in helping the great thinkers make sense of the world. But we cannot quite remember, not all of it. We are very different, my brother and I, as much as we look alike. We try to find our way together to a place that we are not sure exists anymore. Can you help us? Are you here to give us a clue?" He looked at Akim expectantly but Akim just shook his head. He had thought he was merely a spectator but now the characters were asking him for directions. He didn't want to interfere. The little bird chirped that it was time to move on. It told Akim that he needn't be worried about the brothers and their quest as they would find their way when it was time.

The bird led Akim deeper into the forest where it became darker and darker until he was convinced it was night. Then the forest started glowing with an eerie blue light, and he could see what was going on around them. The little blue bird wasn't glowing, but it hadn't lost its visibility. It was as if a patch of sunlight was stuck to it and followed it wherever it went. Akim proceeded with caution, but the little bird sounded happy as ever. He took it as a sign that everything was in order. The forest was on his side, glowing to make things easier for him.

Soon he could see an orange light through the trees. As soon as he noticed it, he could hear music. The little bird stopped chirping for a second, then came to rest on a protruding branch right in front of him. It looked very serious. It emitted a few low chirps, pausing every now and then as if waiting for Akim to confirm that he understood. The sound became more urgent as it continued. It angrily flapped its wings and Akim thought if it could talk it would probably tell him, "You thick-headed human being, stop pretending that you don't understand and listen to me for a second." As soon as the thought entered Akim's mind, the little bird seemed satisfied.

In response, Akim listened carefully to what it wanted to tell him. It chirped that they now had to be careful not to be seen. They were not in danger, but they would be witnessing rituals that were considered very sacred and private. If the ones they were approaching were disturbed, they would cease their activities and be on guard instantly. If Akim was seen, he had to come out into the light and introduce himself as a friend who meant no harm; otherwise he could provoke a hostile response. The little bird told him to pretend that he was invisible because that would decrease his chances of being seen. Akim nodded that he understood.

They moved forward. Akim considered that what he was doing might not be right since they were impinging on the privacy of others without their consent. However, another voice in his head said that he had no other choice but to trust the little bird. The music was getting louder. He felt himself being pulled into it; it was hypnotic and beautiful. All thought left his mind as he was enraptured by the music. Somewhere at the back of his mind he remembered to pretend that he was invisible. It was all that kept him from running to the place where the music was coming from until he merged with it, dissipating in a state of euphoria.

They were moving closer to the yellow light. When they could almost distinguish the source of light behind the trees, the little bird fluttered a few times in front of him before coming to a rest. It looked up at him without chirping. It then hopped onto his shoulder and chirped very softly that he now had to proceed on his own because he would be less likely to be noticed. Since the bird was of their world, it would make him more visible to them if Akim stayed in its presence. Akim nodded that he understood, to which the bird hopped down to a branch close to the ground and watched him expectantly. Akim turned back to the yellow light.

He proceeded again and could soon distinguish the fire that was the source of the yellow light. It was spellbinding. When he laid eyes on it, the music entranced him again, pulsing with the same rhythm that was in the warmth of the fire. He took a few more steps until he could see figures dancing, their hands joined. At first glance they looked like humans, but then he saw animals behind them and wondered if the animals formed part of the celebration. Closer inspection revealed they were centaurs. All of them except one were dancing rhythmically to the sound of the music. They were singing from the bottom of their souls. The one that wasn't part of the circle was walking around behind them, playing a mandolin that provided the lead to their song. Akim wanted to run closer to compliment them on the beautiful music, but he had to stay invisible. He walked a few steps forward until he found a spot where he could watch them comfortably, sufficiently hidden by shadows.

The music became more intense, building to a climax and suddenly stopped. At this point the music merged with the quiet, forming an all-encompassing whole of a silence that contained all the sounds of the song. The song had called forth from nowhere ideas that would match the tone of the song. The silence lasted for a few minutes, after which those in the circle started chanting softly on a low-pitched note. The one on the outside spoke in a clear, formidable voice.

From what Akim understood, it talked about the past and the future, about how mankind and all creatures could learn from the mistakes of the past to create a better future. It spoke of the lost city that the brothers were looking for and how it was time to redeem the loss of what had been destroyed. It foretold a new consciousness that was arising. Human beings and all the creatures on the earth would benefit from it if it was embraced. It said that as much as mankind was on the verge of a great breakthrough that would make living on planet earth easier, so it was also in great danger of being destroyed. The centaur sounded both despondent and hopeful. All the while that Akim was watching him, he was looking at some invisible point in front of him and his hands were held in front of his body in a gesture of receiving.

He ended by saying, "There is hope, but a lot will be lost because they wouldn't listen. Things will be different." His voice faded away and the chanting gradually slowed until it ended in a subdued silence. The one that had spoken let out one last sigh. He appeared incredibly tired. He lowered himself to the ground in a lying position, his face buried in his arms. After a few minutes, the chanting started again. The tone was sad but also grateful and appreciative. It sounded like a song to say thank you, not only for the wisdom received, but also for the privilege of watching over the earth. Akim was wondering exactly what their roles were when he felt an unpleasant sensation of his body being shaken. He was annoyed and wanted it to stop. He was being pulled out of the world of the sky, forced back to the world where he belonged by someone calling him. He knew the voice very well and loved it. Excitement and hope filled his being as he remembered his situation.

Chapter 24

"Akim, Akim, wake up! Wake up now. We have to go." The voice was very urgent and as much as he loved to hear it, he didn't like the sound of the fear it contained. Whenever returning from a dream or a more conscious encounter with another world, he was groggy as he had to become accustomed to the heaviness of being in his body again. He tried to force his eyes open but Matima's face was sliding in and out of focus; the double image just wouldn't merge into one. It felt like he had cataracts on his eyes, preventing him from seeing clearly. The drowsiness weighed on him as he tried to get up and move his body into action. He stumbled and fell back to the ground. Matima knelt beside him and pulled him up. Her voice was now pleading, begging him to pull himself together. When he looked into her eyes, the urgency was enough to bring him back with a shock. He couldn't help himself and threw his arms around her. She accepted his embrace only for an instant, then pushed him away and took him by the arm.

"Come now," she said. "You have to follow me. We have to get away from here as soon as possible. You have to trust me. Let's get out!" She searched his eyes for understanding and he nodded. She started sprinting in the direction of the closest cluster of trees, and stopped only when they were sheltered. She was out of breath, but she continued walking fast. Akim had to struggle to keep up the pace, his body still sluggish. He didn't like seeing her in such a state, but he knew that he had to follow her until she felt safe enough to stop and talk. She knew where she was going. They soon reached a faint path in the woods, along which they hurried away from the city.

Akim started feeling really tired and he thought Matima would need to rest soon, but she kept going at a strong pace. Akim was concerned that she would overexert herself, which would make it difficult to continue the following day. He tried to reason with her, but she kept going. Dawn turned into early morning and still Matima continued at a very fast pace. When the sun could be seen above the trees she collapsed. Akim knew that he had to get her in the shade and find water. He half-carried her off the path to a place where the foliage was thick and she would be well-hidden and protected from heat. He didn't want to leave her alone but finding water was priority, otherwise she could be in danger. Luckily he had a container in his backpack. There wasn't much water left in it. Her eyes were hazy as she sat with her back against a tree. He hugged her and told her to stay where she was and that he would be back soon.

He tried to find a stream. The light made it easier for him to move but it soon became very hot. He had to be careful to identify beacons as he could easily get lost. Soon enough he found a small stream. He drank as much as he could before filling his container, after which he returned to Matima.

She was now lying on her side, either half faint or fast asleep. He didn't want to, but he had to wake her. He dribbled a bit of water over her face and pulled her up to a sitting position. When she opened her eyes, he put the bottle to her mouth and told her to drink. He gave her one sip at a time, waiting a few minutes after the first few before giving her more. He waited until he was sure that it was taking effect. By the time she had finished it, she was looking slightly better.

He knew that she was too tired to talk about all that had happened over the last few days. He tried to act reassuring. He needed to find herbs for recovery and relaxation, but it would have to wait because he didn't want to leave her again. She soon fell asleep and it didn't take long for him to follow suit. All the concern and uncertainty that he had faced was taking its toll. He fell asleep feeling relieved now that Matima was with him, even though he couldn't know for sure that they were actually safe.

When he woke, the sun was high in the sky and Matima was already awake. She was in a good state. She had gone to find some berries from nearby trees. He was thankful to see her physically in good form. However, he had a suspicion that whatever she had to deal with on an emotional level might come up soon now that she was stronger physically. The first expression he could discern on her face was one of happiness to see him, and that was an immense relief. As concerned as he was about her, he had forgotten completely that there might be bad news; he had no idea what had happened in the time that they were away from each other. More than that, he didn't know where they were going. He had almost forgotten about their quest after the commotion of running away. Now that it was coming back to him, the idea seemed absurd. They sat down to eat first before Matima told him everything that had happened in his absence.

Chapter 25

It turned out that what they had had to deal with was no longer Matima's relationship with her father and the question of whether he would give his blessing to her choice of a partner or not. In the course of the few days that they were apart, Matima had found out that things had already progressed long past that point. The king's behavior, especially the way he had treated Akim, had been a reaction to fear. Things were more serious than they had imagined and the freedom of the entire country was in jeopardy. Although the king had initially been reluctant to admit it to her, maintaining peace depended on whether Matima would agree to marry the son of the ruler of Extar. Perhaps "agree" wasn't the right word since those in power generally didn't see the princess as having a say in the matter.

In that sense, the king had conflicting views. Although he leaned strongly towards tradition, he wasn't in favor of coercion. He wanted his daughter to make the right choice out of her own accord. If she didn't want to submit to his will, then by no means would he allow an outside party to command her. That was the way Matima perceived it, although Akim secretly suspected that something deeper than the king's principles had been at work. Somewhere deep inside, the king must have understood that their love was greater than his views. Akim had no doubt that the king loved his daughter and perhaps also loved him in some way. Consequently, he couldn't bear the thought of seeing her with someone, knowing that she yearned to be with another man.

Negotiations had continued. The king begged her to at least reconsider. However, he refused to succumb to pressure to decide on her behalf. Besides, the suitor was obviously not in love with his daughter, either. He had a strong suspicion that the young man was in the same situation as Matima herself, only he didn't have the courage to stand up for himself. The ruler of Extar continued to act as if the marriage would take place. At last the king had to put his foot down. He told the ruler of Extar that his daughter wouldn't marry the ruler's son. The ruler said that he didn't acknowledge her decision as a princess had no power to act in political matters. Any statement made by the king would be accepted as the king's own decision. In that case there would be war since the king had broken a promise. Regardless of the king's protests, the ruler maintained that under international law the king would be held responsible for his behavior.

At that point Matima had to intervene. She agreed to get married to the ruler's son. The king almost stopped her, but Matima acted with an authority she didn't know she possessed. She said that the wedding had to be brought forward in case she changed her mind. The king protested, but she told him to trust her, even though she privately had no idea what she was doing. She was acting completely on impulse. Since the king was in a corner, he agreed. The wedding would be arranged to take place two days later.

Matima kept cool and went through the motions of signing contracts and having dinner with her future in-laws. She smiled often, taking care to act interested and polite. She even got along fairly well with her future husband who looked even more terrified than she felt, or would have felt if she weren't possessed by an illogical sense of calmness. She would have felt sorry for him if her position hadn't been worse. She thought that it was a pity they were stuck in that situation because they could have been great friends, playing important roles in two neighboring countries.

After dinner she excused herself and went to her room. She changed into a dress that resembled that of a servant girl, with a scarf around her head and neck. She exited the palace by the smaller passageways that not too many people knew. She communicated to the garden her need for a solution. She had to find a way to get to Akim with minimal damage to the kingdom. She appealed to all the magic that was available to those in need. Initially, she didn't get much of an answer.

The moon was prominent, shining larger than she had seen it in a long time. A few clouds floated past, looking ominous. The moon was telling her something, promising something, perhaps a way out even though the consequences might not be free of damage. She asked the moon to direct her. It led her to a place not far from where she had found Akim on that first night. It was very dark between the trees, but the moonlight was shining on twigs, making them luminous with the silvery glow of the orb in the sky. She instinctively knew that the twigs would be able to give her information. She picked them up, collating them into a heap where there was a clear patch of moonlight shining through the trees.

What now? She asked herself. She wanted to light them but felt that fire might not be appropriate. She needed smoke, though. She walked off to the magical fountain where she had entered the desert with Akim. Close by there was a watering can, probably left there by one of the gardeners. She scooped up water and returned to her spot. She sprinkled a bit of it over the twigs. In her dress pocket was a box of matches. She lit one and set the pile of twigs alight. Instead of bursting into flames, it started glowing with a gentle white light that resembled the moon. It didn't sound like a fire, either. The sound it made was a low, melodious humming in contrast to the crackling of an ordinary fire.

Soon white wisps were rising from the pile, swirling their way up in the direction of the moon. As Matima watched the slivers of smoke, she started feeling drowsy. Before long she had entered a trance. The smoke was talking to her, pulling her into its language.

She was running along a dark passageway of stone. It was one of the secret corridors below the palace. Not many people knew about them; they were only to be used in the direst of emergencies. The torches on the walls were lit, as if someone had prepared the way for her, knowing that she would need help to get away fast. She realized that the glow of the torches wasn't induced by fire. She didn't have time but still she took a second to stop and look. The wick of the torch was a little glowing fairy flapping her wings. She smiled and nodded when she saw that Matima had noticed her. The garden was showing her that it was on her side. She knew that she had to run as fast as she could. However, since she didn't know where to go, she stopped to ask the fairy for advice.

She didn't use her voice, but explained to the fairy through her mind that she was looking for a message. The little fairy continued smiling excitedly, as if Matima weren't in a dire predicament. It pointed to her pocket and told Matima to open it and read it. Read what? Matima felt in her pocket and touched a piece of paper. When she touched it, she remembered having written something. It was vital to deliver it to the right person in time and get out afterwards, before someone could stop her. She pulled it out quickly, almost tearing it in the process. She took more care when opening it, her hands trembling. The fairy flew over and came to sit lightly on her shoulder to illuminate the letter. Her touch was a strange combination of lightness, heat and coolness. The light that she emanated lit the page perfectly with a soft, white glow. She smiled at Matima when she turned her head to look at her. With the fairy so close now, Matima could hear her giggling. She was indignant because her situation wasn't funny, but she couldn't get angry at a fairy just for being a fairy. She thanked her and started studying the letter. It was written in her own handwriting.

Dear Father

I hope this is not goodbye. I am so sorry about everything I have done to you. I didn't see any other way out. I am alive and hopefully I'll be safe, but you must not allow anyone to find out that that is the case. I hope that relations will be as peaceful as they can be with me being away. Hopefully, I might be able to return one day. I hope that you will continue to rule our beloved land as justly as you have always done, and that your son-in-law, joined to your daughter by law, will be a good and reliable man to work with. I also hope that the son-in-law you couldn't acknowledge, joined to your daughter in heart and body, might return one day by my side in his rightful place, not as my companion in office, fulfilling a role that doesn't suit him because he is in a relationship with me, but as a companion in spirit, fulfilling the purpose that partnerships are intended for. I sincerely hope that things change in my absence and that one day we will be reunited. I ask your forgiveness. I love you.

Matima

When she had finished reading it, the vision faded out and she returned to the garden, staring at the smoke that had given her the message. She wanted to know more but could get no information. She wanted to scream with frustration but she knew she had to act instead. The information she had been given had to be enough. She knew what she had to write to her father and that she would need to escape very fast at some point; that was a good place to start. What else was there? She would need to get married to the ruler of Extar's son. And she would have to find a way to feign her death. She also had to meet Akim at the appointed time, otherwise it might take forever to find him again. She couldn't bear the thought of that with everything else she was going through. In the space of a day or two she had to accomplish all these tasks. Her head was racing. How would she *kill* herself?

She felt panic creeping in, but she forced herself to remain calm. There had to be a solution because the smoke had shown it. The best she could do was to ask it to reveal itself instead of trying to invent it. Inventing it would be willfulness, whereas requesting it would be acknowledging its existence, which would bring it forth in some way. She walked back to the palace. The solution hadn't come to her by the time she reached her room. She went to bed knowing that she would get up early to begin preparations, even though she didn't know what that entailed. Thankfully, she fell asleep the minute her head touched the pillow.

She woke up early feeling pressured, and it took her a few seconds to remember why. She had two hours before she had to attend breakfast. Following that would be a window of about thirty minutes before preparations for her wedding would begin. She immediately sent for Landa, who had a tendency to come up with brilliant ideas. Other than that, she didn't have much hope. If Landa's nerves failed her, then Matima's own would be more likely to do so. Luckily, her right hand woman had a spine of steel and a cool temperament—a deadly combination.

When Landa arrived, Matima could see a spark of mischief in her eyes. This usually meant that she was ready for adventure, which was a good sign. Matima discussed her dilemma with Landa. By the time she had almost finished talking, she could already see a light going up in Landa's eyes. It was one that she knew and it meant that Landa was inspired.

"It's really easy," she said. "That showy future father-in-law of yours has arranged for caged tigers to be on display. Apparently, they will be kept in the second courtyard, not far from your room. Everybody knows you love animals, so it would be easy to imagine that you came too close while admiring them from the balcony and accidentally fell in. Or, more likely, that you were in so much despair about getting married to a man that you don't love, that you opted for throwing yourself to the tigers."

"Are you crazy?" Matima asked her. "Everyone will be able to see that there are no remains, and that wouldn't make any sense!"

"Don't be silly," Landa answered. "Nobody would want to see the leftovers. I just have to pick the right men to find what will remain of you. They will keep everyone away from the sorry sight until they have managed to remove your remains from the cage, to be wrapped in proper linen ready for the casket in which you will be buried. Your father will most probably figure it out. If he doesn't and insists to see, then he can be given the letter that you will write to him now. In that case I will make sure it is given to him on or before viewing. He will be able to choose between co-operation and telling the truth, which would put you in danger. He wouldn't even have to lie; the show can go its own way. If there is doubt, they wouldn't be able to prove that you ran away. The official report would have to be accepted as *dead by accident.*

"In the light of the tragedy that would have befallen your father and the country, the gentlemen from Extar would find it difficult to be aggressive without someone protesting, be it people in their own country or governing bodies of neighboring countries. They wouldn't want to lose support and put their own reign in danger—that would defeat the purpose. They might suspect something, but with the right people in place, they wouldn't be able to use it as a cause for conflict.

"All that you would need to do would be to escape from the room you will share with your groom tonight, preferably without him noticing. If he does notice, then you have to make sure he doesn't follow you. I don't think he will be likely to alert anyone too soon in case he gets concerned. Being rejected by your bride on the first evening you spend together would be too great a humiliation to share with the world." Landa's eyes were shining as she shared her version of events. Matima could tell that she was enjoying the drama. The nerves would probably hit her later, but in her dull day to day life of being a servant, Matima wasn't surprised that she was eager for some action.

Landa left, taking one of Matima's night dresses with her so there would at least be some evidence in the cage. They would use it to dress the real prey that they would give to the tigers. The plan was in place; all Matima needed to do was leave it in her capable hands. Next, Matima wrote the letter to her father and hid it under the cloth covering the table close to the door. She probably wouldn't see Landa again until after her escape so she would take it with her when she left. She would escape alone, but would meet Landa at the end of the passageway. There she could give her an update on whether all was going according to plan. It was all touch-and-go and she wouldn't even be able to take anything with her other than the few things she had already given Landa. Now she had to get ready for her "big day" and enjoy her wedding as much as a bride that didn't want to get married could. She had to remain calm as far as possible. The fact that nobody seemed to care about how she felt made it easier. If she looked nervous, it would only be natural. Now she just had to go through the motions.

The day went fairly smooth. She had breakfast with her father, his advisors, and the future in-laws. The free thirty minutes she had after breakfast were spent in the garden, praying to all the spirits and gods she had ever met to guide her on her path walking into a future that she didn't know. The spirits didn't talk back much. The moon was a gibbous, still visible in daylight as it sat quietly above the horizon, hiding in the blue sky in a way that it could not hide in the blackness of night. It didn't say anything, but she imagined that it was pleased with its own silence after all it had shown her the night before. She now had to trust that her path would be guided as the moon would continue sitting safely in its place in the sky.

The garden was just quiet enough to appear unconcerned about her. She couldn't blame it, though. It had given her enough magic and guidance in the past. If it appeared not to care about her now, then it probably didn't think that she needed its input. She couldn't help feeling afraid that there was more to it. If the garden was in no position to help her, then it would be reason enough not to talk to her. Maybe it was time to move on and let go of the magical garden she had grown up with. Although she felt annoyed with it, she thanked it for all it had provided. She told the garden and all its inhabitants that she loved it. She cut off a small piece of her hair which she left as a gift at the base of one of the oldest trees she knew. She prayed quietly to the tree, asking the garden to reveal its magic to others who are worthy of the knowledge. She hugged the tree, feeling its energy restore her. It was time to go, and she walked back to the palace.

***

The rituals of a bride getting ready for her big day began. The bride was uninvolved, showing neither happiness nor unhappiness. Matima concentrated so hard on visualizing her escape that she had little energy left for anything else. She wondered how other brides in her position, but without the escape route, felt and how they coped with it. She thought that they would probably react in a similar way that she was acting now—with detachment. After all, what could a woman do if she had no control over her circumstances? Matima imagined that she would disassociate entirely from herself to be able to endure giving her body to a husband that she didn't love. Perhaps a few other women in her position would opt for trying to make the best of it. They might try to convince themselves that they would eventually fall in love with their husbands, or that love wasn't a feeling of physical desire but a relationship built on choices and actions. If she couldn't have what she would choose, then she might as well choose what she had and continue doing so until she really wanted it.

Matima felt tears in her eyes when she thought of the unfortunate few who might think there was something wrong with them for not being happy on their wedding day. It was an easy trap to fall into considering the hype surrounding marriage, especially where a princess was concerned. These thoughts came and went. When she grew tired of thinking of her escape, she simply yawned with boredom at all the excited talk of the women surrounding her. The time came for her to line up to be fetched by her father. He looked like most proud fathers when their daughters got married: tender with happiness yet sad that his beloved little girl would now be leaving her place from underneath his wing. Matima felt a small rush of affection for her father but was more annoyed by the fact that he was acting as if this was a normal, consensual wedding.

She wasn't even apprehensive any more. Other than boredom at the tediousness of the ritual and impatience for it all to pass soon, she felt almost nothing. Her father delivered her to her groom who, apart from a generally pleased expression when he saw her, looked almost as unfazed as she was feeling. She guessed that he had also walked into the day with detached acceptance, not knowing what would come, but not in the mood to stress about it either because it would be a waste of energy. His initial acknowledgement of his new bride soon gave way to an empty facial expression, as if his head was in a different place. This lifted Matima's spirits for two reasons: firstly he would be less likely to try to make love to her after the ceremony and secondly, it would make running away from him easier, knowing that she wasn't breaking his heart. She even felt a hint of affection for him, certainly compassion. She said a quick prayer for his future happiness, praying that he would find and be able to live with the love of his life.

The priest's sermon was all about the vindictiveness of God. He droned on about how women had to be obedient to their husbands and how men had to look after their wives. Matima's first instinct was to yawn, but then she frowned. Where did her father get this man? She looked at him questioningly, but he looked away, looking slightly guilty. When she continued to stare at him he finally looked back at her and shrugged, nudging his head in the direction of the groom's father. The ruler of Extar was looking very pleased with what he was hearing. Matima turned to the groom, who now looked not only uncomfortable but also afraid. A little trickle of sweat was running down his temple, and the room wasn't even very warm. Matima was disgusted. Did the ruler have no sympathy for his son? She looked at his wife, her future mother-in-law. Now that she wasn't interacting with others socially, her pleasant manner had left her and she looked haughty and self-righteous. Underneath it all Matima could sense fear, not only of her husband, but also for threats to her social standing. The poor groom. Matima felt even more compassion for him and gave his hand a gentle squeeze.

When the sermon was over, the priest announced that the groom could kiss the bride. He gave her the tiniest peck of a kiss that was so devoid of passion that it would make the brightest flower wilt in an instant. They signed the papers with the witnesses, after which they made their way to the reception hall. The guests were infected by the listlessness of the couple; the party was dull enough to put anyone to sleep. The usual ambitious lot were putting up a show of enjoying themselves with intelligent conversation. Everyone else just waited for the evening to pass, wondering why they were feeling so indolent. Matima didn't even try to pretend that she was excited. The groom sensed her mood and adjusted his behavior accordingly, for which she was grateful. She handled any attention from guests with polite interest, allowing them to do the talking to avoid taking the onus of directing the conversation upon herself. Most of them babbled away in an attempt to avoid awkward silences.

When the evening had passed, it was time to show her new husband the room that was now theirs. This was the part that she had feared most. Everyone knew what happened on one's wedding night, regardless of whether it would be the first time or not. She didn't know the groom well enough to be able to guess how he would handle it. She prayed silently for guidance as to what to do in case he wanted to show physical affection.

They entered the room and she showed him around, careful to avoid eye contact. She didn't want to spur anything on by looking him directly in the eye, but it was also difficult to gauge his inclination if she didn't look at him. The urge to avoid him overpowered the urge to assess the situation. She hoped that he would get the message and be too afraid of rejection to make any unwanted moves.

Alas, the public perception of what happened on a wedding night was too strongly ingrained for Matima to get away without incident. When he touched her shoulder, she still didn't turn to face him. Her body froze and she started panicking, not knowing what to do next. Too much resistance might set off alarm bells when she would try to escape the room. She didn't think the groom would be likely to want to imprison her, but he might go after her to try and reason with her. She couldn't take the risk. Once again she called to all the spirits and gods she knew to give her guidance. She turned to face her new husband.

She was surprised by what she saw in his face. The tedium in his eyes had given way to a vulnerability which she guessed he hadn't felt until now. He was after all alone in a room with a beautiful woman who was his wife, even though he didn't really know her. He tenderly touched her face before withdrawing his hand to drop it by his side, letting it hang there just like the other one. The gesture made him look terribly defenseless. Matima couldn't help feeling a string of her heart being moved. Her fear dissipated. For a few moments there were no barriers and she could see straight into his soul. She saw the depths of a creative personality who would have preferred a quiet life rather than one on the public front. There was a need to be understood without having to fight for it. Those eyes showed a longing for something more profound than what this world had to offer. She understood. In a way they were birds of a feather, except for the fact that her interactions with the invisible might be more practical and less serious than the complexities of meaning that he longed for.

He said, "Look, I know you don't love me, but I just want to get to know my lovely bride. Perhaps we might learn how to get along and make each other happy after all. Maybe we can understand each other and walk this path together as husband and wife." He looked at her hopefully for a second or two, then the barriers returned. He looked ashamed of what he had just said. She took his hand and pressed it gently.

"I understand," she said. "I know that this is also not the life you would have chosen for yourself. I am still very young, or so it feels even though most people don't see me as too young to get married. I sometimes feel that even though biologically I am old enough to bring forth children into this world, my soul is still that of a child trying to find her feet. I have never even been too far away from my father for a long time. I don't understand how one can be expected to make such serious decisions when you are still learning who you are. I sometimes look around with wonder at many young women like myself, dreaming of the day that they would get married. They believe that they would be fulfilled when it happened. When I look inside myself, I find mostly fear. The security that others consider to be the ultimate happiness to me represents imprisonment. I wonder if I am terribly immature for not wanting to bear the responsibility of marriage, for always wanting to be free, even though it makes more sense to share my life with someone I love." Matima realized that she could be opening up too much and she didn't want to hurt the groom's feelings. She refocused her thoughts on where she wanted the conversation to go. Ultimately she wanted him to be at ease.

"I can see that it is difficult for you to be pushed into something that you are not ready for with a woman that you hardly know, never mind love. I appreciate your kindness towards me. I admire the courage you show in wanting to make the best of it and will do the same, but please understand that I am overwhelmed. My new role will take some time to get used to. I will need the space to ease into marriage. I don't want to make it more difficult for both of us. I hope that we can spend some time talking tonight and that it might be a good start."

And so they did. Matima discovered that he had a pleasant disposition, and she regretted the unfortunate circumstances under which they had met. She hoped that he wouldn't succumb to the pressure of becoming an alpha male ruler as he would only grow in power if he cultivated his sensitivity. If that would be what he chose, she could foresee a more harmonious future for the two countries operating side by side.

Eventually she told him that she was tired and wanted to go to bed. She changed into her night gown in the designated dressing area as she didn't want him to see her naked. She went to lie on one side of the bed, not too close to the middle, signaling for him to do the same. He didn't try anything, which was a blessing. She waited until she could hear his breathing becoming more regular, fighting the urge to fall asleep herself. She waited a little while longer, just to be sure. It was a risk since she didn't know how light a sleeper he was. When he started snoring slightly, she took it as her cue to start moving. Paradoxically, she felt awful, as if committing a massive betrayal. She said a silent prayer to his soul, imagining him to be listening as she asked for his forgiveness. Then she visualized herself becoming one with the night air, merging with it completely so her movements wouldn't be noticed by anyone. When she left the room, she could still hear the groom's gentle snoring.

From there everything went fairly smoothly. The trapdoor to the secret exit was unguarded. She was one of few people who had a key. She unlocked it and locked it again behind her. The torches had been lit by Landa, or it could have been fairies, she wasn't sure. She forced herself to walk slowly, saving her strength for later. The tunnel seemed to continue ad infinitum and she had to resist breaking into a run every step of the way. At long last the downward slope turned to start inclining upward. The gradient became steeper towards the end, which made her glad that she had saved her energy. At long last the tunnel became wider and lighter and she knew that she was close to the end. She met Landa, who had been waiting there for her to take the letter for her father and give her a few things she might need. Matima had a fright when she saw her friend's eyes widen with anxiety. Then she realized that she had probably upset Landa because she looked so frightened herself. She once again forced herself to slow down when she realized that she had been running.

Landa confirmed that everything was going as planned. She looked very nervous and only then did Matima appreciate fully that her friend was taking great risks on her behalf. If she had to be caught for such a conspiracy, the consequences would be so immense that Matima didn't even want to think about it. She felt a moment of intense fear together with immeasurable gratitude. The mixed emotions bubbled up, making her want to cry and laugh at the same time. She hugged her friend tightly, thanking her for all she was risking for her own freedom. She wished that she had had more time to tell her how much her friendship meant to her. But since there was none left, she expressed her wish that it wouldn't be long before they saw each other again. They said their goodbyes. Landa had to rush back to the palace to make sure she was in her proper place when the commotion would erupt. Matima hurried ahead, only a few meters away from the final exit.

She emerged from an old watchtower, which was cleverly disguised as a cabin in the woods. It was about two kilometers away from the palace wall. Looking up at the sky she could still see a few stars. The sky was now a gradient flowing from black velvet with sparks of light on one side to deep blue with a tinge of green on the other. For a moment she allowed herself to appreciate the beauty of an early morning in the forest. It was still quiet as the birds hadn't started singing yet. It was only her, the forest and the sky with the aurora still hiding behind the horizon. Matima imagined a playful young woman at the edge of the world, giggling as she got ready to announce the arrival of a new day. She was filled with gratitude as she pondered the thought of her life now being her own.

She no longer had the blanket of security in the form of the identity she was born with and she would no doubt encounter many obstacles along the way. She imagined that there would be times when she would have strong doubts about the path she had chosen, possibly even regretting all that she had left behind. But now, more than ever before, she felt the life force flowing through her veins like blood that was charged with electricity; the desire to go out and explore the world, to *live*. She thanked the heavens for sending her a difficult situation in the form of Akim to wake her up, for the sea of possibilities that awaited her. She imagined her life to be a clean canvas on which she, together with Life and a few other players, would conspire to create a work of art. Although she might not like some of the strokes that would come out, there would surely be many beautiful ones. She would cherish all of them as part of a sacred thread of something she couldn't possibly comprehend.

She greeted the first morning of her freedom thus, breathing in the freshness of life. She prayed for safety and the strength to persevere. She wanted to ask for happiness, but it was somehow irrelevant. She firmly believed that it came to those who had the courage to seek it above all else, because it was the most natural thing in the world. This was why anything that went against it felt so sharply uncomfortable. She envisioned happiness as a deep sense of communion with the universe, a certainty that one's place in it was right and that all things worked together towards a greater purpose.

These thoughts went through her mind as the idea of freedom engulfed her. Then she remembered all that she had gone through and the great risk she was taking, as well as all the other people she had put in danger. The momentary sense of ecstasy left her and the full impact of the fear she had to face hit her like a blow. She fled, running to meet Akim without looking back at the palace once.

Chapter 26

All this Matima relayed to Akim. When she had finished, she looked calmer. He could see a flickering of the light she had felt when breathing in the fresh morning air on the first day of her freedom. She even looked younger.

They gathered material from the woods and built a shelter like the one Akim had made for himself earlier. Since temperatures weren't extreme at that time of the year, they didn't need much other than food. A few days were spent enjoying one another's company, not thinking about the way forward. They were now in the state of simplicity that they had so yearned for while caught up in the world where everything was serious. They avoided dealing with the matter of what to do next because they didn't know. At the back of their minds, both realized that their blissful state of isolation couldn't last forever. They would need to move on to avoid that shriveling state of the soul: stagnation. If they kept from interacting with the world, their peaceful bubble would eventually be destroyed, not by an outside agent, but by themselves.

For both of them knew that they were born to seek growth. Their souls yearned to leave their mark in the world, spreading the joy it drew from nowhere in particular. Ultimately, a bubble of delight was selfishness that would turn on itself if contained. Love and happiness, two of the most special things that life gave for free, could be reversed in an instant if hoarded. It called to better the world, not see what one could get at the exclusion of others. People didn't come to earth to prove their worth or evade challenges.

Matima, perhaps more than Akim, was close to despair after a few days. All she had wanted was to be free to be with Akim, the man she loved more than anything. That was exactly what she had got. Although happy with her newfound freedom, she now felt like a prisoner of a different kind. She couldn't move around freely for fear of being recognized. She missed the small things, not so much the luxury of the palace life, but the people she talked to every day, the magical garden she knew and loved, the freedom of the security she used to have. She missed being the daughter of a well-loved king. With Akim now all that she had, she realized more than ever the falsity of the notion that a woman's complete happiness lay in finding the one man that would love her forever.

It wasn't about the need to be with more than one man. The light that she felt so strongly in Akim's presence came from a source greater than either of them. It was true that she felt at home when she was with him, but he didn't complete her. If their love were to thrive, she had to share this light with the world. It didn't belong to her, but was a gift that came through her. Conversely, if her love for Akim meant anything, it had to help him shine his light brighter into the world, not prevent him from doing so.

It was time to start moving again, but where to? Where could they go if they didn't know whether Matima would be safe? Akim was sure that his mother and Asteodor would receive them, but that wouldn't be the most sensible thing to do. Not only would it be their most obvious hideout if either of them were under suspicion, but Akim had left behind the life he once had there. Everyone he knew would have moved on with their life; there might no longer be a place for him. Besides, they wanted to move forwards rather than backwards. Beside their old homes, they didn't have many other options. Both of them had traveled in their official capacities, but it might now be dangerous to return to the same places. This meant that they would have to take an unknown direction, and hope to find clues for where to start.

***

Now that they were on the lookout, it felt as if the universe wasn't talking to them. They got up each morning and would ask the universe to show them the next step to the Golden City. The more they tried to understand the language and be open to the signs, the more frustrated they would become because they didn't get it. It was as if the answer lay right behind a veil; they couldn't access it because the veil itself was invisible. It was maddening. Both of them experienced times that they wanted to give up. What they had set out to do seemed so senseless that they couldn't believe their own stupidity.

They were becoming lonely. Although they had each other, the dreadful isolation that grew from living in their hideout was becoming too much to bear. They didn't miss the problems in the world, but they missed the love that could always be found somewhere, no matter how harsh the circumstances. They missed participating in small acts of kindness when people cared about others.

One evening as they were sitting quietly next to the fire they had made, they finally got a clue. They could have made it up or it could have come to them, neither was sure. They had been quiet all evening, simply focusing on the tasks of preparing food and cleaning up to keep despair at bay. Their world was monotonous. They were so preoccupied with finding direction that they had stopped noticing the small things that used to give them joy. On the odd occasion that they still heard birdsong, it sounded empty. The early mornings when the sun peeped out from behind the edge of the world went unnoticed. If they were awake at all at that time, they would desperately try to get back to sleep in an effort to escape waking life. They stopped caring about the sunsets as well; they were only a sign that another day had passed without a solution. Matima was particularly despondent. She couldn't believe that this was what she got for being true to herself. How could God be so cruel? She knew that she was responsible for her actions, but it felt as if all the options available to her were dire.

Akim wasn't in great spirits, either. He had long since learned that one might not always be rewarded for being true to oneself, at least not immediately. It wasn't hardship that was bogging Akim down—he had experienced enough to know that the road wouldn't always be smooth. What overthrew him was seeing Matima in such low spirits and being unable to make her feel better. She had to learn to be strong and he couldn't do that for her. Still, it was excruciating to sit and watch while her light was shining so dimly.

They were sitting in silence. They had finished their tasks and were now staring at the fire. They had long since lost track of time; each day was the same. Akim felt that he might as well have been alone since Matima was so withdrawn. He couldn't take it anymore. He had consulted his symbols a few times but they hadn't given much direction, other than telling him to wait until they knew where to go. They had also given some practical advice on how to cope with their situation. He now took them out again, thanking them for their wisdom. He asked his guides to give him courage despite his feelings of frustration and anger. He told them that he and Matima were approaching rock bottom and asked them to help him find the gift there. He expressed his willingness to hand over the reins to a force greater than himself since he couldn't know what was best. Love and truth had called him to act in their service and now they had to show the way.

The answer came slowly, not with clear, precise signals, but as one would look in a mirror and see nothing but one's own reflection, until after careful examination a small trickle of smoke became visible in the background. The smoke would have been missed easily by someone looking for something loud and apparent in the foreground. Instead, Akim found it by zoning out, relaxing, almost resigning himself to the idea of not receiving an answer at all. The minute he gave up, the smoke made its way into his mind, at first obscuring his vision, but then taking form to show him something. Look up, it told him, look at the stars. But be patient because the sign is subtle. Akim wanted to jump out of his skin with excitement but he restrained himself, fearful that the sign might not be what he had been looking for. He thanked the symbols for their guidance and thanked his spirit guides for their presence. He prayed that he and Matima would know how to use the information wisely.

He turned to Matima and asked her to help him find a place where the sky was clearly visible. She didn't even answer, but just got up to follow him. When they had found a suitable place, he asked her to sit down and make herself comfortable. He knelt down next to her and hugged her, hoping that his love would wake her spirit. He talked to her quietly, telling her that he knew she wasn't feeling very well. He beseeched her to please engage with her surroundings for the night. He asked her to look up at the sky and imagine that the stars were alive and talking to her. She didn't even have to take it seriously but she could approach it as a game just to humor him. He asked her to listen and see if there was anything that caught her eye. She nodded, disinterested. He looked into her eyes, trying to communicate to her soul that it was important to him that she played along. Somewhere within those listless eyes he could see something moving. He felt that she grasped it and that she was willing to put in some effort. Then he sat down next to her and did what he had told her to do.

Matima was dead quiet so he didn't know what she was experiencing. For him the process was tedious. The sky was alive and the stars were like fairies in the black velvet night, giggling because they had been noticed but not showing any more of themselves because they were shy and didn't see the urgency. Akim sat patiently, watching and appreciating the little lights of the night. He soon became tired and felt the sky world pulling him in like it had on the night when he had fled with Matima. He fought the urge to succumb to tiredness. If he fell asleep, he would be pulled in too far and forget what it was that he had wanted to find out.

He thanked the night sky politely for wanting to share its secrets with him. He told it firmly that tonight his purpose was to find direction and he would stay on the ground until he found something. The heavens sighed like a mischievous child, determined to keep on playing hide and seek. Akim was determined to fulfill the night's mission so he remained watchful. The pull was becoming stronger. As it increased in strength, his resistance also became stronger. At last he came to a point where he could no longer bear it. He wanted to give in, but then he found a point inside himself that was even stronger. With one last effort of resistance he told the night sky, "Okay, you win. But I won't be pulled in until you show me the next step on the way to the Golden City."

Silence. For a few seconds Akim thought that the sky would unleash its wrath on them because of his unwillingness to be carried away. The silence continued for a few minutes, then the sky assumed a more subtle disposition. It turned into a peaceful, ethereal sea that would show seekers the way if they could look between layers of existence. Between the many layers of air, a very wispy and elusive image of a horse became visible. It was white with a purplish silver glow. It was shy and picturesque. When it became aware that he had noticed it, it snorted, acknowledging his presence. It started running across the plains, expressing its freedom. Its power and lightness were so contradictory, yet they complemented one another beautifully. Akim was awed and didn't want the vision to pass. The horse told him it was time to go and that he now knew the location of the magical portal. She would be present with them even though they wouldn't easily see her. Mark the place in the sky, she said. She lifted her head as if in greeting and ran away, disappearing between the veils.

Akim thanked her vanished image. He regretted losing the vision, but remembered what she had said and marked the place in the sky in his mind. When he looked at it, he could see the horse in a formation of stars. He stared at it until he felt that it was ingrained in his memory. He also located the place in relation to other familiar constellations, making sure that he would find it again. If nothing else, then at least now he knew the direction they had to move in.

He turned around to look at Matima. She was fast asleep and looked peaceful. He assumed she had been pulled into the world of the sky, just like he had been on the night she had returned to him. Now it was his turn to wake her up. He didn't want to disturb her, but he had to find out if she had received any information. If she wandered too far then not only was he afraid that she might get lost, but she could also forget what she had come to know.

He shook her gently, but she remained slack. He shook harder—this time anxiety was tugging at his throat. When she opened her eyes, he could see that it was a good thing he hadn't waited longer; she had wandered quite far. He asked her gently but firmly to stand up and walk with him. Back at the camp he used twigs and stones to ground her. Her energy was returning, but she wasn't feeling well. He thought it best to wait till the morning to discuss what he had seen.

Chapter 27

When they woke up, Matima looked slightly better than the last few days. He asked her what she had seen. She couldn't remember everything. It sounded like she had traveled through many levels, eventually reaching the desert they had walked through on the first occasion when they had met. The sun had come closer, but it hadn't scorched her. She had reached two large gates, on the other side of which was a vast empty space from which a light shone. She had wanted to merge with the light, but Akim had intervened. She had seen a white horse, but more strongly than that she remembered an eagle. She felt that she had to follow the eagle because it would show her the way. Akim then told her what he had seen and said that he knew the direction they had to take although he only knew it by the night sky. It wasn't ideal, but Matima was delighted that they would be moving somewhere. She said that she might be able to navigate by day if the eagle appeared.

They moved on. Although their spirits were lighter now that they had a sense of direction, being on the move made things difficult from a practical perspective. They could only travel so many hours a day before they became tired. Sleeping in a different place every night meant that they didn't always know where to find water and food. They were becoming fairly skilled at reading the environment, but the journey was still harsh. They had no indication of what would happen next or how long it would be until they received the next sign. They didn't even know whether they were in danger. They mostly crossed uncultivated land, occasionally passing a town in the distance. They never went through one as they stuck to following the horse in the night sky and the eagle in daytime.

They had no idea how long they had been moving when they reached the next phase of their journey. They were close to reaching the same point of despair they had felt before. Moving around made the uncertainty a bit easier to bear because things were constantly changing. However, the routine of packing up every day and moving on, only now and again remaining in the same place for a few days, created its own kind of monotony that eventually became soul sucking.

The next stage of the journey was introduced by a gaudy elephant, not one found in a booklet, but in real life. Neither Akim nor Matima knew how they had stumbled into the gypsy van. It was quite large and with an elephant at its head it was hard to grasp how they hadn't heard it. Maybe the band of women were very skilled at being quiet, or maybe somewhere at the back of their minds they had been hoping to be discovered just so they could be in contact with some form of human life. They were extremely tired when the encounter happened. Even so, the parade of bright colors that materialized from thin air didn't fail to surprise them. They had a fright because they didn't know whether the newcomers were friend or foe. Also, the women were behaving quite unusual, which made Akim and Matima wonder whether they had been out of contact with humans for such a long time that they had forgotten how to read body language and respond appropriately in return. There wasn't a man in sight.

The elephant was nonchalant; it was chewing on some form of vegetation and looking around with its head bobbing. It appeared to be both interested and bored at the same time, if that were possible. All the other women were watching them, smiling, not saying a word, but not appearing bashful either. Especially the one at the front, who Matima thought was probably the leader, seemed very self-confident. Matima felt pride emanating from the woman, as if she were challenging Matima to show her own strength. Her body language wasn't aggressive; the challenge came through the air or her mind—Matima wasn't sure. She wanted to cower, especially being tired and confronted with the unexpected. Yet a part of her didn't want to concede. She was no woman's inferior and wouldn't bow down before anyone, especially not someone who had no reason to challenge her. However, she didn't want to waste energy on battles of strength. She reminded herself of her convictions and decided firmly that that would be her response to any challenge, real or imagined. I politely refuse your invitation to prove my strength, she told the woman in her mind. I prefer to greet you as a friend. As these thoughts went through her head, the force of the woman's mental probing relaxed and her essence pulled back into herself. Only the friendly smile of a stranger greeting a newcomer remained.

Matima's attention moved from the curiously silent front woman to her followers. Not all of them looked as friendly as the leader. Matima got the impression that all the women were sizing them up. Measuring them for what, she wasn't sure. She had no doubt that they couldn't look rich, in case the women were thieves, or dangerous, in case the women were afraid. The thought made Matima almost snort with laughter—they didn't look afraid at all. The word that came to mind was once again strength. The women were scrutinizing them to gauge the strength of their will and the magnitude of their understanding. A few of them were staring at Akim hungrily, as if they wanted to eat him alive. As Matima noticed this, a trickle of jealousy stirred in her. She quickly took control of her emotions as she didn't want to lose face.

Their undisguised desire for her partner was only a compliment. She had to feel sorry for these women who were obviously deprived. They might have an elephant and a brightly colored gypsy van, but they didn't seem to have men to give them pleasure. She would proudly flaunt her man, for whom she knew she would always be first choice. She smiled at them in a controlled manner, mirroring the leader woman's behavior.

She looked at Akim to determine his reaction to this unexpected encounter. He seemed confused, partly amused, but not afraid. She realized that he was aware of some subtle dynamic going on between the sisters of womankind. He didn't understand it, so he waited for the flow of energy to run its course.

Everyone was waiting for someone to break the ice and greet each other in the way that was customary—using one's voice. Akim understood that this wasn't his terrain. It took pressure off him as all he had to do was fall in with whatever lead was given. If he had known what was to come, the thought wouldn't have given him relief. Even though he understood that destiny dealt the cards, he might have changed tack if he had been able to see the bigger picture.

The leader woman walked forward, straight to Matima. She put out her hand and introduced herself as Melista. The smile, which never left her face, was radiant. This time Akim understood that she was displaying territorial behavior, establishing right from the start that whatever this meeting would evolve into, she would be the one to call the shots. He watched Matima with interest. She was friendly and determined to be herself. She introduced herself but didn't introduce him. He suspected that she didn't want to acknowledge that the woman had singled her out. She continued to smile in a friendly way, looking at the band of women with expectation.

Next Melista walked over to Akim. Her smile was almost metallic—he wasn't sure whether with friendliness or aggression. Her facial expression turned to neutral as she looked him up and down. When she was satisfied, she silently put out her hand to him as well. He knew that she was waiting for him to introduce himself, but he simply took her hand and said, "Nice to meet you." He wasn't sure why he was acting that way. Perhaps he wanted to challenge her in a way that Matima refused to, or perhaps he didn't like her dominating behavior towards his woman. He didn't mean to be malicious, but he couldn't resist the temptation to inject some mischief in his manner.

She raised her eyebrows expectantly, asking the question with her expression rather than her voice. He wouldn't, however, let her get away with using her eyes to command people. She could talk like any normal person meeting a stranger in the middle of nowhere. He pulled back his hand and gave her a friendly glance before he returned to studying his surroundings, trying to merge with it so as to be invisible. He tried to forget about the woman standing in front of him, rendering her invisible, too.

It almost worked, but then she asked in a cool, yet friendly voice, "What is your name?" He wasn't apologetic, but answered her question. She seemed amused by his attempt to evade her. She caught his eye and he could see a hint of being impressed. She held his gaze for a second or two. A veil lifted and she showed him a little bit more of her heart; he knew it was an attempt to seduce him. He could see that she had the power to bewitch men. He just smiled back at her. He had known the love of a goddess, which meant that his curiosity wouldn't easily get the better of him. Although he admittedly found her attractive, he was with the woman of his life. This weakened the power she normally had over mortal men.

Since neither Akim nor Matima would give much away, Melista took over. She introduced her band of women, nine of them. They greeted Akim and Matima with friendly smiles, then returned to their silence. Melista said that they were always delighted to meet travelers on the road to nowhere. She said it jokingly, but Matima wondered whether perhaps she knew something about their destination. She told them that hospitality was one of the rules of the road. Since they had something to offer and she could see that Akim and Matima didn't, she invited them to spend a few nights with them. They could partake of their food and other facilities. All they had to do in return was assist with chores. Matima turned to look at Akim questioningly and he could see that they were on the same page—both of them were starving for proper food and neither would mind a bit of company, albeit an eccentric gathering. He nodded to her and they gratefully accepted the offer. The women welcomed them into their circle and before long they were feeling at home.

Chapter 28

Melista invited them into her partition of the van while the other women busied themselves with preparing food. She made them a cup of tea while they waited. The potent, exotic flavor of it made them feel peaceful. She stirred a few teaspoons of honey into each cup. At the back of Matima's mind she wondered whether the tea could be trusted, but she tasted it nevertheless. She felt good memories being stirred up. The tea opened a door in her imagination to visions of things she wanted to create. She looked at Akim, who seemed to enjoy the tea while remaining unaffected by its curious character.

Melista smiled at them expectantly and asked if they were enjoying it. Her tone and body language were no longer dominating. She evidently enjoyed the company of strangers. These women must become lonely too, Matima thought. She returned the friendliness and said that she liked it. Akim agreed, now also more at ease.

Melista's demeanor turned serious. She removed the teapot from the little table that they were sitting at. She walked over to a sideboard, opened one of the cupboards and took out a map which she placed on the table in front of them. Akim and Matima leaned closer, gripped with curiosity. The map was clearly magical. The part of the map that they were looking at would come alive, assuming a life sized form in their imagination the moment they laid eyes on it. The first thing that jumped out at Matima from the map was a range of snow-covered mountains. When she looked at the drawing closely, the room around her momentarily disappeared to be replaced by a view of endless white mountains stretching up to grab a clear blue sky. The sound of the wind was overpowering. Even though she couldn't feel the temperature, she could tell that it was extremely cold. She experienced a moment of confusion. On reminding herself that she was looking at a map, the image disappeared. The map resumed its normal size until she turned her attention to the next graphic. Looking at Akim, she could tell that the map had the same effect on him. Melista now started to speak.

"Do you know where you are, travelers?" She asked them. They were not sure whether she was referring to their position in physical space or on the map. The answer to both would be the same, they realized, so they told her that they didn't. Besides, the map didn't bear any resemblance to the country that they knew. There was no spot to mark the capital city or any other city they were familiar with. They couldn't see any connection, so they waited for her to explain. She asked them to look on the map again, her tone mysterious. She was treating their discussion as a great adventure.

Matima decided to play along and started studying the map again. This was an adventure in itself, whether it had any relevance to their situation or not. She looked on the side where the sea was and saw a little boat which was deserted. There was a town of wooden houses where the people busied themselves with different kinds of manual labor. In another place she saw an old mill surrounded by goats and flower fields. There was also a temple on a hill and a monk sitting in front of it, praying. Finally, she saw an exquisite garden, surrounded by mountains and containing numerous old, wise trees.

She had looked at most of the map, but thought that she still hadn't seen what she was supposed to see. Two little figures caught her eye. They were hidden in the woods, which explained why she hadn't seen them initially. When her eyes landed on them, the figures jumped out and she was looking at herself walking right behind Akim, the fatigue and tedium evident in the way they carried themselves. She let out a gasp in shock. It was a strange feeling to look in on oneself, knowing that the other you didn't know that a different you was watching. She felt confused as her attention returned to the flat map. All the other places on the map definitely weren't in their country, nor in any place close enough to it that they could have covered that amount of distance in the time they had had. The sea was supposed to be much further away from them, for instance, and nowhere close were there mountains that were high enough to be covered by snow.

It was a magical map, but still, if it couldn't be applied to real time and space then the fact that it had looked in on them was eerie. She looked up in surprise, first at Melista, who was oblivious to her distress. Next she looked in Akim's direction. From the way he was still studying the map, partly bored, partly focused and slightly puzzled, she could tell that he hadn't made the same discovery as she. When his face finally assumed the same expression of surprise that she must have worn, he came out of his map-induced trance and looked questioningly at Melista. Matima could see that he was now on his guard towards her. The map was just too strange and she hadn't earned his trust.

Melista leaned closer, as if wanting to discuss a secret. Matima was sure that it would be wise to treat the map with reverence, but she wished that Melista would stop being so dramatic and explain what was going on. Melista lowered her voice and told them, "This is the Map of the Threshold. It is in our possession because we are the Guardians of the Threshold. We know that you are on a sacred journey, because all travelers that come our way do so for a reason. It is because we have to assist them to cross the boundary between what they used to know and what still needs to be revealed to them: the Sacred Unknown." At this point Matima wanted to interrupt and tell Melista that they hadn't sought them out, having forgotten her resolve not to challenge Melista. She opened her mouth, but Melista continued as if she hadn't noticed. However, it was as if she could read her mind. "I repeat, all travelers that come past us require assistance in accessing the unknown land." Again Matima wanted to protest, but she was too tired to question Melista. "Not all travelers are aware that they are on a sacred journey. But we know. We also know that your journey is intentional.

"The Land of the Threshold is, for many, not a nice place to be. It is the point of no turning back, and it could be that the strength of your resolve will be tested here. You might have come here because you need to visit memories of past lives that you haven't been able to access, because they have been too painful to deal with. These memories might have haunted you, interfering with all your efforts to become emancipated. The Threshold brings you face to face with karma, trying you to find out if you are strong enough to see what you cannot bear to see, put it behind you and move forward, or otherwise if it would destroy you. The answer, which only you can determine, would either open the door for you or cause you to be swallowed by a black hole.

"Your experience of the Land of the Threshold might conversely be agreeable. It might give you a gentle passage, either because you have proved yourself worthy of the challenge in past lives or because it was your choice not to be tested so much. It could also be that the Threshold allows you to pass without testing you because it doesn't think you are ready yet." Melista paused and looked at them meaningfully, first at Matima, then at Akim. Her gaze was penetrating, as if she were searching their souls for memories of past lives to see what the Threshold had in store for them. Matima felt that she was also searching for courage.

"Occasionally, a traveler is sent for special apprenticeship, which involves accelerated learning. The apprentice has to take a vow to serve a sacred purpose, otherwise she might not be able to return to the world where she has come from." She looked at them almost as if expecting to be challenged before resuming her secretive tone. "We don't always know where the travelers are going to, because not all of them have the same destination." She looked sad. "It depends on the traveler's intent. Some want to find out about magic for personal gain and to hold power over others. These are the sad cases. We cannot stop them. It is not our place to judge or interfere with free will. Ultimately, they emerge with their souls blackened, and it takes many lifetimes to restore them to a state of purity. It's not necessary to go where they go in order to learn what they need to learn, but they do not grasp it. Ultimately their activities will lead to their own demise as well as those of others who are not strong enough to protect themselves." She took a moment of silence to meditate for the lost souls. "We pray for them and beseech the Great Spirit to call them back to the light. We have to continue loving them. The world will not be harmonious until all our brothers and sisters are united.

"While encounters with these kinds of travelers do happen, the other kind is more frequent, those whose search is about bringing light into the world. All of them travel with more or less different destinations in mind. Some can be categorized in groups, depending on the tradition from which their search originated. While many may search for the same place according to their mythology, the place will be a little bit different for each of them because of the picture they had built in their minds. Each individual's experience of the road to get there is also different, regardless of the tradition. That is the beauty of the Sacred Path; it shapes the traveler as much as it is shaped by the traveler. The paradox is this: even though people from different cultural traditions look for different places, their end destination is ultimately the same." She smiled with the pleasure of imparting this wisdom.

"'So what is the map all about?' I hear you ask. It is a sacred object, passed down to us through several generations. The map is an entity in its own right. It is the Map of Now and it shows the truth, whatever needs to be known. The sisters don't know the secret of the map and neither do I, but we have sworn to honor it. The Map calls for reverence, but it will not force anyone to obey it. We, the sisters, have had to find a way to honor the map without taking away the freedom of choice of the traveler.

"The map shows what needs to be done to pass the Threshold successfully. We give the traveler an alternative, which might not get them to where they want to go but will ensure that some knowledge is gained. The traveler can choose one of these two if they want to move forward. It is very unlikely that the traveler would find both alternatives unacceptable. If that is the case, however, she can turn back, but she must know that there is a price. Having made it to the Threshold will mean that her soul has grown. Getting to this point demands courage and perseverance, not all that a person has but a good amount of it. If the traveler chooses to return, he will have to go back to a life and identity that no longer suit him. Because she has become too large for it, the confinements will be painful.

"Once again the traveler will be faced with two choices: either bear the pain of entrapment, or diminish her soul in order to fit the old container. The latter is what normally happens because a soul can only bear the pain of confinement for so long. While the second alternative sounds more peaceful, it is, in fact, direr. For when someone willingly makes himself small because he refuses to grow, perspective becomes flat. When the light can no longer flow freely, it becomes sticky, eventually turning into illness. The worst part is the emptiness in their eyes ..." Her voice trailed off, as if she were seeing it in front of her. The darkness of it perturbed her.

Matima wasn't impressed. Who was this woman who wanted to deal the cards of destiny? Did she have the right to decide what was allowed and what wasn't? She wanted to get up and leave immediately, but the woman was their host. For the sake of courtesy she would hear her out. She said, "Please tell me more about the alternative that you offer. Could you also explain to me why the map showed our recent past if it is the Map of Now?"

Melista didn't seem to notice Matima's cynicism. She continued with enthusiasm. "The map is the Map of Now because it shows whatever truth is relevant to the Moment of Now. It might show your very recent past or a fairly immediate future. It doesn't often show anything older or further ahead than that. This is because when the traveler has come to this point, he is in a position to choose. The future is very much editable and he has shed most of the past layers that have held him back.

"The traveler holds destiny in his own hands. It gives him power because he can now call the shots. The map might have shown a greater spectrum of points in time if it were consulted in the place where you came from. On the other hand, it probably wouldn't be anything other than an ordinary map there; the layers of reality are too heavy." Matima looked at her wearing an expression that was close to disgust. Melista had just told them that the map would decide where they had to go, then she had said that she and the sisters would give them an alternative. They only had those two options or they had to turn back, where they would also have two options, both of which were undesirable by the sound of it. Now she was telling them that they had power over their own future and that they could call the shots. She wished their hostess would be more realistic. Melista still didn't notice her resistance.

She continued. "The alternative is something that I decide with the sisters after consultation with the runes that speak the truth of the Great Mountain. We talk to her about the wishes of the travelers and impart our intention to give them the best alternative. She then gives us information on a likely outcome to expect if the travelers travel with honesty and grit. After the ceremony we give the travelers the option and they can choose." She smiled, looking at them expectantly as if waiting for praise. Matima's attitude hadn't changed, but still Melista was unmindful.

Matima asked, more for the sake of irony than anything else, "How do we know that you carry our best interests at heart? And that there is in fact a Great Mountain that you talk to, or that she is a traveler-loving entity?"

Melista wasn't bothered by her sarcastic tone. She simply answered, "You don't know. You just have to trust. This is where the road has brought you. Now you have to continue." Her smile was radiant as ever; she wasn't concerned in the least about the distress of her guests. Akim thought that she had probably gone through the motions enough times not to detect it anymore.

He felt exhausted and just wanted to go to bed. He would worry about it in the morning and make up his mind about whether the woman was authentic or not. He thanked Melista for the evening and the hospitality and asked if he could please be excused. She wasn't remotely offended and showed them to the room that she had prepared. Without further ado they passed out, sleeping many hours in the comfort of a warm room and a soft bed.

Chapter 29

It was midday when they awoke. They were still overwhelmed by the information they had received the previous night. Neither felt like discussing it yet. They just wanted to enjoy being in a hospitable environment for a little while, regardless of how nervous they felt. They walked to the front room where they had entered the van, hoping that Melista would show them around.

When they arrived, there were two places set at the table and breakfast was ready. It looked like they had been expected at exactly that time, for one of the sisters walked in with a pot of steaming hot tea even before they had had the chance to sit down. The smell of food came invitingly from the van kitchen. The breakfast was delicious. At the end of it they were feeling lazy enough to go back to bed. They did so and only woke up again in time for dinner. Feeling human again, they realized how much the journey had exhausted them.

They hadn't seen Melista all day. In fact, the only sister they had seen was the one who had served them breakfast and dinner. Over dinner she spent some time with them, telling them some stories about the creatures of the woods. They didn't have much else to talk about and Matima realized that the woman couldn't tell them anything about herself because she didn't have a past. She didn't want to admit that Melista had been right, but she was also feeling progressively more like a person without a past. She felt lighter, more movable, as if she had shed some of her weight. She was losing her containers of meaning. She couldn't say whether she preferred this state of neutrality; it somehow had less depth. However, it also had more potential, which could be dangerous if proper intent wasn't applied. It was a central point from which their choices and actions would ripple into effect. The waves would be felt on multiple levels and in different time zones. The thought frightened her.

After dinner they thanked the sister, who had introduced herself as Latina, and went back to bed. Upon waking up the next morning, Matima knew that it was time to act. The longer they stayed there, the more they were losing themselves. She felt frightened to discover that she was having trouble recalling details of the life she once knew. She realized that if they delayed making a decision for too long, they would start thinking that they had been there forever and that where they were was all there was. She wasn't sure whether knowing that they were in the Land of the Threshold would remind her that they had been on their way somewhere. However, she didn't want to find out. Living meant moving and experiencing. If she didn't have a direction to move in, she wouldn't have a means of defining herself. In that case, happiness would lose its meaning. She wouldn't be like one who was dead, but like one who didn't live. She wasn't sure which one was worse.

The place didn't have as strong an effect on Akim. He felt flatter than usual, but wasn't quite forgetting himself. He could still remember his mother, his past and Asteodor. He hadn't forgotten the day when he had visited the pool with Asteodor and neither had he forgotten the eagle and all it had taught him. He knew that he had a mission to fulfill and he could feel it burning in his chest. The will to find out what it was and share it with the world was too strong for him to lose his footing. He knew what was at the core of this will: love. He had seen and experienced love in different dimensions and with different people, yet the thread remained and it was what bound him firmly to the earth. Not only that, but curiosity inspired the need to find out how he could best be of service to the world in his current identity.

Knowing that they had to leave didn't make it easier to know what to do next. Especially Matima wasn't keen to play Melista's game. They didn't want to be rude, however, and they had to admit that thanking her and leaving politely could be dangerous. Since Matima was already close to forgetting all she had once known, they could get lost in both the woods and memory. They didn't want to be stuck for ever, and they weren't even sure that they would die in this place. They were becoming less aware of day and night. Neither of them could recall seeing the sun since their arrival. While they still had a notion of when they arrived, it might be wise to follow the instructions of the self-proclaimed guardian of this strange land. At least it sounded like there would be more or less a favorable outcome. They decided to ask Melista to state her case, after which they could always try to move forward on their own regardless of her ultimatums.

On the day that they were ready to hear her proposition, she appeared at breakfast, as if she had anticipated their move. Matima asked Melista why they hadn't seen her for a few days. Melista answered that she and the sisters had been preparing for their ceremony to talk to the Great Mountain. They had consulted her and found out her will, and they were now ready to offer them an alternative. She smiled the radiant smile that they knew well by now and waited expectantly. Matima still felt reluctant to give in immediately, so she asked, "What would happen if we didn't want to go with anything you offered us? Meaning we didn't want to go back either, we simply wanted to move forward and go away from here, see where the road would take us?"

Melista answered, "You can try to get away from here without taking either of the choices that we offer you. I will not stop you, but you will not be able to do so. You will find that whichever direction you choose will lead you back to the choices you are faced with now, unless you choose to go backwards. This is not because I am imposing my will on you; we are simply the Guardians of the Threshold and I am the leader. You didn't stumble upon this land by accident, it was your choice to walk a certain path without knowing where that path would take you. On a level that you don't understand, the choices you are faced with are what you want to experience.

"You cannot choose wrong, although moving forward is certainly more advisable than moving backward. Moving backward would simply mean going against yourself. If you choose not to make any choice out of the options that are available to you then what will happen is this: nothing. That's right, you will stay here and nothing will happen. Eventually we won't be here anymore, either, and the nothingness will consume you. Your mind will become blank, for you will see that we were merely your creation: what you have brought into life to help you move forward. Do we exist if you don't exist to perceive us and communicate with us? I doubt it. On the other hand, it could be the other way round and we will continue to exist whereas you will cease to exist, eventually disappearing from our memories as one who had erased her identity because she had refused to make a choice. Feeling confused?"

Through the course of her speech, Melista had transformed. She was no longer the friendly yet powerful hostess. She was a malicious, cruel witch who worked her wicked magic to frighten Matima and cheat her into believing that her mind was playing tricks on her. Matima stopped her spiral of thought in its tracks. It's you, she told herself. You don't want to own up to what you have created. You are projecting this evil image because you are afraid of moving forward. Trust in the choices you have made; the universe is on your side.

Melista had an inkling of what was going on in her mind. When Matima realized this, Melista changed back into the powerful, independent woman that she had been measuring herself against. Maybe Melista was just a mirror of herself, someone that she envied because a part of her yearned to be like her. Maybe she was projecting the image outside herself because she was afraid of owning up to it inside her. Maybe she feared that she might lose things and people that were important to her if she showed her true power. She admired Melista's unabashed confidence that made her more of a woman, not less so. She wanted to be that person who always knew what she was doing, who had many friends even though she didn't need anyone, who had no man in her life and didn't care about it because she knew that she was beautiful and that any man would give his right arm to have her. Maybe she just desired to be a woman whose identity was set in stone because she was an archetype, a persona that had a place in the universe for the purpose of performing a certain task. She was sure Melista didn't feel any unhappiness with herself or her destiny, because if she didn't perform the task, she would cease to exist.

Only then did it occur to her that Melista might not always have held the position that she was in now. Perhaps she had had her struggles as a woman, learned her lessons, and had become tired, after which she had resigned herself to the will of the gods and willingly entered their service. The thought made Matima soften with appreciation. She resolved to treat Melista with more empathy, not because Melista needed it, but because she understood that Melista was a part of herself that she had to acknowledge if she no longer wanted to feel challenged by her.

She turned to Akim and didn't even ask Melista to give them privacy so that they could discuss their decision. She knew that what Melista had presented to them was all that there was to it. It would be no use feeling uncomfortable about her presence as she most probably could see right through them. "I no longer want to waste any time," she said, looking at Akim. "I don't want to go back and I don't feel like going in circles trying to escape. I say let's hear her out before we decide."

Akim nodded. He didn't feel that Melista and the band of sisters couldn't be trusted, regardless of how strangely they acted. His symbols weren't giving him clear readings; he suspected that it was because things were so fluid in the Land of the Threshold. Perhaps it was the place from where the symbols picked up information to pass on to earthlings. Being there, the symbols could not indicate what wasn't that dense yet. He no longer felt like he needed them; their communicative capacity had moved to a place within him. Whereas he used to be the recipient, he now was the channel who could control the flow of things. He was a step before the point where they had taken sufficient form to be captured in a reading. His inner compass was telling him that Melista was authentic. They had to go with what she would offer them because there were no other avenues. He agreed with Matima and nodded at Melista.

"First, I will consult the map. After it has shown its truth, there will be no second chances. We will know when the map has spoken. It will show what it will show and it is up to you to interpret it. I am not the map's spokesperson, for I can promise you this: the map tells your story and will speak to you directly. I am more than willing to offer my insights, but understanding the message is your responsibility. If you listen from the heart, the message will be clearer than anything you have heard in your entire life. If you have trouble interpreting it, it will mean that your mind is clouded by fear. In that case, I would advise you to go with the first meaning that comes to mind. Akim, I believe that you are skilled at reading omens. You will understand what I am talking about."

Matima was already feeling afraid. The idea that some mystical object held power over her destiny disturbed her. Akim simply nodded that he understood and waited for Melista to continue. "After consulting the map and discussing it if you want to, I shall offer you the alternative, which is the truth of the Great Mountain. You then have to decide. Having come to this point means that you have indicated that you want to make a decision, therefore, being forgotten or ceasing to exist is no option. If you fail to decide, I decide for you. More often than not my choice will be that you have to go back. This will not really be my choice, but yours." Akim and Matima nodded that they understood. "Are you ready?" She asked. Again they nodded their agreement.

She lit a candle which she had placed beside the map. Next she said an incantation in a language that they didn't understand. She asked them to bless the map with their purest intentions and call forth the forces of light to guide and protect them. She extended her hand over the map and said, "Let us walk forth in light and be guided by the truth." She withdrew her hand and asked them to find themselves on the map.

Chapter 30

Matima looked. At first she couldn't see anything; the map looked ordinary. However, she could see that Akim had been taken by the map. His eyes were looking into another dimension. She looked questioningly at Melista, who was also confused. She tried to shrug off discomfort. If the map gives me an option that I have connived towards, she thought, then there is nothing to be afraid of. Surely it will show me my heart's desire. She looked again. Instead of finding herself on the map like she had the last time, she closed her eyes involuntarily and saw the moon. She was in the world of the map and the branches were partly obscuring her view, but behind them the moon was bright and large. Its normally gloomy aura was transformed into a sparkling energy. It felt as if she were holding the moon, worshipping it. She was asking for her blessing so the land might be fertile and the crops would grow. Within the moon she saw the Great Mother, the one who gave life and nurtured it, providing comfort to those who were weary. She bowed before her, feeling the moon stroking her back and kissing her neck.

The view zoomed out and now she could see herself standing on a raised dais, her hands extending into the air. She wasn't alone. Around her were a dozen or so women dressed in similar attire as her. They were all facing her, their hands also extended, facing upwards in a receiving gesture. They were receiving blessings from the moon. She could sense, rather than see, the spirit of the wolf being present. She started dancing a slow, sensual dance. The women around her followed her lead. They were entranced in a sacred dance to thank the moon for the fertility and abundance it brought to earth. The wolf was happily moving between them, enjoying the energy that the dance awakened.

Matima could sense the earth being wakened. From where she was observing, it was mesmerizing. A curtain closed on the image and she returned to her surroundings. She was slightly out of her depth; she had almost forgotten that she was in a gypsy van in the middle of nowhere. Melista asked if she would like a glass of water. She gratefully accepted and drank it quickly. She was dizzy and nauseous. She leaned forward so her head could rest on her knees, hoping that the sickness would soon pass. She wouldn't make any decisions now. She would leave it to Akim.

He looked pale as a ghost. Matima wasn't sure whether it was because he was also feeling ill or whether he had seen something he didn't like. He was concerned about her, but Melista called them back to the present.

"Tell us about what you saw, Akim." Her voice was firm, almost authoritarian. Akim was trying to avoid the situation by still doting over Matima. Realizing this, Matima also looked at him questioningly. If he had seen anything he was hesitant to tell her, then she'd be interested to find out what it was sooner rather than later. He conceded, pulling away from her.

"I saw myself walking a very narrow path to go over a range of mountains. The weather was horrendous; it was windy and the rain blew into my face. I had to struggle not to fall. It was dark, not because it was night time, but because the storm clouds were gathering. The gods were showing their wrath with lightning bolts flying from the sky. I didn't see much more than that, but it wasn't easy. I just knew I had to keep moving forward. There was something I had to find within the mountains. I knew that the road would be clearer after that, perhaps a bit easier to walk even if it wouldn't be without danger. It didn't look like an easy journey." He started fiddling with his hands, seemingly nervous.

"Is there anything else you saw that we need to know about?" Melista asked again in a resolute voice.

Akim looked up. Matima could see that he didn't want to hide anything but that he was confused. "It's not about what I saw. I didn't see much more than what I told you. It's what I didn't see. Matima wasn't there. I'm not sure if I just couldn't see her because the map only shows what the future holds for me. But I also wasn't aware of her presence; it didn't feel like she was supposed to be there. It felt like I had to go through it alone, but it didn't feel wrong." He resumed his fidgeting and looked down again. "I don't know if that means that she's not coming with me, according to the map's truth." He looked squarely at them. Matima guessed that her facial expression told him that what she had seen didn't contradict his vision. Realizing this, he was both alarmed and more at ease.

Once again Melista took the lead. "Now tell us about what you saw, Matima." So she told them about her vision of the moon dance. Even Melista looked puzzled. Matima wasn't sure whether she had had an inkling of what the map would show before they had consulted it. Her guess was that Melista had known something of the map's plan, but not all of it. Melista's surprise probably had something to do with the details that had been shown to her rather than the outcome itself. Matima still felt disassociated. The fact that Akim wasn't present in her vision, either, didn't upset her as much as it did him. Admittedly, prospects looked more pleasing for her than for him. At least she wasn't alone, which made it less daunting despite the fact that Akim wasn't by her side. She felt ready and excited to experience what she had witnessed. Akim was looking at her almost pleadingly. He turned to Melista.

"Could you please tell us more about the alternative?" he asked, his voice despondent. Matima felt a surge of sympathy. She wanted to lean over and hold him tight, tell him that he didn't have to go through it all alone. Instead, she visualized her love to surround him, offering a layer of protection. She silently whispered to his heart to remember her love for him no matter what happened and to keep believing. She turned back to Melista, who had now started speaking again.

"Let's close the ceremony of the map first." Putting her hands over the map as if in blessing, she said, "Map, we thank you for the truth you have shown. May these travelers walk forth in courage, remaining true to themselves and honoring the truth in others. We honor your wisdom and guidance. Thank you for the opportunity you have given them. May they be protected through grace." She turned to them and said, "Please ask the map for its blessing." Akim and Matima both did as they were told. Using an incense stick that she had lighted, Melista passed it over the map, chanting under her breath. She blew out the candle and clapped her hands together three times above the map. She folded the map and put it away. She lit a new candle to start the ceremony of the alternative, which was courtesy of the Great Mountain.

She thanked the Great Mountain for its wisdom and called in her guides to assist her with imparting the wisdom. She acknowledged that even though she and the sisters had received guidance, it was up to them to offer the alternative. She expressed her best will for the travelers, stating that she and the sisters had their best interests in mind. She admitted that they didn't know what was best for them. Since they had to fulfill their task, they had made a decision trusting that all would work out well without knowing whether they were right. She beseeched the travelers to do the same: trust without knowing and accept the alternative as it was, perhaps not perfect, but well intended. She was quiet for a second or two, waiting for them to agree. They simply stared at her and waited for her to continue.

"All right," she said. "We have decided that should you wish not to go with the map's advice, Matima has to leave tomorrow morning. It doesn't matter which direction she takes or what she does. Our sole requirement is that she leaves. We would offer advice, though. Since you are already close to losing yourself in the Land of the Threshold, Matima, we suggest that once you choose a direction, you continue in that direction without fail, keeping your mind fixed on where you want to go to. This is the only way that you will make it past the Threshold. If you falter, you will slip into forgetfulness. You will not only forget who you are, but you will also be forgotten. *By everyone,* including the people who love you most: your father, your friends and the one person who can never forget you, your lover. It is a very dangerous journey to undertake, but you have the ability to see it through, otherwise it wouldn't have been offered to you.

"The alternative for you, Akim, is that you stay with us until it is time for you to go. Another way of looking at it is that you will stay with us until we decide to release you. You cannot go according to your whim. We have your best interests at heart, but you have to know that it will be a commitment. We cannot tell you everything we plan for you. Suffice to say that you look like a good candidate to be one of the very few men to be initiated into the way of the goddess. It might sound absurd to you, but occasionally we find a man whom we deem worthy of gaining insight into his polar divinity.

"Since you came to us together, you will be treated as a unit. That means that one of you cannot go with the map's advice and the other one take the alternative. You have to decide together, and it will have to be no later than tomorrow morning. I would advise you though not to wait until the last minute. Matima is already close to forgetting who she is. Each of you has to take full responsibility. Do not blame the other for the choice you have made in case you don't agree initially. It is best not to look back and to simply trust that you have made the right choice.

"I shall give you a few minutes to talk. If you haven't come to an agreement by the time I return, we shall postpone your choice until tomorrow morning. Once you have indicated your choice, all shall be put into action." With that she blew out the candle and got up to leave the room, closing the door behind her.

Akim turned to Matima, who was still pale. He took her hand and said, "Matima, I don't want you to be in danger of losing yourself and be in danger myself of forgetting you. I don't believe that you could be forgotten. My heart would lose a part of itself for ever if you would disappear from memory. I say we go with the map." She just nodded. He took her by the shoulders. "Matima, please say something. I know you are not feeling well, but I have to know that you are consciously making the decision." She nodded again. It looked like a lot of effort for her to talk, but she said, "I leave it to you, Akim. I know that you love me and have my best interests at heart, more so than anyone else. I am not sure what the map and the Great Mountain are all about, but I trust in your ability to make good decisions. If you say we go with the map then that is what we do."

The moment she had finished talking, the door opened and Melista returned. She looked at them questioningly, without even coming back to sit down. Akim nodded to indicate that they had made their decision.

When he had told her, she said that he could stay until breakfast the following morning before leaving. She couldn't point him in any direction; he would have to bear in mind what the map had told him. There would be clues, but he would have to keep his eyes open. As for Matima, she continued, she would stay until she felt better, after which she could decide how to pursue her vision.

Melista walked over and hugged Akim to say goodbye. He thanked her for the hospitality. His feelings towards her were ambivalent. He knew that she genuinely believed that the map's truth was outside her control, which it probably was. However, he still felt resentful towards her. In his mind she was the agent causing him and Matima to part ways. He didn't even want to think ahead about what the future would bring. From some place inside him he had to trust that they had embarked on the journey together and that they would find each other again. It was all he could do; he couldn't turn back and he couldn't stand the thought of losing her, either.

It was late in the evening when Melista had left. Since Matima still wasn't feeling well, they went straight to bed. Akim knew that he had to rest well on the last night that he could sleep in a safe place. He didn't want to miss out on holding Matima close to him for the last time, not knowing when he would see her again. He hugged her sleeping body tightly, burying his face in her neck. An infinitely sad feeling overcame him. He felt that he had the weight of the world on his shoulders, a world that he had lost and didn't even know where to find again. His tears were rolling down his cheeks and Matima's back. As he wiped them away, the touch of her skin warmed him up from the inside. He thanked the universe for knowing such love and prayed that it wouldn't be the last time he slept next to her. He fell asleep, lost in dreams where he was but a little baby again and his mother comforted him while he was crying.

Morning came and it was time for Akim to embark on his unknown journey. It was incredibly hard to leave Matima behind as fragile as she was. Since she didn't even make it to breakfast, he went alone. He finished his meal, thanked the patron and returned to Matima.

Her eyes looked hazy, as if she weren't quite present. He didn't understand her illness since he had gone through the same process without experiencing similar symptoms. Since he could no longer be there for her, he had to withdraw. At least that way he didn't feel the pain of his powerlessness.

All that was left to do was trust that the sisters would look after her. He felt like a traitor for leaving her behind, even though he knew it was preferable to the risk that she might lose herself. Looking into her eyes he could barely see a trace of the Matima that he knew. He understood that she had also withdrawn to make the parting easier for both of them. Being already so close to forgetting who she was, it was easier for her soul to find a gap and escape until it was safe for her to come back. The effect on her body was evidently more than she could handle. However, if the sisters were giving accurate information and the map had indeed been telling the truth, then she would soon come back and grow in strength.

When he had kissed her goodbye, he gathered his things and walked away in a direction that he didn't know. He wanted to pause at the doorstep to wonder if he was doing the right thing. But he pushed on, determined to find a way forward. Soon he was in the middle of nowhere again, just like before they had met the women in the gypsy van. The only difference this time, apart from being alone, was that he was aware of being in the middle of nowhere and the dangers associated with it. He decided to embrace it, because it was all that he could do. He walked on until darkness swallowed him and the stars came out, showing a different night sky from the one he knew. It was cold and fatigue made him stop to find a tree and a decent place to rest. He took out his blanket and a pillow and snuggled underneath it. Being in the land where things moved fast, he was engulfed by dreams almost immediately. It felt good. Forgetfulness was what he wanted and needed. He would sleep for as long as he could. Only when he was thrown out of the sleep world would he consider where to go next.

Chapter 31

Akim was dreaming. The dream world was so much closer in the land of the Threshold. He only had to take a step through the veil into a world where everything was less dense. The most noticeable difference was in how he felt. While being awake he had felt tired and discouraged. Now that he was no longer trapped in his body, he felt unencumbered. It helped that the place where he found himself reminded him of heaven, the one where he had been told good people went after death. He hoped that he wasn't dead yet. He missed the earth and all that he loved about it. The dream place was enjoyable, but he wanted to go back to make a difference. He needed to bring the heaven of his dreams into a world that needed healing.

The place reminded him of the palace gardens. It wasn't like its wild aspect that always caught one unawares, but rather like the flower garden where Matima had informed him of being the king's daughter. It also resembled the place in the sky world where he had found his symbols. Still, the place in his dreams was different. Here he was engulfed by such a deep peace that sadness was irrelevant. It came from deep within him and was everywhere around him. He felt connected to a Source much greater than himself through the center of his heart. Source expanded through him, encompassing him, containing him. The sense of calm was more stable than anything he had ever experienced in the dream world.

The wind was whispering softly through the trees. The flowers of the plants were massive and a soft shade of violet. The bees were much larger than those on earth and were humming quietly rather than buzzing. The clouds were silky, looking like spongy beds that would provide a welcome resting place for a tired traveler. The blue of the sky had the same intensity as the purple of the flowers. A few meters away from him was a pond with a surface as smooth as a mirror. The water flowers floating on it interspersed, forming a harmonious picture.

Matima was there and yet she wasn't. He felt the peace that he felt through his love for her. He tried to picture her there, but as soon as she appeared the image would evade him and only the heavenly garden would remain. His contentment was so complete that he didn't need to physically see her. The moment when he would stop trying to call her to the garden by imagining her there, she would show up somewhere, even if he only saw her through the flowers or clouds. She was part of the garden just like she was part of him. Their love was everywhere, engulfing them rather than being a stream between them. The world around Akim faded out as he merged with the Great Idea where nothing was everything and consciousness was all there was.

He drifted into more dreams, the random, unpredictable kind that made him feel like he was back on earth. He was just a small boy who didn't have a care in the world and whose dreams meant nothing. He had no responsibility because he didn't have the power to make a difference. He embraced these dreams, enjoying the condition of not having much freedom of choice nor understanding of the effect of his actions.

Morning came and he had to continue his journey. Despair washed over him. He was lonely, afraid and had no sense of direction. He closed his eyes, blocking out the world where his body found itself just for a second or two. He slowly opened his eyes again, determined to move on even though he didn't feel ready. He picked the first tree he laid his eyes on and asked it for a sign to show him which direction he had to take. Next his eyes fell on the moon. The sun was coming up as the moon lowered itself to the horizon to eventually drop behind a range of mountains. It brought to mind the orb that had hung in the sky in the world where Samuel came from. That was his sign, he knew, for mountains were also what he had seen in his vision of the map. He set off in the direction where the moon was sitting, resolved to find himself as the map had shown him in the lonely mountains which seemed so impossibly far.

Chapter 32

The journey was long and dreary. Akim lost track of time more the further he went. He could see his physical surroundings but it was losing its relevance. The world inside his head became louder and more prominent as he proceeded, at times driving him insane with nagging thoughts. The world around him came to reflect what he was going through internally. While Matima had been forgetting herself, Akim was plagued by memories from the past, things he wished to let go of that were now showing up from where they had been lurking in the corners of his mind. They were mostly fears: fear of rejection, fear of isolation, fear of insanity, all at the forefront of his psyche.

The tedium of the journey was intensified not by its duration, which could hardly be defined anymore, but by all the little parts of himself that he didn't like and had to face now. It was only his desire to reunite with Matima that was driving him to continue. Several times he stopped, asking himself what the point was if he didn't even know where he was going, how long it would take or whether he would get there eventually. He didn't even know where "there" was. He sometimes asked himself where he intended to get to and wasn't able to answer his own question. The only thought that would come up was that he had to get to Matima. He would remind himself that he was wrong because he was actually moving away from her. After searching his mind for some time he would remember that he and Matima had set off to find some place which they didn't know, but he couldn't remember why.

The random memories of his past continued to haunt him. He surrendered, observing them and accepting them. The temptation was there to forget that he was on his way somewhere and let the stream of thought take him, swallowing him until he believed that the memories were his present reality. At times he could almost physically see himself in his past. The memory would be a layer of visibility covering the physical layer of existence where he really was. If he would believe in it too much then he would always stay stuck where he was, never passing through the difficulty so as not to be controlled by it anymore.

There was a depressing quality to all layers of his reality, as if they were enshrouded by a heaviness of the mind. All the central parts of his being—his heart, his mind, his body and, most importantly, his will—felt cloudy and blocked as he fought the metaphorical demons. While he had no idea what time of day or night it was, or even whether there were still days and nights, his only escape came during the occasional moments when he was able to fall asleep completely. He would then escape to a world where everything was light and experience a little bit of heaven.

To pass, or rather survive his trial, he kept his eyes on the mountains, at least whenever he could see them. When he couldn't, he tried to conjure them up in his mind's eye, focusing on the image to make it stronger so it would banish the ghosts of his past. Sometimes he was more successful than others. When he became exceedingly tired, the memories would go away, leaving nothing except blankness. It was an empty peace, a stillness consisting of nothing and nobody. In these moments, he would lose all thought of himself and, paradoxically, be firmly grounded in the physical world where he was.

When he had been empty for long enough, he would find a fraction of hope returning to his heart. Next would be the courage to move forward. Akim generally rested only during the quiet spells, when he had no strength to put in any kind of effort. As soon as hope showed its face, he would get up and start moving again, determination pushing aside the tiredness in his being.

As grateful as he was for the return of hope, there was also a downside. It would inevitably invoke its polar opposite: despair. The two flipsides of the same coin would rival for the upper hand and the feud would continue until he became too tired to move forward again. As soon as he rested and assumed neutral, the coin would be perfectly balanced until it eventually merged with the ether, only to return to existence when he resumed his journey.

He found himself wondering by how many years he had aged since he had left the gypsy van, if indeed there was such a thing as age in this place. At other times he wondered if he had only left the van a day or a week before. Would he be stuck on a journey to nowhere forever? Where would it end? He asked himself if he would ever just be Akim again, in a world that was a world in itself, not one that was ruled by whichever thought came to his mind and whichever suffering happened to torture him on the day.

At long last he could take it no longer. He had reached the point where he was about to give up for good. He was in a place in the woods next to a stream. Normally the enclosure would have soothed him, but the woods were so dense around him that he felt trapped. The infinity of obstacles in the form of vegetation that he had to push through stifled him. Once he reached the mountains, he would merely be a shadow of the solemn traveler that he had seen on a magical map, walking in the rain, pushing on despite the uphill climb. He couldn't even imagine further than that, and what he had seen on the map definitely wasn't a worthwhile destination. What was he doing it all for? There was nothing to look forward to. He had no destination, no light and, most importantly, no Matima to encourage him. He might as well be dead.

A few hundred meters away he could see a spot of light in the woods. He instinctively moved towards it, despite his resolve to discontinue. If nothing else, it would at least be a spot for him to hopefully sit down and see some sunlight while beholding the destination that he would never reach. The spot turned out to be a clearing before a cave. At peace, he looked up at the mountains that never came closer. The cave lured him. It was a good spot to return to nothingness, he decided. Let the universe take him and maybe some other lone traveler would find his skeleton in a million years from now, wondering what the story behind the forlorn remains was. Yes, he would sit there and wait for the end to come. This time he wouldn't get up again. He had no motivation left if everything always turned to dust and all that hope ever did was fail him. Why was he alive if suffering turned out to be his ultimate milestone?

The cave was the perfect place. It reminded him a bit of a womb; it was the womb of the earth. As life had been given to him through a human mother, so life would be taken from him through the earth mother, who took all life as mercilessly as she gave it generously. He didn't even feel sad about it anymore, he was ready to go. Even Matima had faded from his resolve. She was the happiest memory he had ever known, and yet all happiness turned out to be insubstantial. Their love was a fluke that made no sense in a world ruled by despair. Love wasn't real, it was simply an illusion and it was time for him to face up to it.

Even walking the distance to the cave seemed like a lot of effort. That promising black hole, that gap of nothingness, if only he could reach it. It was all he could see. Not even the splendid mountains that had always talked to him were alive anymore. The woods were invisible, dead. The sky that used to signify aspiration was now just a dull, empty space, depressing to behold. The black hole was the only thing that attracted him. He had to get there, rest, merge with nothingness. Was it even possible, he wondered, to stop existing once you have existed? Could consciousness be killed once it had woken up and seen itself?

Consciousness was such a strange thing, Akim thought. It had not chosen to become what it was. It was driven by some inexplicable force that the bearer, the one that existed, couldn't get away from. Human beings hadn't created themselves, and how many didn't at some point in their life either think of ending it all or otherwise wish that they had never been born in their present identity. They would yearn to go back to sleep without making the decision to be the agent that would send them to oblivion. They simply wanted to escape the responsibility of having to make decisions and define themselves through what they thought, said, and did. Not only that, but especially in the eyes of the world through what they had, in which case they often had no control, left to the mercy of a social system that had been created based on a consciousness of limited resources and survival of the fittest.

Akim thought that existence was as strange a phenomenon. The difference between humans and animals was that animals instinctively fought to survive, whereas humans fought to survive unless they didn't want to anymore and opted for killing themselves instead. Another remarkable difference was that animals never tried to be something else than what they were. Humans, on the other hand, were hardly ever happy with themselves or what they had. They always wanted to have more and be better, no matter how splendid they were in the eyes of the world, measured by whatever standard was prevalent in a given social context.

Akim wondered, did humans have the capacity to create happiness? Or was the only way that they could bring happiness into their lives to accept that they couldn't create it, but believe that it was natural and would be given to them in abundance if only they were open to receive it? Was happiness a birthright, not because people had the capacity to create it, but because there was an existential responsibility to honor the gods by being the best they could be? But humans insistently interfered. Instead of allowing themselves to be splendid as they were created to be, just like all other living things, they created misery. How ironic, he thought. The beings on earth who were supposed to be most awake were most asleep, miserable and out of balance. It was actually so easy and yet they made it so hard.

Those who wanted to create a world that they were born to create suffered the most, because the world of their dreams contrasted too sharply with the real world that they lived in. Their ideas were often rejected by a world in which beauty and harmony had no place. What if humanity had it all wrong? What if those we considered unimportant played a vital role? What if those whose ideas were thought to be insane were actually closer to hitting the mark as far as creating a better world was concerned? Or was it the case that those in positions of power didn't want to create a better world; they wanted the world to act in the interest of their personal gain and would promote any agenda that would serve that end? Maybe a better world would mean that they were no longer stronger or richer than anyone else and they didn't want to let go of their stronghold.

Who are our heroes? Akim thought. Looking at the world it seemed to him that the liars, cheats and psychopaths stole the limelight. He couldn't lose his faith in the human soul, though, for those who lived in favor of peace, love and tolerance were remembered. Ultimately, they had the power to return others to themselves. The artists who expressed themselves from their souls were the ones to be remembered for being original. What the leaders and oppressors had forgotten all about was the power of love and joy. One person who consciously intended to spread joy in the world had the power of a tornado to wake people up. One expression of sincere love could be all that was needed to stop evil in its tracks.

The mouth of the cave was coming closer now. I have given my best, Akim thought, but now I am tired. What was the point of having a mission if the universe and the spirits weren't there to support him? He might as well bury himself in darkness, waiting for a day when there would be light before he came out. He no longer cared. All he wanted was darkness so the darkness itself could no longer threaten him. He entered the cave. It was pitch black inside. He sat down and waited. He waited for a very long time. It wasn't even painful, there was just nothing at all. It was probably what people felt like when they weren't awake to their heart's deepest desires and when they chose to believe whatever they were told about the nature of life and the universe, rather than finding out for themselves. Maybe it was what being dead felt like, he thought. Eventually all thought ended and there was only blackness, like being asleep, except he didn't want to or plan to wake up.

Chapter 33

"Hello, are you there?" The voices penetrated his consciousness, but he couldn't see anything. Something was different, he was different. What was his name again? Were they looking for him? It sounded like a boy and a girl who were trying to find someone. Judging by the sound of their voices and the nature of the conversation he estimated them to be teenagers. The boy could be younger, early teens or pre-teens. He froze. He hoped that they weren't looking for him; he wasn't ready to go back yet. Wait, yet? Had he just thought "yet"? He wasn't ready to go back ever. He wanted to remain asleep.

He tried to move but his body was completely rigid. Why was it all so black and why couldn't he see anything? He could feel, however. The wind was whispering through the woods. The strong physical sensation made him think that perhaps he was no longer in the land of the Threshold. Maybe things would be different here, better, wherever he was. Had he passed his ordeal successfully? Had he moved past the place where he was stuck by giving up? No! He wouldn't succumb to the temptation that hope offered him: the yearning to move forward again, lured by the possibility that things could after all be better this time around and maybe even work out. He had to suppress the will to find out. Hadn't he already done what he could? Wasn't the answer clear as it could be, set in stone? He refused to be called back to life. He would stay where he was, even though he wasn't entirely asleep. He definitely wasn't entirely alive either, and he couldn't move, even if he wanted to, which he didn't. That suited him perfectly. Now he could stay just where he was forever with no responsibility. The voices he had heard eventually became softer until they faded away. It sounded like the children had only walked past, looking for someone who wasn't him.

***

He felt uncomfortable being entirely still, trapped in a strange form that he didn't know. It felt as if he wanted to grow; the urge was becoming too strong for him to continue resisting. It was almost painful to refuse it. As soon as he relaxed, he would become aware of his hands, or his top, whatever, stretching upwards, always trying to reach the sky, looking for sunlight, trying to touch the stars at night, drinking in its light to be nourished by it. He would receive the fluid light and would cherish it, allowing it to flow all the way to his roots, where his feet drew sustenance from the earth. Gratitude. He loved the feeling of the sky showering him with light, blessings entering through his fingertips and moving to his heart, energizing his being. Conversely, he also loved the strength the earth gave him, the solidity of his foundation, the sustenance that the Mother provided, looking after him so selflessly. The earth and the sky, two such different entities and yet they worked together in perfect harmony, blending in this way to transform energy and enhance growth. In the region of his midriff the two polarities came together and spun in a wheel of electric light, turning possibility into potential that would eventually become great power if used correctly. If only he could move.

Where was he? He wondered. And why was he trapped, even though it didn't feel wrong? Was he still who and what he was or had he transmuted to a different life form because he had refused to be human any longer? More than that, he had refused to be Akim and live Akim's life. Would that account for the fact that he could no longer see with human eyes, only feel the energy of the universe flowing through him? Would that be why he couldn't move unless he was moved by an outside agency? Would that explain why he had been feeling all along that he couldn't walk, only grow?

Maybe he could see after all, even if not through his human eyes. As he attempted to sense what was going on around him, the spirit world opened up. What he could see wasn't so much the density of objects, but rather the light that appeared in the spaces between particles. He was in a forest, he realized, a very dense one that stretched out for many acres around him. He couldn't perceive a city or any other area that was frequented by human beings too close. It was quite amazing to be able to see a forest in this way. There were millions more organisms appearing as little lights than anything he could imagine with his human mind, even for a forest. He himself was sturdy and high, one of the tallest in the forest. He could stay in this shape for ever. It was peaceful, the best feeling he had ever known. Maybe even better than …

He had known something that might have felt a little bit better, even if only by a fraction. As much as this state was close to perfection, it didn't feel right, nor would it ever, at least not for more than a very limited time. He had to go back and finish what he had started. He had to know, find out, become all that it meant to be Akim. He had to live in a world as a being that could act as a way of defining himself. No matter how bad it could be at times, no matter how many mistakes he would make, no matter how many times he would cop out because he was too tired to move forward, he had to keep on trying until he did it right. He probably wouldn't ever get it right, either, but wasn't that what living was all about? At least then he would have gained some experience, passed some tests and learned a little bit about himself and others. At least he would be free, to a certain extent, to choose what he wanted and who he wanted to be. At least then he would have known what it felt like to be powerless against life's twists and turns.

Maybe there was nothing more worthwhile than to get up from the ashes, look life and the world in the face and say, "Despite your efforts you couldn't get me down. I am still me. Regardless of my failures, I choose to make the most of what I have. I may have been rejected, ridiculed, and even tortured, but I'll be moving forward again soon. Beware, life, there is a hard core traveler who is ready to have another go. He is stronger than before with all his scars, for now he knows his capacity to love." Silence as the world faded out again.

"Are you ready to come out now?" a voice asked in the blackness. He was no longer caught in the body of a tree. It was still dark, but it felt more like the womb; his energy was looser and his soul could float around freely. He was still angry, so he hesitated. Was he ready? Nothing, no answer.

Chapter 34

"I guess I am." It came from within him, faintly. No reply. Had he forfeited his chance? Or lost his mind? Was he still asleep? No, please no! He didn't want to be lost forever. "Help me," he shouted, but the panic only produced a maelstrom of blackness. If he still had a body that could get nauseous he would have felt sick. It felt like the whirl was pulling his insides apart, that all the bits that made up Akim were scrambled and torn in different directions. He would have thought that he was dissolving except that it was too gentle a description; what was happening felt far more violent. Please, can I just remain intact, he prayed. He didn't want to fall through cracks and be spit out into a place that was not the universe, consisting of darkness and discord.

It felt like his skull was cracking open as his head hit something hard, like a rock floor. Surely the blow should have been hard enough to kill him? But no, he was assembling again, all his different bits and parts coming back into his body, flowing through the crack in his skull. It felt uncomfortable. He was weak and limited again, confined within the boundaries of being human. His body was too small a container for the amount of light that it had to accommodate. Enough, too much. He started vomiting all over the rock floor of the cave he was in. He was shaking as he retched until there was no longer anything to come out. His fingers were tingling as if they were still the top of a tree reaching up towards the sky.

He wasn't in the same cave that he had been in when he had given up. This one was lighter, brighter. When he walked out there was an entire forest stretching out below him until the point where it met the sea. The forest was shimmering and ... *solid,* unlike the dismal darkness of the wispy world where he had felt so stuck. It was beautiful. The birdsong gave it a happy feel. Although he couldn't see the birds, he imagined them to be colorful and friendly. The sun was hanging over the ocean. From the fresh feel of the environment, he surmised that it was probably morning. He breathed in the cool air. Despite the fact that he was still adapting to his body, he was renewed, as one who had gone through a process of purging. Appreciation bubbled up inside him. It was good to be alive. But where to now, seeing that the mountains were missing?

"Looking for something?" a voice asked behind him. Akim turned around. There had been someone with him all along and he hadn't even noticed. It was a fairly old man, not old enough to be weakened in body, but not young enough not to be associated with wisdom. His face wore the imprints of experience, giving him a kind and understanding look. His hair was long and grey and tied back into a ponytail. He wore black robes tied at the waist with a strip of braided brown leather. Around his neck was another strip of leather decorated with feathers and stones. His sandals were made of the same leather.

Akim was startled by his presence, but the man didn't inspire fear in him. In a way it felt like Akim had known him for some time. It was unexpected and he was at a loss for words. "Beautiful, isn't it," the man said. He wanted to put Akim at ease.

"It is beautiful," Akim said. "But how do I get to the mountains, the ones that will take me to the Golden City?"

"The mountains were just a figment of your imagination," the man said, "something you have conjured up to signify your deepest fears. Because you have moved past them, they no longer threaten you. By isolating yourself, you have conquered your fear of isolation. You have proved that you can and will survive because your love is greater than your fear. That which you have feared turned out to be peaceful and hold its own kind of comfort, like the eye in the midst of a hurricane. But it just wasn't you, so you decided to move forward. You deserve a medal for that, by the way.

"Take a look at this place, for it is one of the only real places you will ever know. Breathe deeply and remember what it feels like. Keep the image fast in your mind for the moments that you will need it. It is your place of love, victory and beauty, born in your sorrow but coming from a place beyond it. It is the strength within you. When you move forward, bring this world to whatever aspect of space and time you may find yourself. You will not only be helping yourself to deal with life's challenges, but you will also help others to find the same place inside them. Now close your eyes while you are carried to the next phase."

Akim didn't want to leave, but the image was fading out so he didn't resist. He closed his eyes. There was a sound of large wings flapping, then he was lifted from the ground by talons gripping the back of his shirt. There was a sensation of the world passing underneath him with the wind in his ears. He didn't open his eyes. The movement slowed as the creature, which he imagined to be a massive eagle, lowered itself to the ground and gently put him down. His feet hit the ground first and he stumbled slightly to land on his knees and hands.

When he opened his eyes, there were a few sandy dunes in front of him. The sun was high and bright in a clear blue sky. He looked behind him. It didn't make much sense, but there was a range of massive white mountains looking like they were covered in snow. To the left behind the spot where he had been put down he could see a cave. Although the surroundings looked completely different from the forest he had seen while standing at the exit of the cave, he knew that it was the same one that he had just been in. He knew that the mountains could no longer threaten him, but he also now knew the direction he had to take. They were behind him and he had to walk away from them in order to move forward. Whether the way would take him to the Golden City he wasn't sure, but there was only one way to find out.

Chapter 35

He walked across the dunes ahead. They looked like the kind that one would find by the seaside, covered with small shrubs. However, when he came to the top of what seemed to be the last dune in the series, a vast, empty desert stretched out in front of him. The temperature had been moderately warm up until now, but as soon as he laid eyes on the desert, it was extremely hot. Now what? He thought. One man couldn't possibly make it alone across a desert, not without at least a lot of help. His backpack had somehow made it through with him. In it he had one medium sized bottle of water, which was full, and a rather small blanket. Was it enough to protect him against the extreme temperatures of a desert? Not a snowball's chance in hell, he thought; he was already dehydrating as he stood wondering what to do.

He had to decide and act fast. Don't look back, something inside warned him, but desperation got the better of him. When he turned around, all he had seen behind him a few seconds earlier was now immersed in a dark cloud—what looked like an enormous sand storm. He quickly turned forward again. He had about ten seconds to figure something out or the sand storm behind would catch up with him. His instincts told him that he would be safe as long as he kept moving to the best of his ability. If he faltered, then the bedlam behind would no doubt consume him.

Deserts were unforgiving, he thought, but they were part of the earth and the earth looked after all that lived on it. He thanked Mother Nature for giving of herself so freely, not only sustenance, but also beauty, tranquility, and joy. The earth also took her dues since Nature was a powerful force that couldn't be tamed. Mother Earth, Nature, he talked to her. You give and take life. You sustain and destroy. I have no defense against your power and I stand humble before your supremacy. I am but a young man who wants to reunite with his beloved so we can be safe, enjoy each other's company, and serve the world together. I honor you as the one who always has the final say. Please hear me out; I am not ready to leave my current body and this world behind without having held my beloved in my arms again and spent many years by her side. I will now be at your mercy, so please guide me along safe places. I believe that the impossible can be achieved. Please help me and let it be so.

With that he put his backpack down at his feet, bowed over it and took out his blanket, leaving the water inside. He tied the blanket around his head and neck as best he could, leaving breathing space for his eyes and nose. He picked up his backpack again and started walking.

The desert was a living organism just like everything else. One had to get to know and understand her before one could win her trust. One had to tell her what one wanted, but be careful not to demand it. The traveler had to tread carefully on sacred ground so as not to lose the favor of one who could be ruthless. When she was appreciated for who she was, she would guide the traveler to survival.

Looking out over the sands, Akim could see a slight dip in the desert surface towards the front right. It looked like it was becoming less sandy and stonier in that direction. That was his only hope, so he walked there. Within minutes he felt so hot that he thought he would die before the day was over. To counteract the heat, he conjured the image of the beautiful world of forest and sea that he had seen from the mouth of the cave. He would continue talking to Mother Nature, reminding her of his plea and asking for protection. He would only take a sip of water when his mouth was feeling exceptionally parched.

The water in the bottle was diminishing slowly but surely. Show me where I can find water, he asked the desert. As soon as he had finished his last bit, the sun touched the horizon. The desert was now ready to change her gown and temperature; twilight was the only chance he had. He still hadn't found a sign of water, but he couldn't lose hope. Keep walking, he told himself. You might not have a solution, but it's imminent.

The light was rapidly dimming but he could see that the surroundings were changing. The color of the sand was turning from beige to grey and there were more stones around. The dunes were becoming flatter as he descended. His eye fell on a rather prickly-looking stone. Interesting, he thought, his mind foggy with fatigue and dehydration. He walked closer to investigate. It was prickly indeed, and well-shaped, just like a plant. His eyes could be deceiving him in the dark, but the color of the stone also looked suspiciously green. His eyes were telling the truth. It was only a small, singular plant, but it meant that there had to be water somewhere. It was a gift from the desert to show him the way. He knew now that water was on its way to him, so he got up to move ahead.

Sure enough, a second plant soon came within eyesight. It was another prickly succulent, and it was beautiful to behold. The plant held all the secrets of the stars in it, representing the Milky Way in its shape and containing its magic in its leaves. It was shining from the inside, illuminated by the light of the stars on which it was modelled. Akim looked up. The stars were talking to him as always. He loved feeling that the universe was on his side. He had to work with it and find ways in which he could be successful. Small and insignificant as he was, it was no use trying to do anything on his own.

Looking at the stars, Akim thought that the universe didn't need to be explained. All that had evolved had done so without being aware of how the process worked. Looking back, humans believed they could explain everything. But moving forward was different because the future could not be grasped. Akim thought, it's because we treat the future in the same way that we treat the past, believing that we can understand and control everything, that we lose touch with the life force. It was because of this that humans had forgotten how to see life as magical and instead tried to rely on the world as a dull, predictable place. It wasn't only because they were afraid, but because they had become lazy, refusing to stretch their own minds. Perhaps the best answer in the world to any question was, "I don't know" and, more than that, "maybe I never will," because those were the answers that opened up new paradigms. It was the blessing of consciousness if one remained humble to the fact that there was something infinitely greater going on than what could possibly be fathomed.

Akim kept moving, believing with all he had that water would be found soon, or would find him, depending on which way he looked at it. The plants were appearing more frequently. They were also becoming higher and leafier until he eventually spotted a small tree. He thanked his lucky stars, for he knew that he was now very close. Vegetation was becoming quite dense, although not close to a forest. The sand was still grey and interspersed with stones underneath his feet. So close, he thought, so close.

Ahead of him to the right he could see something solid in the starlight. It looked like a building that was hidden behind plants. This was a good sign; it meant that there were people close by who hopefully wouldn't mean any harm. It was also an indication that water couldn't be far away. He wanted to start running, ignoring the warning lights at the back of his mind that told him he had to make sure all was safe first. He was too tired to run. What he wanted to do was collapse and hopefully someone would come out to save him, give him water and food to eat, a pillow for his tired neck and a bed for his exhausted body. He didn't want to die or stop existing this time; he simply wanted to rest. He would be up again to take on any desert the moment that he felt strong enough to move forward. Right now he was just too tired.

While he was forcing his body to push on to the square building, something moved at his feet. He looked down, but it was too late. How could he have been so careless? It happened too fast. The moment he saw the snake, his foot was almost on top of it. Before he could stumble, the snake had already slithered out from underneath him, coiled itself upwards in his direction and lunged viciously. Next thing he felt a sharp pain in his left forearm. His body refused to react; it was like an anesthetic spreading through his veins incredibly fast although it felt slow, making him drowsy and paralyzing him. It spread outwards from his hand. When it got to his neck, he knew it was over, and the next moment there was only blackness.

Chapter 36

In the meantime, Matima had been on a journey too, although the circumstances weren't close to being as harsh for her. After Akim had left, her illness changed in form. It turned out that the illness was her mind's way of bringing her attention to energy that had become stuck in corners of her mind and body. Realizing this, she acknowledged the illness as a way for her spirit to move to a more wholesome state. She asked it to guide her back to her health, showing her what she needed to become aware of.

The illness was gentle to her. She could sense the flow of energy through her body. In some places it was clear and bright, but there were locations where it was murky, like dark clouds obscuring the view. She acknowledged to her body that the heaviness and the clouds weren't its natural state. She thanked it for guiding her back to health and being a vehicle to experience a wholesome life. As if in answer to her plea, her mind shifted its awareness away from her body and took her on a trip down memory lane.

Looking back on her life from a different perspective, she could now recognize instances where she had blamed herself for doing something wrong even though it wasn't her fault. She could see the times when she had believed herself to be treated with love, although it hadn't actually been the case, instilling in her mind a faulty impression of what love looked like. The insight didn't cause her to blame the people involved. Instead, it led her to understand that although the people who had been close to her had done their best, they were also only people who made mistakes. The realization was painful, but it brought healing.

She realized that she could forgive them for teaching her principles that caused her to become ashamed of who she was. She didn't need to base her beliefs about herself on their views; she could choose to claim the happiness that was her birth right. As she set the old thoughts free, she watched them run away like wild horses, returning to the flow where they could be transformed into something useful. The process continued until she returned to full health. Her eyes were brighter and shinier than before, perhaps closer to what they had looked like when she was a child. She knew, however, that although she was freer and lighter, she now had more responsibility, knowing that she alone had to answer for who she was in the world. She knew that she would have less security since the walls that had signified the boundaries of her mind-set had been broken down. Henceforth, reality would be more pliable, depending partly on how she chose to define it.

On the first morning that she awoke in an improved state of health, the sisters were there to greet her. They seemed less remote than when she had first met them. They were supportive rather than challenging, and she greatly appreciated their presence. She was no longer in danger of forgetting herself. Instead, the memories were now much closer to the surface of her awareness, but she didn't depend on them. She accepted them as a part of herself without allowing them to run the show from a place where she couldn't see them.

Most of the sisters, lovely as they were, still seemed to be unaware of themselves as entities in their own right. Matima found it curious and depressing. She wondered if they were meant to be flat archetypes without much capacity for choice, or whether they had lost parts of themselves along the way. She contemplated whether having the will to recognize options would return them to themselves.

The first few days after her return to wellness were spent absorbing the kindness of the sisters. They cherished her, treating her with so much love and understanding that at times it almost brought her to tears. She felt sad because she couldn't do anything for them in return, at least not in their detached state. She also knew, however, that if she was going to grow through the experience of spending time with them, they would have to do the same, or it would be meaningless. Growth could only take place if the person had an identity. If she had to help them get their personalities back, she would do her best to accomplish it.

Eventually, she felt ready to get up and explore. She wasn't sure what could be done in this land of nothingness. Were they on their way somewhere? She knew where she wanted to head to, but the way there was still a mystery. It was time to find out what she needed to learn. If the sisters were going to help her find her way, then consulting them would be a good place to start. The gypsy van hadn't moved for a few days because the elephant had wanted to rest. It could be an adventure to discover the other coaches that she hadn't seen yet as well as the surrounding area, especially now that she no longer felt inclined to forget who she was.

On that morning, the sisters didn't come to her like they normally did. She got up with the firm intention to go and find them. They at least had some part in deciding that she had to stay there so the least they could do was to help her to the point where she could move forward. The lack of information was frustrating. They had given her instructions while at the same time refusing to take responsibility for what they told her to do. In that case, Matima thought, the Great Truth, or whatever invisible entity was operating through the map, had to take responsibility if she would become a nuisance. If the sisters wanted her to leave, they could once again blame it on the Great Mountain or the Truth of the Map. At least then she would be free.

Free to go where? She thought. She was a fine one to think belittling thoughts about the sisters who were being so kind to her. She herself had simply gone off on a whim, taking her lover with her without an idea of whether it was feasible. Now they had been split up and it was all because of her. She had led them into this mess out of desperation. On the other hand, there wasn't much else she could have done. Fulfilling her civil duties while her soul was waning wasn't an option. She would rather be caught up in a mess knowing that she had made well intended mistakes than be a living dead person.

She knew that Akim would face a harder ordeal than she and was angry at herself for it. Yet, she had to concede that he also hadn't had many options. She had to trust that he would survive.

On this morning the breakfast room was empty. Other than a bowl of fruit, there was nothing on the table that normally was laid, ready for her to eat like a queen. She would not be deterred, however. If anything, it gave her an excuse to move beyond the familiar boundaries and find out what was on the other side. She assumed that the door where the sisters normally came from when serving breakfast was the kitchen. Other than that there were two other doors, one on each side of the coach, leading outside in opposite directions. On both sides she could see through the windows so it wasn't all that tempting. The kitchen, however, lured her.

The door somehow told her to stay away while at the same time inviting her. She was far too inquisitive to heed the warning. It also sounded to her like nothing really mattered in the land of the Threshold. While she was in a place where actions were inconsequential in terms of judgment from others, she might as well make the most of it. With that thought, she boldly moved forward and pushed through the door.

What greeted her eyes was quite different from what she had expected. Instead of another room in the van, she walked into a garden that was mystical and dream-like. It wasn't morning in the garden like on the other side of the door; it was a strong twilight, almost night. The dusk had a substantial quality, like a kind of dust that floated in the air but was not affected by its currents. It was halfway between smoke and light. There were torches set up in the garden, reminding her of those on the way when she had escaped from the palace. She walked closer to inspect the nearest one. A little fairy was indeed the source of light in the torch. She smiled and waved at Matima when she saw her. She had a little bag with a sandy substance in it. She dipped her hand into the bag and threw a handful of the dust up into the air. That was where the light came from; the dust emitted its own luminescence which made the torch glow like a flame. She smiled at the fairy before moving on.

From the door where she had entered there was a paved pathway leading into a clearing amidst a cluster of trees. She couldn't see into the enclosure. Overcome with curiosity, she followed the pathway, greeting every fairy that she walked past. It felt like the garden was holding its breath while she was about to discover some ancient secret.

As she walked closer, she could hear a noise coming from the clearing. It sounded rhythmic, like the working of machines, although it wasn't an unpleasant sound. When she entered the space, she was struck by surprise. The sisters were bustling about, looking stressed and tired. In the midst of the clearing was a wooden constellation which looked like something between the mechanism of an old ship and a machine that would be found in the laboratory of an eccentric scientist. The machine was large enough to take up almost all the space inside a small room. At its top was something that resembled a chimney, except it had a wider opening, like a funnel. One of the sisters was sitting to one end at a large wooden wheel with pedals on both sides. She was pedaling with her arms to make the wheel spin. She was responsible for initiating the movement that would make the entire mechanism work. Her hair was sticking to her forehead and there was a blank expression in her eyes. She looked exhausted.

The machine had a dozen or so outlets: pipes or ditches through which a golden, sandy substance flowed outwards from the machine to land in small pots that were placed around it at the end of every outlet. From what Matima could see, it looked like a substance of light was flowing in through the chimney at the top. It was then churned by the machine, fueled by the person treading the wheel. The machine transformed the light substance into something more solid, dust like. The sisters picked up the pots containing the dust and went to sit by holes around the clearing that looked out onto the world. They appeared to be many kilometers above it sitting in a world in the sky. They then took the dust in their hands, little by little, and blew it out through the holes, chanting prayers and incantations as they were doing so.

They didn't look up when she entered; they were so completely immersed in their work. Every now and then they would change places at the wheel. Matima watched the process until it finally came to an end a good hour or so later. The sisters looked shattered. After a few minutes of resting, they gathered around the machine, looking up at the sky above the top of the chimney. They thanked the sages for providing their input and giving them something to work with. They expressed their wish that their hard work would be appreciated by mankind and that it would make a difference.

When they had come out of their trance, they turned to acknowledge Matima's presence, each in their own turn. They greeted her without looking resentful of the fact that she had walked in uninvited. The clearing looked more like a room and less like a magical garden now that they had completed their ritual. The machine in the center now took the guise more of a useless old object that took too much space than a valuable artifact coming out of a book. Matima looked around, surprised. The magical garden had now been replaced by another eccentric room in the coach with windows that looked out on nowhere land. She looked back at the path she had walked to reach the clearing. It was merely an unstable corridor of narrow coaches that had been strung together. The sisters were now busying themselves cleaning the room. One of them threw a moth eaten blanket over the machine, which made it look even older, sadly forgotten.

None of them was inclined to tell Matima more about what she had just witnessed. Maybe it was because she was used to being treated like royalty that she found their behavior impolite. Where she came from, it was good manners to tell your guests more about cultural traditions that they might not understand. She didn't want to be obnoxious to people who had been kind to her, but she couldn't keep the irritation out of her voice when she asked, "Would anyone care to tell me what that was all about?" Most of the sisters ignored her and continued their tasks. Melista, however, reacted with understanding.

"Let's go and get breakfast, Matima. The sisters and I haven't forgotten about our guest and we apologize for being so busy. Once we have had something to eat, we will tell you more about what you have just witnessed." She took Matima's hand and led her to the breakfast room. Matima gratefully accepted the gesture.

Chapter 37

She was always amazed by the way the sisters conjured up delicious food out of nothing, and in no time, too. While she and Melista were waiting, the table was laid with breakfast muffins that were freshly baked, as well as fruit, bread, cheese and jams. Matima dug in; it was good to have an appetite again after not feeling well for so many days. When she had finished, they eagerly cleared the table and cleaned up.

Matima turned to Melista. "So, do you want to tell me about what you were doing inside that room?"

Melista said, "With pleasure. The machine that you saw is a dream machine. The light coming through the chimney is the substance that dreams are made of. The machine has receptors down below in the world where people are asleep. It picks up what's inside people, not only their hearts but also their minds, what they think about in their day to day activities. It receives the kind of light from the upper world that is needed in the world. With our help it combines the light stuff with information about the individual's inclinations to fabricate a dream that would remind them of what their soul yearns for. We then blow the dreams into the world in the hope that they would inspire people."

"Are you talking about daydreams or the kind of dreams people have when they are asleep?" Matima asked.

"Both, actually," Melista answered. "Not all dreams come from us. Some night dreams are just the mind's way of processing everything that sits in the subconscious mind. Some daydreams are inspired by the ambition to gain material power. Some sleep and waking dreams, however, come from the soul. Those people who have easy access to the dream world because they cultivate their connection with their souls receive light directly from the upper world. However, that mostly isn't the case in a world where the existence of the soul is either confined within certain boundaries or denied completely. Its purest expression that can be seen in the world, apart from the innocence of children, is through sincere art and sincere love. Sincere anything, in fact. Most people aren't aware of much more than their bodies and minds, so we send them a little help."

"Why do you do that?" Matima asked. "What's in it for you? I thought you were the guardians of the Threshold, but now it sounds like you are much more than that."

"We are guardians of the Threshold," Melista said, looking away. "But have you noticed that there aren't many travelers in this land? We just want to matter again. People used to believe in us and look to us for inspiration. Not only those who were serious about walking the spiritual path benefited from our help. People turned to us because they wanted to have fun, or they needed to escape the suffering of the world, or they wanted to express themselves. They turned to us because we were all they had. Now things are quite different in a world where people can keep their minds busy all the time, every day. They prefer to do that rather than stop for a second to consider what their life is about.

"Most people just worry about where their next wage will come from or what they could buy with it that is better than the next door neighbor's latest possession. I know you think that that isn't what life is about in the eyes of people. But a lot of it is, even if it's on a symbolic level. People mingle with certain people to be smart in the eyes of others. When people enter relationships, they ask, 'What's in it for me? Will the other person fit in with my life and strengthen my position in society? Will they make my life more comfortable and secure?' They ask these questions more often than, 'Do I love him/her? Am I happy and comfortable with him/her?' If they consider the latter important then they don't even have to ask the questions, because love takes its own course.

"Nowadays, a few brave souls care to cultivate the inspiration they receive from us. The rest don't believe in it, or they don't have time to do something about it, or they think it wouldn't help them in any way.

"I'll tell you something about the world as it is today: people don't believe in happiness any more. Even those who claim to be firmly grounded in religious values find a way of making material considerations central to their world. They might deny that that is what they are doing, even to themselves, but if you look closely you will see that that is the case. If they claim to serve the will of a god, they will tell you that god put the man at the head of the household and he has to provide for the family. The same god also ordained that a woman has to be submissive to her husband. If others don't judge you according to the material wealth you have amassed yourself, they still rate you in terms of how good a follower of that particular religious mind-set you are. If you pass the test, they will believe you to be good, right and happy. In that instance you might be liked, if you're lucky. Why did the word happiness pop up if it's irrelevant? Because what's important in the world of today is whether others consider you happy. Chase your own true happiness and you will be called naïve at best, insane at worst.

"How many people wake up in the morning and can remember what went on in their sleeping minds last night? How many people take the trouble to think about it, remember it, or talk to someone else about it? That is why we have to work so hard—to restore something that should be people's birth right. If we're not successful, then we'll just disappear further into nowhere land, until we're transformed and hopefully one day reborn, albeit in a different form. In a way we're just fighting for our own survival since the substance of dreams has all but lost its relevance in the world out there."

Matima nodded that she understood. Although she had grown up in a place where the garden was protected by magical traditions, it wasn't what was prominent in the world. Most people couldn't even see the magic in the garden. However, the question of what she was there to do remained unanswered.

"Where do I fit into the picture?" She asked Melista. "I know you claim not to have any say in what the map has shown us. It sounded like you were more involved in the Alternative coming from the Great Mountain. So why then did you decide that Akim had to stay as an Alternative? Was it a chance occurrence that one of us had to stay with you and that we would inevitably be split up, no matter which road we took? Or does it happen on a regular basis that you host travelers as part of the deal and those who come together are separated?

Melista looked stern. "I cannot talk to you about what happens to other travelers. I am not sworn to secrecy, but it has no relevance to you unless you can learn from it. If I talk to you about the stories of others at this stage it will only serve as a parameter of judgment. Purpose has nothing to do with who you are in comparison to others. It is about what rings true for you. If you can learn from other travelers you will meet them at the right time. If you approach each other with openness and honesty there will be no competition. There will only be companionship because you have shared something of yourselves and offered each other support.

"I would encourage you to be observant when you meet people. It would be beneficial for you to become skilled at recognizing others who travel along the same path. They will be few and far between, but if you celebrate your friendship, they will be worth more than gold. They will bring the dream world closer to you and will strengthen your resolve.

"As far as you are concerned, you are here because you want to be here. You want to learn from us because it is the way that you can best serve the world. It is not a requirement to move forward. It is part of the cause you have served for many lifetimes, possibly since the beginning of time. It is part of a sacred geometry which you will never be able to fully understand, but you will nonetheless be drawn to it time after time, lifetime after lifetime. The most important thing to understand is that you have choice. You are not bound to your calling by obligation or because a force outside of yourself wishes for it to be so. No, your calling represents your deepest longing, your roots. If you forget that, you will become heavy and immobile. If you start feeling disconnected, the best way to reconnect to your path is to simply stop caring about anything other than being happy. It is what makes you happy that leads you to your path in life."

"Thank you for the information," Matima answered. "But what will you teach me?"

"We will teach you the mysteries of the Goddess," Melista answered. "For it is She who looks after the earth and Whose essence needs to be reawakened in order for balance to be restored to earth. The nature spirits are still there, but they have been dwelling in the shadows. They are ready to come back and restore peace while the earth herself is reacting to the abuse she has endured for too long. There will be a day when the earth dwellers take their rightful place as magical beings; sons and daughters of that which is All. They will learn how to treat all living things with respect and will no longer resort to violence. That will be the time when love reigns supreme and when heaven is brought to earth; when prevailing consciousness will surpass views of separation, limited resources and survival of the fittest. When that happens, all life will be treated as sacred and the pain and happiness of one will be the pain and happiness of all. Each will be appreciated in his/her uniqueness. Differences will be celebrated as something that makes life interesting rather than shunned as something that defines *otherness*."

That is about all that can be told about Matima's apprenticeship with the sisters. The ways of the Goddess have traditionally been shrouded in mystery, but the moon is there to provide guidance. When her music stirs the soul, the traveler is called to dance the energy of the earth into being.

Chapter 38

Akim woke up, not knowing where he was. There was a sharp pain shooting up from his left hand. He looked around him and couldn't make out much in the strong twilight. There was a rectangular patch of light a few meters away. It almost blinded him. A man was sitting next to him, holding his right hand. Was he on his way out? he wondered. In this land where strange things happened, he couldn't know any more. Perhaps death would not feel much different from traveling to worlds where everything was wispy.

The man looked familiar. He had long grey hair and a beard that was braided. He wore a black cloak and was fairly old, with a face that wore its wisdom well. Even in the semi-darkness he realized that he had seen the man before, and not in the too distant past, either. Was he there to help him pass over to the other side? In that case, why was he in so much pain? Surely death had to bring a sense of freedom, he thought. Not that he wanted to die yet. Please take me back, he thought. I'm too young and I still have my life ahead of me. The man squeezed his hand and smiled down at him. All went white before going black again.

When he woke up again, someone was holding a cup of water to his lips. He drank eagerly, thirstily. The pain had subsided a little although he was still quite far from feeling better. He couldn't see as well as the last time he was awake; everything was slightly blurry before his eyes. His body felt very weak and numb.

The man in black was by his bedside again, still holding his hand. The surroundings looked the same as the last time he had had his eyes open, but it was lighter this time. The room gradually shifted into focus as his eyes adjusted. He was still out of depth and his vision was unstable. He was feeling so tired, so uncomfortable. He wondered if he would ever feel at home in his body again. He turned to the man at his bedside.

"Have I been asleep for a long time?" he asked.

"Long enough," the man said. "A few days. It's a miracle we still have you, although it couldn't really have gone any other way. Your will to come back was too strong."

"Where am I?" Akim asked.

"In a village right outside the desert. To be more specific, in the home of an eccentric old man who lives a little bit outside the village," the man answered.

"Who are you?" he asked the man.

"I am your patron," the man answered. Akim was too tired to talk anymore. He liked the fact that the man was holding his hand. The physical connection brought warmth, which helped his body to recover. The man let go of his hand and put his hand to Akim's forehead instead. He felt the same sensation, but this time it was stronger. A warm glow started at the point on his forehead where the man's hand touched him and spread downwards. It felt as if the poisonous reaction in his blood was being reversed. As the energy flowed through him, his cells were restored to vibrancy. He wished that it could happen faster. But the man withdrew his hand. A threshold was reached and he couldn't do much more than that at one time.

The man rose from his seat beside Akim's bed. Against the wall on the opposite side of the room on a counter top were glass jars filled with various kinds of natural substances. Most of them were dried plant residues. Some were filled with stones, animal bones, or the bark of a tree. There was a pot stand with a candle underneath it in one corner. The man took different amounts of ingredients from various jars and added them to the pot. He filled it with water from a can that stood in another corner. He lit the candle and waited for the water to start boiling. A strong, herbal smell filled the room. In his foggy state it looked to Akim like the steam coming from the pot was shining with different colors of light. The aroma was pleasant, but it made him feel drowsy again. He closed his eyes and drifted off to a state where he was close to sleep, touching dreams, but not quite losing awareness of where he was.

He saw his mother in her hut. She looked concerned, like her heart was in a different place. He wanted to reach out to her. It took him a while to realize that she was so sad because of him. She didn't know where he was or what had happened to him. The pain of the realization stabbed him like a knife in the chest. He had never considered the effect his actions would have on her. He had only thought of himself. The insight made his heart break.

The short-lived sensation of feeling better left his body as his heart filled with grief. It welled up in his throat and spilled over, making him sob with regret. The pain pulled him back from the dream into his body again where he only felt worse than before. Although he was now back in a waking state, the image of her sad figure remained, etched in the black behind his closed eyelids. He cried and cried. When he was empty, he had a massive headache. His patron was there by his bedside again. He pulled Akim up into a sitting position and rubbed his back. He put a cup to his lips again and told him to drink. The potion was pungent but not entirely unpleasant. Akim dutifully obeyed, finishing the drink.

The warm glow spread through his body again. He felt slightly restored. He leaned back against the pillow and fell asleep.

He was in a forest and it was night time. Looking up, he could see a sliver of a sickle moon peering through the tree tops. She told him that it was a good time and the omens were favorable. He suppressed the cynical retort that surged from inside him. Nonetheless he told her that it surely didn't look like it. She told him not to worry, because appearances could deceive. Especially in the dream world, things weren't necessarily dire when they looked bad.

"That is what I have believed for most of my life," he told her. "And yet looking back it feels like I have been stuck in the same position for most of my life. I keep thinking that it will be better around the next corner. But as soon as I get there, there is another problem waiting for me. Will this go on forever?" He asked, not even trying to suppress the cynicism this time.

"Possibly," she said. "It depends on which way you look at it." Then she was silent and told him that he had to move on. He didn't have much of a choice.

The path was clear ahead of him. He reached a circle that resembled a labyrinth. It was a spiral, marked out by different colors of stones. In the center there was a small round mound with a flat top, also made of stones. The path in the spiral was laid out with tiny white pebbles and its edges were fringed by small plants. The outside of the spiral was surrounded by a hedge, neatly trimmed to about chest height. It looked like the woods ended against a mountain to the right ahead of him. The mountain was very high and had a pointed shape.

He noticed that in the middle of the spiral there was a tall man in silver robes. He wasn't sure if the man had just appeared or whether he had been inattentive for not seeing him. The man had long white hair and a white beard. He was standing with a lantern in his hand. He looked stern, not exactly friendly but kind nevertheless, albeit not in a soft way. Without talking, he invited Akim to walk the spiral. On the outside of the hedge Akim was aware of the forest nymphs watching him, waiting expectantly.

He started walking the spiral, unsure of what to expect. The man at the center continued watching him, as did the forest nymphs. They were giggling, and he couldn't figure out whether they were laughing at him or with him. The faint moonshine on his face warmed him. He enjoyed listening to the forest sounds: the rustling of leaves, the giggling of fairies. The cool night air on his face and the beautiful sight of the mountain made him feel alive. The mountain was alight, glowing from the inside. That was all there was to the walk. He liked it.

At the center he stopped and waited for the man to say something. From up close, the man looked much friendlier. His face was lined with astuteness and he exuded an aura of power without force. Akim sensed that the man was perhaps much more than a man, possibly a magician, a sage, or a legend. He bowed instinctively. He knew that the man was there to help him.

When facing him again, the man put his hand on his shoulder. He felt the same sensation that he had felt when his patron had put his hand to his forehead. "Who are you?" the guide asked him.

Akim hated it when people asked him that kind of question because he never knew what to say. He gave it some thought before he answered, "I don't know. I don't know how or why I came into existence as myself. My name is Akim and I am connected to this body. I was born to my mother and I think that the woman I love is my soul mate. I have certain personality traits, but I am not sure where they come from. Is it my circumstances that have shaped me or is it the way I was born? I have stopped thinking about it because it's tiring. Perhaps I am just a character in a universal mind, doing my best to love and be happy although I feel most of the time that I have no idea what I am doing. Perhaps I simply exist and I'm free to make of it whatever I choose."

"Good," the guide said. "Now take this light and go and shine it in the world. The light is just a light, doing what it does best. For light to shine, all you need to do is allow it." Akim took it and as he did so, he was transported back from his dream to the place where his ill body was lying in the hut of a stranger.

The next few days were spent recovering. He dutifully drank the herbal mixtures that his benefactor, who called himself Luca, gave him. Luca cooked for him: mostly vegetables and a little bit of meat. Akim didn't know the food. When asked, Luca just told him that it was desert vegetables and desert meat. The meat tasted a little bit like chicken, but it was softer and redder and contained more bones. The fruit that Luca gave him was akin to watermelon, but it was lighter in color and less sweet. "Also desert fruit?" Akim asked Luca. Luca said that it was. Akim was feeling stronger by the day and the pain was becoming less intense. He gradually spent less time sleeping and was more alert during the waking hours. He didn't have the strength to walk very far at one time yet, so he still spent most of the time in bed.

When Luca wasn't around, his pet cat kept Akim company. It was a large, vicious cat with orange, black and white patches. The cat looked malicious, but he knew that it was guarding him in Luca's absence. The curious thing about the cat was that it changed shape at night. In the day it pranced about in the hut, behaving like any normal cat would. In the evening it would lie down outside by the door side, seemingly fast asleep. Akim could see its chest rising and falling as it breathed deeply. No matter how close either he or Luca would walk past it, it wouldn't move or wake up until Luca blew out the last candles and went to bed. By that time Akim was already asleep on most nights. But when he wasn't, he would see in the shadows the cat lifting its head which had somehow become enormous. Its tail would pat on the ground with a swishing sound. The door was left open at night and in the starlight the cat's pelt would assume a different hue, a bit brighter, more orange, and stripy. On occasions when he woke up in the middle of the night, the cat's normal soft purr sounded frighteningly deep.

It happened once that he was woken by a sound outside the hut. It didn't look like Luca had heard anything because Akim could hear him breathing deeply as one who was in a deep sleep. When he looked at the cat, however, its massive ears were erect. A second later it leaped up and pounced in the direction where the sound had come from. Akim was convinced that he heard a low growling sound. A rustling noise followed, which made it sound like there was a struggle. A few minutes later the cat was back by its post, larger than life and more brightly orange than ever. On another occasion it happened that he woke up and really had to go to the loo. The idea of walking past the massive cat was daunting, but he just had to go. The minute he set his foot to the floor, the giant cat bounded from its place into the bush. By the time he reached the doorway the cat was nowhere to be seen. The minute he arrived back at his bed, the cat was in its normal spot, guarding the door to the hut.

Chapter 39

The time eventually came when Akim felt strong enough to continue his journey. Once again he wasn't sure which way to go. There was no storm behind him that he had to move away from. He decided to discuss it with Luca. Wasn't Luca the man who had sent him into the desert in the first place? he asked himself. The resemblance between the man he had met outside the cave and Luca himself certainly was striking. Had he come to his rescue because he had sensed that Akim was in danger? Or had Luca known what would befall him before he had embarked on his journey? Since Luca didn't talk much, it was hard to decipher how all the pieces fit together. He wanted to thank Luca for saving him, but he wasn't sure how. He owed him his life and yet it was so hard to talk to the man who looked after him like he would after his own son.

Luca initiated a conversation before Akim could decide how to approach it.

"You have recovered well. It might be time for you to move on." Akim nodded and said that he knew. He then started by telling Luca that he didn't know how to thank him. Luca only nodded. He wanted to ask Luca more about who he was and why he had supported him, but the words wouldn't come. Luca put his arm around Akim, sensing his emotions. Akim started to cry; he wasn't even sure why. Maybe he thought that Luca was lonely and he felt sad for his sake, seeing that he was such a caring man. Luca comforted him.

"You're lucky to be alive," he said. "The snake that bit you is deadly." Akim was confused. He waited, hoping that Luca would elaborate. He sometimes got the impression that the more questions he wanted to ask Luca, the less likely it was that he would get an answer. Luca continued, "It's not a snake that bites often. You must have walked in on it while it was mating or eating, or you have stumbled upon its dwelling. This snake isn't easily surprised and it's not overly aggressive, either, but you surprised it." He paused again. "You're the only person I know of who has survived the bite of this kind of snake. I know the ins and the outs of the village. Generations of healing lore has been passed on to me, including case studies. You're the exception. I don't know if that makes me a very good healer or if it was the snake's way of giving you some of its power. You have now overcome that which could not be overcome, and because you have done so, you must help others to do the same. The snake is a part of you; you must now use it to your advantage and the benefit of the world. You must teach others about its medicine." He stopped talking, but Akim wanted to know more.

"Was it you that sent me into the desert, knowing that the snake would bite me? Did you conjure up a storm behind me and send me to danger, only to be there when I needed healing?" He regretted sounding reproachful but he had to understand. Luca looked up and Akim thought he could sense a hint of hurt in his eyes. He felt ashamed, but he somehow felt that Luca understood.

"No, I didn't," he said, looking down. "I only helped you along the path of your destiny. I knew about as much as you did about the details of what it would entail. When the snake bit you, I knew that you would survive, even though it was theoretically almost impossible. I had to help you back to health, but I knew you would do it."

"I didn't do anything," Akim said. "You were the one who healed me and looked after me. I just slept, dreamed, and felt the pain."

"Perhaps that was all you needed to do. A healer can only heal someone if they show their ability to be whole. You showed me yours."

"How did I do that?" Akim asked.

"By surprising the snake in the first instance," Luca answered. "By fighting it in the second, even after it has bitten you. You should have been dead already, but you fought it and you managed to kill it."

"I did?" Akim asked, flabbergasted. He couldn't remember any of it.

"Yes you did. I found you just at the right time, but I can guarantee that no snake will ever mess with you again. You are now the king of snakes. Your legacy will live on in the snake world." He said it tongue in cheek, smiling.

"Tell me about your healing powers," Akim asked. "How do you heal people?"

"In the same way that you heal them," he answered. "The ability of a healer depends on potential. A healer must not stare himself blind at what he sees. He must look deeper, below the surface. He must reveal the person's wholeness to them. The healer's success also depends on whether the person in need of healing believes in their ability to recover. If the healer can find a person's power and bolster it, healing is a natural process. If he finds what is wrong and tries to fix it, he will only give the patient more reasons to be fixed.

"The healer has to find the right power for the person, not just any power. If he tries to strengthen the person's heart with a power that doesn't fit, they will feel misaligned. This is where nature is useful, because the way of nature is to restore to wholeness. It usually shows the way, even more so when asked. Therefore, the most important thing a healer could learn is how to communicate with the universe. We have to allow the rest to go its own way."

"Can I ask you one more question?" Akim asked.

"Sure, go ahead," Luca answered.

"Is your cat a tiger?"

Luca just laughed.

Chapter 40

Akim had asked Luca before about his whereabouts during the day, to which Luca had answered that he mostly spent his time assisting people in the nearby village. The square building that Akim had seen before being bitten by the snake was a temple devoted to restoring people to wellness. The villagers consisted mostly of people who loved living in the desert and assisted travelers in passing by. They believed that their home would look after them if they looked after their home.

Akim mentioned the fact that he had been on his way to the village but had never made it there. He told Luca that he wouldn't be able to justify having stayed close to a village in a strange land for a few weeks without having seen it. His plea was partly out of curiosity because he couldn't help wondering why Luca hadn't offered to take him in before. Luca agreed and said that when Akim's few things were packed and he was ready to leave, he would take him to the village. These instructions made Akim even more curious, but Luca said that he didn't want Akim to be tempted to stay there. He could experience what he could fit in in the space of a few hours, but after that he had to honor his journey and move forward.

"Don't forget where you are headed to," Luca warned. "Even though the journey is not only about the destination, it would lose its meaning if one lost sight of one's end goal." Akim understood. He missed Matima, but having been away from her for so long and especially after the terrible ordeal he had faced on his own, he found that she was fading from memory. He didn't love her any less, but it was a defense mechanism to help him cope without her. Matima was his destination and where he was headed. If he would forget that, then the journey without her would lose its color and depth and simply be a chaotic search for nothing.

With this understanding Akim got ready to leave. He had conflicting feelings towards getting on the move again. To start with, he felt that his experiences over the last few weeks or months had changed him. He was still the same person and yet he wasn't the same any more. It felt as if he had expanded and wouldn't fit back into his old shell. If he had experienced the unimaginable, what had Matima been through? He had faith that he would find her, but he couldn't be sure. If both of them had changed through separate journeys, would they still be able to live together? He was afraid of finding out. Being away from her was almost less painful than the thought of reuniting with her but finding that they no longer fit together. He had conviction, but there was also fear.

Over and above that, he didn't know whether at some point his journey might lead him back to the world where he came from. If that was the way he felt about their relationship, what would it be like to return to a world where he hadn't always felt at home to start with, and would perhaps now feel even less so? He would be like someone who had never existed returning to the world as a grown up. Only his mother, and perhaps a few others, would remember him. Maybe Samuel and Asteodor, too. If he didn't have a place in his home country any more, would he be welcome in another? Thinking about it filled him with trepidation. Still, he wasn't sure whether it was worse than the thought of never returning.

The final factor that made him feel ambivalent towards the idea of moving on was the feeling of being tired. He hadn't enjoyed his illness, but at least he had had the chance to rest. His body and mind were now hesitant to make the shift towards being geared for action again. He knew that he could be tired forever if he didn't take action to start moving again, always waiting for a time when he would feel energized. Yet the temptation was great to want to rest just a little while longer, persuading himself that he wasn't yet ready for the next step. Perhaps it was a good thing that Luca was throwing him out.

Akim thought to himself, maybe it always went that way in life: we knew when it was time to move on because we would recognize the signs. The signs didn't necessarily talk to our logical mind, however, so our logical mind overruled the messages we received from the universe. We wanted to move on and yet felt alarmed at the idea of change. Our soul's yearning to experience new things would be pushed to the back end while we allowed our attachment to our comfort zones to keep us where we were. But in the end the universe had the last say. When it was time to move on and we didn't listen and act on it, the current surroundings to which we had become so attached would collapse in some way or another.

Further, he thought that perhaps we privately plotted the downfall of the castle that no longer served its purpose. While the conscious mind was busy justifying our reluctance to move forward, the subconscious mind was preparing us for a more worthwhile experience. The subconscious mind knew that we were greater than we believed ourselves to be. When the conscious mind was still acting in fear, the subconscious mind was creatively conspiring to our demise, urging us to own up to who we really were.

So when Akim had to go, he was open despite his feelings of resistance and fear. He felt excited, not only at the prospect of hopefully seeing Matima again, but also about the next phase of his journey which could turn out to be anything at all. The nervousness combined with exhilaration made his hands tremble slightly when he packed his last few things—the meagre sum total of his belongings with the food and other provisions that Luca had added to his baggage. This included water, a blanket, some herbs, and other first aid tools. He could see that Luca was sad to let him go. He hugged Akim but didn't say much.

First they had to go to the village. They walked for about three quarters of an hour to get there. They passed the place where Akim had been bitten by the snake; it was a little bit more than a stone's throw outside the temple in the village. When they entered the village there were only a few people around, mostly children playing in the sand or women sitting weaving or talking. The temple looked out on the village square, in the middle of which there was a well with a large bell overhanging it. Some of the villagers appeared to be expecting Akim. When he walked in with Luca, they rushed over to greet him and shook his hand. They didn't speak his language, but Luca explained that they were wishing him luck for his journey ahead. He asked Luca how and what they knew about his whereabouts but Luca just laughed and said that it wasn't hard to guess, even if he himself hadn't told them anything. He was much loved by the villagers despite the fact that he was not quite one of them.

Luca took him to the temple. Although the temperature was scorching in the village, it was quite cool inside the building. In the middle of the temple there was a small fountain around which candles and incense were burning. At the opposite end of the doorway was an altar at which objects and little pieces of paper were placed, presumably as prayers and offerings. A few people were sitting against the walls or at the side of the fountain. Some of them were praying while others were writing or just sitting quietly.

A monk in orange robes came over to greet Akim. He smiled graciously and took Akim's hands in his own as a gesture to convey goodwill. He knelt in front of Akim and lowered his forehead to the ground, touching Akim's feet with his hands. Akim was slightly alarmed as he didn't know how to react. He didn't understand what the monk was doing, but Luca put him at ease with his eyes and demeanor. He understood that he had to go with the flow while the monk performed his ritual. The monk came erect again and signaled for Akim to follow him. He led him through a door on the altar's side of the temple. Luca followed.

The doorway led out to a small courtyard with a quaint little garden and two large trees on each side. The garden had all sorts of peculiar objects in it, including gnomes, a Buddha statue, and other strange artifacts. On the other side of the courtyard was another small brick building which would have looked neglected if the door hadn't been decorated with an inviting image of a human being with circles of light around various centers in her body. The monk smiled back at Akim, signaling for him to come inside.

Inside the room there was a low bed with crystals and feathers packed around it. There were also two armchairs. The monk gestured to Akim to take one of the seats while he himself sat down in the other. Luca took his seat on the bed. The monk took out a piece of paper containing a graph of the outlines of the human body. It looked similar to the figure that was on the door except it was less attractive and emptier. The graph was simply a sexless line drawing with no colors or expression. He then took out some crayons and looked at Akim while coloring in the piece of paper in a way that resembled the painting on the door. Energy zones, Akim understood. He waited, afraid to interrupt the monk who was deep in concentration.

Akim was keen to find out what the monk was seeing and if he had any special insights to offer. Some of the circles he drew were subtler in color and size while others were stronger. He drew a small green circle around Akim's left hand—this had to be because of the snake bite as it was the most remarkable difference between the monk's drawing and the figure on the door. Akim rubbed his hand; it was still somewhat sore. The monk noticed Akim's motion and stopped, putting down his crayon. He seemed to have found what he had looked for. He asked Akim to give him his hand. Akim understood even though the language didn't make sense to him.

The monk concentrated deeply while holding Akim's hand. Akim could feel something stir at the end of his fingertips. It felt curious, not entirely unpleasant but not comfortable either. Next it started to feel like a wheel was spinning inside his hand. It became very uncomfortable, almost too much for him to bear. He wanted to pull his hand away. The monk understood and he stopped with whatever he had been doing. He soothingly rubbed Akim's hand. He talked to Akim while Luca translated. He asked Akim to look at the circle he had drawn on the paper corresponding to the place of the figure's hand. He told him to imagine that he was moving through the circle and tell him what he saw.

It was strange. The circle of his poisoned hand was unsurprisingly a portal that pulled him into space, perhaps just to show him that he was communing with the universe. Against the backdrop of the stars and the black velvet, the figure he had seen on the paper loomed in front of him in gigantic proportion. The colors and shapes were the same as what the monk had put down on the paper, except they were brighter and slightly less defined. The circle around his hand wasn't there, however. Next he saw images of things that he had experienced before or dreamed of still experiencing: some moments with Matima in the palace garden; a snake moving up and down inside the trunk of a tree; a beautiful, peaceful garden with Matima by his side, reminding him of heaven. The sky was filled with bright colors. Some of them formed wheels that were spinning in opposite directions. Others appeared as the strokes of a paint brush. The monk touched his arm, pulling him back to the room where he was sitting.

The monk started talking again with Luca translating. "The wound will always have an effect on you," he said, "but if channeled in the right way it will remind you of what you have survived. Because you have fought and killed demons, you are capable of magic. Don't curse your wounds, but don't nourish them either. Don't look to wound yourself, but in case it couldn't have been avoided, celebrate your scars. They are a portal to resources that you wouldn't have known you had otherwise. Just remember that the scars aren't who you are; the wholeness on the other side of the scars is closer to the real you."

Akim nodded and thanked the monk. A moment passed when he imagined that he could look beyond the man's eyes into his mind. The monk's eyes suddenly looked very old and sad, not to mention lonely. It was as if he could see inside the monk's head the entire universe. Although the monk was capable of observing and appreciating magic from one moment to the next, he could also see incredible emptiness in everything. The moment passed and the monk was just the monk again, a wise old man with kind eyes and a disposition to serve. The sadness stayed with Akim, though. In a way it had shaken him.

Being about to embark on the last stretch of his journey, Akim suddenly felt strong resistance. He had had enough of suffering and disillusionment without getting anywhere. He had forgotten why he had started the journey anyway. It probably had something to do with wanting to be with the woman he loved, or with feeling out of place in the world. Was this just a personal drama he had staged for himself? Wanting the princess so badly even though he wasn't close to her caliber? If that was the case, why did he want to make it so hard for himself? Was it just because he wanted to escape the tedium of his life? He didn't know, but he was tired of hardship, misunderstandings, rules that made no sense and danger. Most of all, he was tired of people leading him in the wrong direction, and he felt like saying it now.

"Wait a minute," he said, not even sure whether he was talking to the monk or to Luca. "Why did the snake bite me? You can tell me I am a miracle because I survived it and you can tell me that I am stronger than I used to be. But it wasn't very nice. I had been through enough when I was alone in the cave and when I turned into a tree. I was on the verge of madness. Wasn't that enough? Yet you," and now he turned to Luca, "or someone like you sent me here. Why didn't you help me? I know you did, but you sent me into the claws of the enemy first, and then you pretended to help me out so I would honor you as my savior. Was it just some ego trip for you?" He knew that his words hurt, but he was past the point of thinking carefully before saying what he felt.

Luca didn't want to look at him. Akim wasn't sure whether he was feeling embarrassed after having been exposed. The monk intervened. This was surprising since Akim had been under the impression that the monk couldn't understand him. He must have got the gist of it just by listening to his tone. He started talking and Luca translated, still looking away.

"A path is not a real path if there aren't lonely times, utter despair, and pain that you think is close to unbearable. But hope will triumph in the end. You don't always have to believe it but as long as you believe it most of the time you will be okay. You might come to a point where you will embrace hope and faith because it will be all that you have left after everything else has failed you. Hope and faith cannot fail you because they don't promise anything. Therefore, they carry you through the times when you need them most.

"Every person you love will at some point or another hurt you. The question is whether you will continue to love, not because you owe it to the world, but because you owe it to yourself to serve as best you can. That is when you are happiest. Take responsibility where you need to; in that way you can make better decisions in future. Where no responsibility is due to be taken, lift your head and move forward, bearing your pain with pride. You are more interesting because of your challenges."

Akim nodded. He wasn't satisfied with the answer but he understood that it would be about as good as it got. He had to continue without asking too many questions. Trying to find answers was futile, because knowing everything, or even anything, was the surest sign that one was missing the mark. He could only know with his heart, because it didn't depend on certainty, but on experience and subjectivity. It implied faith, the greatest tool to create something better. Every magical experience lost its magic at some point or another. He might as well accept it and move on rather than cling to it and injure himself in the process. If he moved on, the magic would have enriched his soul. If he tried to confine it, he would only destroy its mystery.

Chapter 41

Despite his anger and confusion, he liked Luca and he knew that it would be better to acknowledge it. Love that was denied could wreak as much havoc on one's soul as darkness that was denied. He hugged him and wished him all the best of luck for his future. Luca looked sad. Akim wasn't sure whether it was because he would miss Akim or because he felt hurt by his hostility. Akim resisted the urge to try and make Luca feel better. Luca had to deal with his own distress in the same way that Akim had to live with his uncertainties. He told Luca that he would miss him, after which he thanked the monk for his blessings. He looked around at the village one last time to imprint it in his memory, but not long enough to be tempted to linger. Next he walked off in the direction of the desert, his water bottle full but once again without any idea of where he was going. He focused intensely on the Golden City and Matima, hoping it would pull him closer to it.

The desert turned out to be friendly to him this time. There were long stretches of dunes on end. During these stretches he would conserve his energy in every way that he could. He felt fear at times but more often he trusted that he would be looked after. His water bottle was never empty for very long before he would find some vegetation and, not too far away, water.

He didn't encounter any more people or signs of civilization. It was only him, the desert, the sun, the sky and whatever plants he could find. He didn't see many animals, either. When it happened that Akim saw an antelope in the twilight of dusk, it felt like a magical moment. In his eyes, the antelope was sent from heaven to be his guardian angel for the night, bringing him a special message that he would soon reach his destination. He wanted to thank it for being there for him. The antelope stared at him for a minute or two. Akim slowly, carefully, gave one or two steps closer, stretching out his hand. When he did so, the antelope started and trotted away. Akim wanted to cry. He then proceeded to try and find a decent-sized shrub to sleep under.

Being completely alone for a long time did strange things to one's mind. This time it was different from when he had just left Matima and the gypsy van. Back then he had to face fear and uncertainty, knowing that the journey would be hard. This time he was certain that he would get there, not because there was any reason to believe it but because it was all he could do to survive. If he couldn't escape his ordeal of existing, he might as well direct it; deciding what he would like the outcome to be and willing it into existence. Now that his mind was focused on where he wanted to go, there wasn't much space for doubt. It didn't mean that he didn't feel it at times, but the thought of arrival being imminent overrode all the others, which meant that they lost their energy after some time.

He experienced something else that was strange to describe. His will was a focal point where everything started; a little space of light where intention was born. This intention then expanded, moving outside of himself until it filled the entire universe. He became one with the universe, not sure whether the sun and the sky were outside or inside of himself any more. He was no longer sure whether his breath was his own or the breath of the universe, or whether his body was something inside him or something that contained him.

Despite his loneliness and isolation, or maybe because of it, he enlarged, becoming one with all that was within reach of his perception and all that wasn't. This made him feel terribly lonely, magnificently quiet and also strangely fulfilled. The entire universe was within him as much as it was outside of him, expanding in every direction. He was the center of the universe as much as any other point could be if one imagined that point to be expanding without ever reaching a boundary. Infinity was too large to fathom and it made him tired, so he settled with the idea of the universe being inside of his own little body. Whatever was in his field of perception was working with him to create whatever he imagined himself to be. Hopefully one day it would be merciful. If he died in the meantime then he would just return to where he came from.

His thought processes gradually became less defined. He became quieter, and the space inside him turned into a place of being and appreciation rather than an endless chatter of thought. He believed that what he put out to the universe would eventually come into being. Survival became a matter of instinct and knowing rather than one of panic and thought. Only at the back of his mind could he remember that he was still Akim, a lonely boy turned man coming from a harsh world, just looking for a more harmonious life with his beloved. Other than that he was simply a light, an energy being in the world for no reason whatsoever, existing to make the most of it and to know whatever happiness he could find.

He was the happiness, he realized, simply seeking expression. Wasn't that the miracle of conception? Wasn't it a state of ecstasy born out of desire to merge with another person and that desire being satisfied? He speculated that we didn't really desire to become one with another person through sex; we desired to feel the energy of the universe flowing through us, the original bliss where we came from. The energy was more powerful when the other person's energy was a bit like our own and yet they were a person in their own right, not confined by our desire to have them. We had come into existence as ourselves mostly because there had been enough happiness to bring us here. The energy of sex was mistaken with and misused by force, perversion and security all too often. But there would be a time when we remembered sex as an expression of the joy of who we were, just like work and pretty much everything else.

When one day he could see something gleaming on the distant horizon, it didn't even come as a surprise. It came as the sure manifestation of where he had applied all his energy and focus. It appeared out of the middle of nowhere; something that came out of nothing. Even in his mind it had come as something out of nothing. Although he had heard about the Golden City, giving him an idea, he couldn't actually have conceived it if it hadn't been for his ability to imagine it. Or maybe it had existed first, making its way into his mind, presenting itself as his own idea while it could have had a will of its own, wanting to manifest in the physical world and looking for a mind that was open enough to serve as a gateway. Akim didn't care. He was as happy to see it as it could or could not have been to see him. He knew that Matima would be there waiting for him, not only because that was what he hoped but because he believed it without an atom of a doubt.

As he moved closer to the Golden City, it felt like he was finally coming home to a place where the universe was an extension of himself. Having been through what he had, he now knew that he carried the universe inside him. Whatever was going on around him didn't matter. In the same way that the outside world affected how he felt internally, he could also bring the joy and harmony of the universe inside to the world around him. It would never be perfect and he would never quite get it right, but that wasn't the point. He was alive and free to explore. Adversity wouldn't get him down because wholeness was his natural state. Whenever it was impaired he would return to it sooner or later until he died, which was the only sure outcome of life anyway. In the meantime he was free to love, work, and create whatever he chose to.

Chapter 42

The Golden City was just as he had imagined it and yet it was nothing like it at all. In terms of how he felt, it matched his imagined vision, probably because he had focused on the experience for such a long time. However, in terms of its size, proportion and physical dimensions, it was completely different from the image he had had in mind. The closer he moved to it, the more obvious it became that it wasn't pure gold everywhere. The buildings were mostly white stone but were decorated with mosaic and a strip of gold here and there. It's probably the same as with life, he thought. When we imagine and experience something wonderful, it's never only marvelous. Rather, it has elements of the magic we imagined in it. As for the rest, it has a will of its own with a unique character that makes it interesting. If things always turned out exactly the way we had hoped then life would be uninteresting and we wouldn't learn to adapt along the way.

From far away he could see that the city had a pointed hill at its center. He knew that he had to go there—the mountain would have the answer that he had been looking for about his place in the world. On the other side of the city the landscape changed. It became greener and the dunes turned into hills. There wasn't any sign of roads or other human activity on them, which made him wonder how the city sustained itself and whether there was any other way in and out of it except if one crossed an entire desert. There had to be at least one other way, the one that Matima had come by because she was waiting for him by the gate, as he had known that she would.

He wondered how she had known he was coming. Could it be that he had also appeared at the right time for her in the way that she had done for him? She looked sparkling and strong. She was positively a goddess. Something had changed in her, but it wasn't quite that she was different from before. Maybe it was her eyes that were shinier; the tiredness had left them. Maybe it was the aura of self-confidence whereas before she had known her own power but not fully believed in it. There was something else. She was larger, much larger. Not only did she look taller because of her stronger aura, but her stomach had a massive bump. He asked himself, had they been apart for less than nine months? It had felt like years. Unless ... His heart sank.

His shoulders must have slumped when the thought struck him. He almost wanted to fall to his knees and turn around. She was now only a few meters away, close enough for him to see her radiant eyes. Her face fell as she realized what he had to be thinking. She ran up to him clumsily with her tummy shaking. He realized that he had in fact fallen to his knees because she picked him up, hugging him close to her bosom which was larger than he remembered it. Her tears fell into his hair as she sobbed with happiness and grief at his reaction. "It's yours," she whispered in his ear, eager to comfort him. When he pulled himself up, she pulled away. "What were you thinking?" she asked angrily. Then she softened again, still looking hurt. She couldn't blame him for the thought crossing his mind when he had had no inkling.

"You're different," he said, happiness and tiredness now overwhelming him. He just wanted to find a place called home where he could rest and sleep.

"I know," she said. "Maybe I'm just a bit more myself, or a bit less myself, I'm not sure which. Look at you. You're tired. What have you been through? For your sake I hope we can just go home and relax, live a happy, quiet life without being too worried about anything, as long as we have each other." He nodded and laughed with a slight note of cynicism.

"If only life were really that easy," he said. She obviously had no idea of all he had experienced.

"Perhaps it could be," she said. "We can always hope and believe. Maybe if we stop believing that we have to struggle for everything that's important to us, we'll no longer make things harder than they need to be. We love each other and have found each other again despite the odds, isn't that enough to be grateful for? Isn't it a sure indication that we are meant to be happy and that the universe will support us if that is what we pursue? The happiness is right here, inside us, looking for expression. If we give it action, it will multiply. Isn't it the expression of our joy and love that has caused new life to grow in my body?" He smiled at her, the light in his eyes still dimmed by the hardship he had been through. Maybe he would feel better after taking some time to recover. Maybe he would even be able to see things from her perspective, knowing that all was well. But for now he was happy to lean on her. He pulled her closer to him, allowing the warmth of her body to lift his spirits. They stayed like that for a while until Matima pulled away, gently nudging him.

"We have come this far," she said. "Now shall we move on and see what it was we were after?" He was too tired to persuade her to stay where they were for just a little while longer, so he nodded and followed, his hand in hers. He would keep his eyes on the mountain in the center and feel gratitude for his love being back by his side. In that way he would hopefully be able to complete his mission.

Chapter 43

The Golden City was surrounded by high walls. The only visible entrance on their side was a massive wooden gate with inserts of gold. The gates were wide open but there were guards on either side who stopped them, wanting to know who they were and where they were going. The guards were wearing mail and their faces were not visible. They had swords with golden hilts by their sides. The hilts were elegantly shaped and supplemented with various colors of gemstones. Akim was really glad that Matima took the lead in dealing with the intimidating guards.

"We are travelers from far away who have come to see the Golden City. We would like to go to the mountain at the center to consult the oracle," she said without any hesitation. Akim was surprised. How on earth was she so confident in the face of armed men?

"Very well, young lady," the guard said. He lifted the visor to reveal striking blue eyes. Akim was surprised to see that the eyes looked young and friendly, about as sparkly as Matima's were at present. He found it even harder to believe that the guard accepted her answer without further ado. He stepped aside and made way for them. Matima turned to smile at Akim. Her eyes were saying, see what I told you?

They entered the city. It was ordinary and exceptional. The first part was a street leading straight in the direction of the hill. There were buildings on either side, which could be people's homes. The sidewalks on both sides were tidy with plants and trees arranged in the way of an orderly little garden. The impression it created was one of elegance. There were street vendors, mostly selling fruit or other food from quaint stalls. A few other people walked past them. The vendors and other pedestrians were amiable, just like the guard at the gate.

Matima was enjoying the walk down the street. Akim felt more energized, but he couldn't help wondering if the place was too good to be true. It probably was, he thought, if only by virtue of the fact that they couldn't stay there forever. If they did, they would be sad because they would be disconnected from where they came from. They would also be missing the people they loved. He couldn't help wondering if too much prosperity would make them bored. What would there be to strive for in this perfect little place? Would expressing themselves be as meaningful as it would in a place where the world needed them?

Perhaps Matima was right; maybe he was making things difficult for himself by believing that he was in the world to fulfill a certain mission. Maybe it didn't matter what he was up to or even who he was with, as long as he was fully himself. The thought felt like a release. If he cultivated his own happiness, his mission would take shape naturally. His spirits were already lifting, no doubt at least partly thanks to Matima being by his side. Her positivity was making an impact on his mood. The vibe of the city was also contagious. With everyone being so happy and friendly he felt his eyes filling with the same sparkle and his body with the same energy.

They reached a point where the buildings ended but the streets continued between parks and gardens. A few birds could be seen and there were squirrels running around, collecting acorns and chasing each other up and down the trunks of trees. Matima was having fun watching the squirrels frolicking. Akim silently thanked the universe for bringing this joy into his life. He felt his spirits lift more and more as they walked in the direction of the mountain.

The gardens gave way to plants that grew more wildly, gradually turning into forest landscape. Both Akim and Matima sensed the energy of the earth becoming stronger. The forest turned into an organism that was alive, anticipating them. The more they walked upwards, the narrower the street became until it was no wider than a footpath. Its cultivated surface ended, turning into a subtle path in a dense and magical forest. Akim couldn't fathom whether the forest was friendly or unfriendly towards them, but he knew that they had to respect it. Since it could play with them if the whim took it, they had to make their intentions clear and ask for its help. Matima was quiet, which indicated that she sensed the atmosphere.

The path was winding and becoming steeper. Akim had to stop to help Matima several times. What had looked like a hill from far away turned out to be much more than that—closer to a very steep mountain. It also wasn't quite a single pointed mound of earth and rock. On occasions, when the dense foliage wasn't blocking their view, they could see a gorge below them on the opposite side of which there was the sloping side of another mountain. The fissure became narrower, leading up to a point where the two mountains met, becoming one single mass of majestic earth. The point where the two mounds met was where they were heading. They instinctively knew that it was the center of the place.

The higher they moved up, the cooler it became. They were entering fog, which impaired visibility. It was dark in the gap; they wondered if it was getting close to dusk. The mountain and the forest path were deceitful in that sense and they lost track of time. They couldn't even roughly estimate how long they had been walking or what time of the day it was. The feeling increased as they moved deeper into the forest and mountain center. They didn't feel tired after what had been a long walk. They drank water from streams and ate of the forest fruit—whatever they could find that looked edible. It was refreshing. The thought crossed Akim's mind that they had to be careful of eating the fruits in this strange place. However, since it was too late to worry about it, he pushed the thought away.

When they came to a point where they could no longer continue due to low visibility and difficult terrain, they finally saw a light ahead between the trees. Akim wasn't sure whether he should be happy about it or not. Either they had reached their destination and would find what they had been looking for, or the light meant danger, and he had had enough of that. He walked on, leading the way. He quietly talked to the forest, telling it that they were travelers who had come from far away to experience the Golden City and learn from it. He asked it to guide and protect them as their intentions were sincere. He imagined that the forest accepted his plea.

The light they saw turned out to be numerous lights. As they moved closer they could see torches along the way to where the two mountains met. Through a gap in the foliage it looked like a cave, the outside of which sported gemstones and inserts of gold, just like most everything else in the city. Where the torches began, there was a tall old man standing in the middle of the path with a lantern in his hand. He had very long grey hair and beard. He wore a wizard-like hat and a long cloak with pictures of moons and stars on it. As they moved closer, he could see that the man's body language showed power. In no way did he look feeble as would have been expected from someone of his age. Moving close enough to distinguish his facial expression, the man looked friendly, slightly amused and a bit severe.

Akim and Matima stopped when they reached him. Akim instinctively wanted to bow before the man. However, he felt foolish doing so physically, so he bowed mentally as a way of acknowledging the old man's influence.

"Welcome," he said in a deep voice. He put out his hand first to Akim. Then he put out his hand to Matima and kissed hers. Akim was surprised by the gesture of gallantry with a hint of flirtation coming from such an old man. He could see that Matima was flustered but enjoyed the attention nevertheless. The man's age only added to his aura of wisdom but didn't reduce his virility. "Please introduce yourselves," he said.

Matima introduced herself first, after which Akim said his name. The wizard nodded and introduced himself as Lamka, keeper of knowledge. He applauded them for traveling such a long way and not giving up on their mission, despite facing hardship. He said that he believed that one of them had faced more adversity than the other, but that it had served his soul to grow. His experiences would come in useful for his future mission. He then invited them to follow him to complete their journey.

They walked ahead in the semi-darkness. The path was now easier to follow. The torches along the way gave an eerie sense of mysticism. When they reached the cave, Lamka came to a halt. He turned to face them and said, "You now enter at own risk. I hope and believe that you will find what you have been looking for." He walked away before either of them could say anything, vanishing in the shadows. When he had gone, neither of them could tell where he had disappeared to so fast. They looked at each other, astonished.

Now that there was nobody to direct them, all they had left to deal with was the massive opening to a cave that was pitch dark. When Akim squinted, he thought he could see a glimmer of light much deeper inside. Matima looked bewildered, confronted by the unexpected. Akim, on the other hand, had learned along the way that it was best to be open. That way one was more likely to notice the beauty of things, which would have been missed if one had had a fixed idea in one's mind of how things should look.

Chapter 44

Akim knew that the best they could do was to keep moving. But first he wanted to take a deep breath to appreciate the beauty of where they were. Hopefully, the scene with all its sights, smells and sounds could be imprinted in memory. He wanted it to have a place in his insides where he could return to as a reminder of how far he had come. He drank it all in and asked the surroundings to stay with him, giving him strength and courage in the moments that he would need it most. He turned back to Matima, who now looked worried, confused and tired. He took her hand.

"Let's go," he said.

They entered the cave. It was cool inside. The feeling reminded him of the first day when he had gone up the mountain and found the tree with the cool aura around it. It was dark enough that Akim could only just perceive the cave walls. Ahead of them there was only pitch blackness. When his eyes had become accustomed to the darkness, he could make out a small, dim light far ahead.

The walk in the cave proceeded slowly. Akim could sense anxiety on Matima's part and he realized that she was extra careful because of her unborn infant. The idea was still so strange to him that he could hardly grasp it. In some ways he still felt like a boy himself, as if his arrival on earth had been very recent. Now he had to take care of a new soul arriving. He had to believe that infants had intended to come here on some level, keen to experience life as themselves. Children were, after all, children of Nature. As a father he would do his best, but the universe would have to take care of the rest.

As they were walking closer to the light, he could see that the cave was more like a corridor; a very wide and high one. Walking still closer, they could discern a person sitting at a low slab of rock. In front of the slab was a burning torch. The cave came to an end right behind it. They were now close enough to see that the person was a woman. She was bent over the rock table, her thick dark hair spreading out over it. Akim held Matima's hand firmly as he could feel her wavering. He knew that they had to be clear on their intent or otherwise risk being tricked. They walked ahead and stopped in front of the rock table.

The woman sat upright. Her eyes were closed in a trance. Her fingers were held in the lotus position and Akim could see a blue light shining from her forehead. She opened her eyes. "Welcome," she said. Her voice was clear and sounded loud in the silence of the cave. "The spirits are excited to see you. They know that you have come a long way and they applaud you. If you are ready to work with them, they hail you as messengers of light. They want to make it clear that there will be many times when you might lose faith, when you will be ridiculed and when you will ask yourself if there is any meaning to what you are doing. If you are ready to accept the duality of being in a physical world while trying to live out a dream, they welcome you as partners in your quest of doing what you want to do. That's what life is about, they say, serving the world in your own particular way, always aware that the most important thing is to be true to yourself. Are you ready to go ahead?"

Akim and Matima nodded, saying that they were.

"Good," the woman said. "I am the High Priestess of Malta and I guard the door for travelers who have successfully passed the Threshold, ready to move on to new realms. I give you a choice. The runes tell me which is the better way for you to go, but you still have choice. I will only advise you if you ask me to do so. If you would like to choose first and hear my advice afterwards then you can do that. Otherwise, you can hear me out before choosing. There are two paths: one that goes up and out of the mountain to the top and one that goes down and eventually comes out in the valley. The one is more chaotic than the other but neither is better. Do you want to choose now or would you like to hear my advice first?"

Akim was tired of hearing advice so he said he wanted to choose first. He said he would go with the one that would lead to the top of the mountain. He had expected Matima to do the same, but she was more cautious and said that she would like to hear advice first.

The woman came out of her trance. She knelt down and picked up some sand from the floor of the cave, which she sprinkled over the rock slab. Akim only noticed now that it was inscribed with runes, just like the one he had seen in the world of Montana. The woman asked Matima to give her hand. She took Matima's in her own and held it for a little while, sensing Matima's energy. Then she let it go and put her own hands together in prayer. She blew over the sand which she had sprinkled over the slab. It scattered in every direction. She inspected it carefully, observing the way it lay over the runes. Then she turned back to Matima.

"You are very special, my dear, and so is the little one inside you. The chaotic path is the one for you. When you reach the valley, you will find the beauty and peace that are needed to put your mind at ease. What you have learned through your journey so far will come full circle and the way will be paved for a new phase of your life. I recommend this one, but if you would like to accompany your partner to the top of the mountain, then you are welcome to do so. It would also be good for you." Then she turned back to Akim. "Don't worry about being split up; you will be re-joined soon and it will not take as long as the last time you were separated." Addressing Matima again, she said, "What is your choice?"

Matima said that she would go the way that the priestess had suggested. The woman nodded. She then stretched out her hands in the air above the table and said something in a language that Akim didn't understand. Behind her in the wall two openings became visible. It was the same as with Lamka disappearing. They didn't actually see anything move or change, but when they looked it was there.

"Akim, your entrance is to the left and Matima, yours is to the right. Good luck to both of you. And don't worry, the last stretch will not be so hard." Akim turned to Matima and hugged her goodbye. Then he turned to the priestess and bowed before her, thanking her for her help. Without further ado, he faced his entrance and walked on.

Chapter 45

The path was steep, but otherwise not too hard to walk. He could see well enough, although he wasn't even sure where the light was coming from. The faint blue glimmer could have emanated from the rock wall itself. As the priestess had advised, it wasn't too long before the climb became easier and the plane flatter. He soon came out on top.

The bright sunlight was blinding. He sat down on a rock near the exit to orient himself and become accustomed to the light. He wasn't at the top yet, but very close to it. Right above him there was a mound of large rocks which formed the summit. To all sides he had a breathtaking view of lush forest. In the distance he could see the city and down below on the other side he could see the valley where he assumed Matima was. On the other side of the city was the desert he had just crossed. He chuckled quietly to himself. In this land all things were possible, even forest and desert existing side by side.

When he had caught his breath, he made his way to the ultimate top. On arrival he noticed that the large boulders formed an indent which created a sheltered area with rock on three sides and a ceiling. Instinctively, he moved to this container. He could hope to find something special that would indicate what his mission in life was.

There was indeed something. It was an object that looked like a mirror in a stand. When he moved closer he saw that it was golden, or gold-plated. Expecting some sort of explanation if not a miracle, he inspected it carefully, looking for clues. It was circular in shape and tilted slightly. Its face was perpendicular to the sun, which was now fairly low in the sky. It was very bright and he had to shield his eyes. The object was strange and looked out of place, but it didn't give him any clues. There was no magical answer, no explanation. He went to stand in front of it, hoping that it might show him something.

It didn't. It was simply golden, exceptionally bold and bright. He looked around but there was nothing else. He stood in front of it again, imagining that he could see his own reflection in it. In his imagination he looked dirty and tired, perhaps a little bit older than the last time he had seen himself in a proper mirror. His eyes were also different—less innocent, a bit deeper, and more concerned. Was that all there was to see? he asked himself. Only an interesting object with no explanation of its purpose? For the rest he had to fill in the missing spaces using his imagination.

Maybe that was what he had come to see and perhaps it was the same way with life. Akim mused to himself, we perceive interesting things and we want to know that there is a reason for it. We expect clues that would lead to an aha-moment, hoping that we can be better off than before. But perhaps that isn't what our quest in life is all about. Maybe it's about striving for something and only finding ourselves in the end. The best we can do, Akim decided, is to do our best, work with love and enjoy the ride while allowing our quest to unfold. When we find our mission, we might not understand it, but the imagination is there to guide us.

He sat down next to the golden mirror and looked out over the forest in the direction of the city. He looked at the desert, on the other side of which he could now see a range of mountains that appeared infinitely far. Looking back over his journey he couldn't believe that he had survived it. The splendor of the view filled him with gratitude. The earth gave so much beauty that most of the time it was enough to be there and experience it. The best things in life were indeed free, he thought. Tomorrow things would be different, he didn't know in which way. Whatever would come, he would meet it with as much courage as he could.

The sun lowered itself to the horizon, reflecting the quietness of Akim's state of mind. The scene changed its hues when the sun touched the earth, giving it a different ambience. Night fell and the stars came out like cheerful little sparks. The new scene was as peaceful as the former one. Although he couldn't see much, the night sky kept him company and the golden mirror glowed with a faint light, reminding him of a journey complete and a quest fulfilled. He didn't want to miss out on the moment, but sleep overcame him and he effortlessly slipped into its landscape, where his dreams were quiet and happy.

Chapter 46

It was dark and he was walking down the mountain to the valley where he knew he would find Matima. It was easy, despite the fact that he had to make his way through the forest. The plants made way for him, moving out of his way when required and providing stability for his feet whenever he needed something to step on. He could see well enough, not with normal daytime vision, but with eyes that enabled him to see in the dark. Everything, especially the plants, glowed with a blue light. He was more aware of their essence, the vibration that kept them alive, than their physical forms. They reassured him quietly that he was on the right track.

The lower he descended into the valley, the darker it became, although he could still see clearly. The blue light of the plants was becoming stronger. The slope was also becoming less steep, which told him that the valley was close. When the blue light started dimming and he could see spots of a different color light ahead, he knew that he had arrived somewhere.

He walked into a charming garden. There were a few large trees in some spots, their branches forming a dense roof to the little haven. There were lanterns and flower beds with pink, orange, yellow and red flowers, the light of which contrasted with the blue light of the other plants. The lawn was strewn over with something that resembled fairy dust—small particles of light like glowing snowflakes. The tree close to the center of the garden was the largest. There he saw an even stronger light that attracted him. It was Matima.

She didn't come to him, so he walked over to her, not sure if she was aware of his presence. Her hands were against the trunk of the tree as if she was drawing strength from it. He watched her from a few meters away as he didn't want to interrupt her ritual. She turned to the light of the moon shining through the trees and put her hands together in prayer. A light point on her forehead started glowing, resembling the shape and color of the moon. He could almost see a thread of light connecting the one on her forehead with the one in the sky. She bowed down, touching the earth with her hands and head, giving thanks and asking for guidance. Her ritual complete, she got up and walked over to him. She took his hands into her own.

"I am glad you came," she said. She smiled and pulled his hands to her heart. Her breasts felt soft and sensual. Her eyes were serious. "Do not think that because you perceive me as beautiful and strong that I am not afraid. I am unsure of myself. I do not always have a lot of courage.

But I have been given a task which I take very seriously: to restore the divine feminine to her rightful position in the hearts of men. I hope it will turn out to be worthwhile, for I undertake this task at great risk. I invite you to walk alongside me, fulfilling your own mission in life rather than only supporting me in mine. I hope that our paths will enrich each other's lives and that when one of us falls, the other will be able to restore them to dignity. I hope that our love will shine together as a beacon for those intent on fulfilling their heart's desires. I hail you as my lover, my friend, and the father of my child. Would you walk with me?"

He fell in next to her and she led him along a path of pebbles, which was also sprinkled with the fairy dust. They arrived at a spot in the garden where there was a pool, the surface of which glimmered and reflected like a mirror. There were a few purple flowers in the pool. Surrounding the pool were seven women dressed in white robes. They were smiling at Matima affectionately as if they knew her well. He wondered if they were the sisters whom she had stayed with. He couldn't remember what they looked like. She nodded at them and said that she was ready.

Akim looked at the surface of the pool. The reflection of the moon was now clearly visible, larger than life. If he hadn't known better, he would have thought that the moon was housed in the pool. One of the women had a staff in her hand. She stepped forward and touched the moon in the pool with it. The entire surface of the water assumed the color of the moon's reflection, and a vapor of the same hue rose from it. Feeling sleepy, he lowered himself to the ground and lay on his back. The women were around them but he didn't care; he was hypnotized by the moon. She enchanted him, drugged him while the women were fussing over Matima.

He was on his own blissful planet when a sharp and unsettling noise suddenly pulled him back to where he was. It was the sound of a baby crying. He looked next to him where Matima was holding the infant in her arms. She looked happier than he had ever seen her. He leaned over to greet his son, beholding the little miracle that had come into the world as a result of their intense desire for one another. He was convinced that no man could be a prouder father.

Epilogue

That was the *end* of the two travelers' journey. Having experienced what a magical country looked like, they were given the option to stay there or go back to where they came from. Between the choices of inhabiting a place where things were mostly right and returning to their original lives where they would face many challenges, both felt that it was more appropriate to go back. They wanted to at least attempt to live out their visions despite the limitations imposed on them by others. Akim felt the need to serve the world and he couldn't do so by dissociating himself from it. Matima didn't want to lose her connection to her roots, because she had been born a princess for a reason. Her safety could be at stake and she might have to face up to being in disgrace. But she had hope that her material position of hierarchy would give her the opportunity to transform the rules. So the sisters transported them back home through magical means.

The sisters had been right and the challenges they had to face were massive. Both of them expected that things would be easier in the world after their journey. They felt that the lessons they had learned had strengthened their spirits and would provide them with the tools they needed to achieve victory. But the growth that they had experienced put the world outside in such sharp contrast to the world of their inner visions that the disparity was particularly painful.

The harshness of the world at times put a lot of strain on their relationship. There were times when each of them felt uncertain of whether their relationship was still good for them. All they could do was trust that their love was strong enough to keep them together, and it always turned out to be. Going through difficult times strengthened and matured their bond. They learned how to take care of one another while maintaining their own individuality and freedom.

When Akim and Matima had arrived back in the world that they knew, they settled in a small town, raising their son as a normal child while remaining as anonymous as possible. They got to know their neighbors and became friends with them. Matima didn't exactly hide her identity, but she didn't announce to everyone that she was the lost princess, either. By acting like a normal peasant mother who did her best to raise her child, she disguised herself well. If she would be discovered then she might make an effort to reclaim her position of power obtained by birth. When that happened she would deal with the legal aspect of her marriage. For the time being, she just worked in the village as a teacher. In her own time she busied herself with creative expression such as painting and weaving.

Akim resumed his job as a carpenter and occasionally performed services as a healer, much like Asteodor. He was in regular contact with his mother, who was overjoyed to see him again and meet her grandson. Matima didn't contact her family immediately on her return. She knew that at some point the tension of living in the country ruled by her father without having any contact with him would be too much to bear and she would make amends.

Whether king or carpenter, the paths taken are many, but the destination is the same.

About the Author

Experiences early in Mia's life have led her to search for true healing. In the process she discovered the shamanic way: a relationship with the essence of all things. In the worlds that opened up to her through shamanism, she found the stories of the unconscious that often take expression in myths. Through her writing she hopes to give the reader access to these otherworldly realms.

She grew up in South Africa in an environment that she describes as religious, patriarchal and academic. After school she studied psychology and classical literature at the University of Stellenbosch in South Africa. She worked for a business in customer service for five years, during which she continued her studies of healing and spirituality in her own time. In 2010 she did a course in cross-cultural shamanism with The Four Gates Foundation, following this up with a course in African Tree Essences in 2013. She moved to Edinburgh, UK in 2013, where she did a master's degree in classics, focusing mainly on mythology and ancient civilisations. She currently works as a healer in Edinburgh.

ALL THINGS THAT MATTER PRESS

FOR MORE INFORMATION ON TITLES AVAILABLE FROM
ALL THINGS THAT MATTER PRESS, GO TO
http://allthingsthatmatterpress.com
or contact us at
allthingsthatmatterpress@gmail.com

If you enjoyed this book, please post a review on Amazon.com and your favorite social media sites.
Thank you!

Lightning Source UK Ltd.
Milton Keynes UK
UKOW06f1828030516

273505UK00008B/223/P